THERE ONCE WERE STARS

Melanie McFarlane

Month9Books

THERE ONCE WERE STARS by Melanie McFarlane
All rights reserved. Published in the United States of America by Month9Books, LLC.
No part of this book may be used or reproduced in any manner whatsoever without written permission of the publisher, except in the case of brief quotations embodied in critical articles and reviews.

ISBN: 978-0-9968904-0-3

Published by Month9Books, Raleigh, NC 27609
Cover design by Paper and Sage

Month9Books

To my mother, champion of make believe, and fan to all my stories.
To my husband, who is good at keeping the little ones busy so the fantastical can be created.
To my father, who always said I should be a writer.

THERE ONCE WERE STARS

CHAPTER 1

I stretch my arms across my bed, running my fingers along the same sheets I've had since I was a child. The stiffness was beaten out of them long ago, but they still carry the memory of my mother carefully stitching the first tear back together when I was seven. The tiny *x*'s remind me of her long fingers, moving the needle back and forth with the same care as when she worked with samples in her laboratory.

I trace the row of stitches, squeezing my eyes shut as I make a wish; it is my eighteenth birthday, after all. But when I open them, the same scene shows from my bedroom window that always does—the grid of our dome. Nothing changes. It doesn't matter how many birthday wishes are made; I always wake up trapped inside the dome. The grid of thick glass and steel arcs far above our apartment, stretching to where the great Axis, a tower of government offices, meets the peak of our home—Dome 1618.

I crawl out of bed and let my gaze trail down the Axis to the rooftops of the other apartment buildings, row upon row of housing for blue-collar workers. Closer to the Axis are the townhouses of business owners, hidden from the rest of us, but that's not where I long to be. My eyes drift to the base of the dome, far away from my window where the Outer Forest stands tall—my only saving grace. It's forbidden to hike among the trees, but sometimes rules need to be broken.

"Natalia!" Grandmother's piercing voice comes from the other side of my bedroom door. "Get up. You're wasting the day away."

The clock on my dresser reads eight o'clock in the morning. It's been nine years since I moved in with my grandparents, and saying Grandmother and I have differing opinions barely touches the surface. Her rules are sometimes worse than those of the Order, who police the dome. With any luck, I'll be assigned my own apartment soon, and will finally be able to restart my life again.

I run a brush through my long brown hair, which matches my eyes. I don't know why I bother—by the time I go outside it will look unruly once again. It's my curse; I have thick hair like my mother, with waves that look more like oddly-placed kinks, unlike the smooth-flowing locks worn by some of the other girls at my school. But I won't have to go back to the Learning Institute again. Today I'm an adult.

My jeans are on the floor where I left them last night, and I manage to find a clean T-shirt in my drawer. Both have the same tiny stitches as my sheets, covering up the wear and tear over the years, but I sewed these back together myself. Grandmother is firm on the fact that if I don't take care of what I have, I don't get a replacement. There's no point in arguing when her opinions are as deep as the wrinkles on her face, and honestly, it's hard to tell which she has more of. Before I leave my room, I grab my mother's notebook. It's filled with her sketches and work notes on different projects she was involved in. But my favorites are the tiny notes, squeezed in the margins, excerpt of her personal thoughts, hopes, and dreams. The biggest of these was to move her family outside the dome.

"I know you were out last night," Grandmother says, eyeing me suspiciously between the milk and dry toast as I slip into my seat at the table.

"Must we have this conversation every morning?" Grandfather speaks up.

"You know the ramifications!" Grandmother shrills, and he shrinks in his chair. "Do you want to let her stroll around at night past curfew? One day she won't come home, and then we will be questioned." Grandmother redirects her attention to me. "What are you doing out there that's important enough to risk everything? Haven't I warned you? If the Order catches you, you will wish you had listened to me."

"That's my problem." I fold my arms across my chest. She always makes me back down with her words. If I'm going to be an adult, I need to learn how to take a stand.

"If your parents could only see you now," she says unsympathetically. "They would wonder how they got a daughter so determined to get herself detained. You know what *they* do with little girls who don't follow the rules."

"Yes," I say through gritted teeth. She's given these lectures many times. Girls who don't follow the rules are sent back to the Learning Institute for retraining, where they come out all prim and proper, ready to take their place as functional residents of the dome. I'm not going back there; I know how to stay under the radar.

"Come on, now." Grandfather finally steps in. "It's Nat's birthday."

"Yes." Her tone softens. "You're eighteen now. Hurry and eat; we got you a little something."

I gobble down the toast, stale as it is, but fresh food is not something that our dome has had in a long time. Since the accident that caused my parents' death, the Order stopped all excursions for scientific research, completely cutting off the outside world. Prior to this, there were plenty of rations from the farms due to uncontaminated seeds the expedition teams found, along with new plant life for supplementing the crops. But those stockpiles have slowly depleted.

When I finish breakfast, I look at my grandparents in anticipation. Grandfather's face is beaming, and though Grandmother looks like she is trying to be serious, I can see a small sparkle in her eyes as she hands me a tiny green box with a little purple bow. The bow is smooth, made from fabric nicer than anything I own. I gently untie it, and put the silky strand safely in my pocket, before opening the box to see what is inside.

A silver, heart-shaped locket sits on top of fine tissue paper, so delicate I don't dare touch it in case it rips. An image of two hands holding a smaller heart is engraved into the center of the locket. This is the most beautiful thing I have ever seen—I've never owned jewelry of my own. My hands are shaking so bad I almost drop the box.

"Careful!" Grandmother's voice snaps me from my awe. She grabs the box from me, and it takes all my inner strength to let it go.

She removes the necklace from the box and opens the locket, revealing a photo of my parents on their wedding day. Photos are luxuries. I only own one other— a photo of me with my parents when I turned three—and it stays safe on my nightstand. But this locket—I can take it with me anywhere. I hold up my hair, allowing Grandmother to secure it around my neck, then grasp the tiny keepsake in my hand. I will cherish it forever.

"I'm going to show this to Jak and Xara," I say, leaving the table.

"Don't forget, you have to report to work today." Grandmother reminds me.

"But it's Saturday." I groan.

"You're eighteen now," she says, her eyes vacant of the compassion they held only seconds ago. "Your time to contribute to the dome begins today. Plus, any experience is good to have if you want to be a scientist one day, like your parents."

"I don't see how cleaning toilets at the Axis will do me any good in the future," I complain. "And I never said I want to be a scientist."

"You'll find where you're meant to be." Grandfather smiles. "Understanding everything from the bottom-up will help you make a better decision about what you want to do to make your contribution."

I sigh as I lace up my sneakers, now feeling the pressure of the future. I have no idea what I want to do today, let alone the rest of my life. But it definitely does not involve cleaning up after those in the Axis. I wave good-bye as I leave the apartment, but only Grandfather waves back. My number one fan; he always tries to keep the peace between Grandmother and I. But no matter how close we are, I still have to lie about where I'm really going. No one can know about my secret place.

Outside, I stretch my arms up toward the top of the dome. The sun shines through the dust covered glass of the dome, with sections of blue sky showing here and there. I sneak around the back of our apartment building, and begin my stealthy weave through alleyways. I have hours before my first shift starts at the Axis. Hours to spend somewhere the Order can't find me.

When I reach the Outer Forest, I sneak through a break in the fence and move between the trunks of trees, inhaling the last of the old world. The rich combination of musk and earth fills my lungs as I run as fast as I can from the fence. Running is one of the few things that make me feel free. When I reach my destination, I'm out of breath, but exactly where I belong—a hidden clearing at the edge of the dome.

I crawl inside a hollowed-out tree I've claimed as my own. How did the Order miss this lone tree, dying amidst the perfection of the Outer Forest? It should have been torn down long ago, to make room for larger, healthier, oxygen bearing trees. Decay doesn't coincide with the Order's pursuit for perfection and efficiency, but it's ideal for me: hidden, empty, and alone. I accept this tree's imperfections and it offers me solace.

I clutch my locket again, this time removing it from my neck so I can look inside. A twinge of pain prickles my throat as my parents' faces stare back at me. They look so happy and in love. I remember that about them. The *in love* part. I haven't thought about people in love for so long.

I lean back, holding the locket against my chest, intent on enjoying the morning sun. Unfortunately, the heat of the sun doesn't penetrate the cold glass of the dome, but something about that glowing orb in those blue skies makes me feel better. Mom wrote in her notebook about the first time she felt the sun on her skin: warm, and bright, as if it gave her a new life with its rays, just like it did to the world, after the Cleansing Wars. I close my eyes, imagining myself bathed in sunlight, and finally give in to the peace of the forest.

I wake up, feeling something sharp poking my side. I can't believe I drifted off. My hand shoots behind me, to find the source of the pain. My mother's notebook is jutting awkwardly from my back pocket. I stand up to tuck it back in, and my gaze slips above a line of bushes growing wildly along the base of the dome. At the same time, something flashes above them, and my breath catches in my throat. My reflection stares back at me from the glass, revealing my locket shining in the sunlight. *Relax, Dacie, it's only you.* A nervous laugh escapes my throat, as I finish putting the notebook away.

Another light flashes, but this time it's in the distance, on the other side of the glass. I lean forward, focusing on the light, and see a shadow move on the other side. My entire body goes rigid, and my heart beat thunders in my ears. No one could be out there—unless—could it be an Infected? No, that's impossible. They were all killed by the Cleansing War—everything was. If the nukes didn't kill them, the nuclear fallout afterward would have.

Something moves again—closer this time. A gasp escapes my lips, as a shudder rips through my body. That's when I see it—the faint outline of a person standing in the open. He's camouflaged by a layer of dust, blending him into the barren landscape that surrounds the dome. The figure's shadow stretches across the ground, reaching toward me.

I rub my eyes, as if something in them could be making me see the figure, but when I open them I'm startled to see the figure again, only now there are two. One stays farther back, toward the rockier land, silhouetted against the foothills in the distance. The other stands a short distance from the dome. My heart skips a beat—they're both human, and they're both staring in my direction.

CHAPTER 2

I creep toward the glass, slowly forcing my feet to move, not wanting to draw attention. But as I try to control each inhale and exhale, my entire body vibrates in rhythm with the electricity of my adrenaline. This can't be happening. I must be still asleep.

The man closest to me looks up in the direction of the peak of the dome, and my tension eases. They haven't spotted me. I take this moment to check him out; his clothes are covered in the filth of the dust outside and a hood hides his hair. His face is disguised by goggles above a bandana that hides the rest. Everything about them blends into the surrounding wasteland.

They can't be infected. They're much too interested in our dome. At the Learning Institute we were taught about the virus that destroyed most of mankind. People who weren't immune, changed—marked by the telltale scarring of the infection on their skin—a blackened spidery rash. The virus attacked the nervous system, making those infected jerk involuntarily. But the worst of it all was how they viciously attacked anything that moved.

I know it's foolish to think something outside could be an Infected; there hasn't been a sighting since my great grandmother's generation. But I've never seen anyone on the other side of the dome, because of the dangerous radiation left from the Cleansing Wars. I can't tear my eyes away from these mysterious Outsiders who defy all the teachings I have known my entire life. How can they survive the same radiation that killed my parents almost a decade ago?

The hood blows off of the figure in the distance, revealing messy, dark hair on a boy close to my age. He doesn't rush to lift his hood back up. Instead, he removes his goggles, and then does the unthinkable … he takes off his left glove and points a finger right at me.

I gasp out loud as his partner turns toward me. There's no way they can see me; a foot of shock-proof glass, spotted in dust, stands between us. I'm on the inside, under the broad cover of the dome, protected behind the tinted façade, while they stand on the outside, open to the harsh world that was destroyed long before my time. But still, against all odds, our eyes connect. A smile breaks at the side of the man's mouth as another gasp escapes my lips. My hands jump to my mouth to hold my screams inside. *They see me.*

He steps toward me, removing his hood and goggles as he approaches the dome wall. His eyes are dark. I expected them to be entirely white, from a combination of sun blindness and radiation. When I was little, I saw an expedition scientist come back like that, skin raw and blistered; her white eyes staring into the nothingness of death. She died soon after, but the memory of those eyes was burned into my brain.

From the other side of the glass, he stares me down as he gets closer. Fear ripples through my body; I am exposed and defenseless. He is firm and unyielding with a determination unlike anything inside these walls. I force a swallow, unable to make myself run or move away.

As he walks, he kicks up the sandy dirt with every step, creating tiny clouds of dust around his boots, and footprints behind him along the undisturbed terrain. When he reaches the edge of the dome, he lifts his hand and places it on the glass in front of me. As if it has a mind of its own, my hand leaves my mouth and reaches out toward him, revealing my fear in its tremors. Our palms touch on opposite sides of the smooth glass, and I brace against it, feeling its security as I stare at the Outsider. His skin is weathered from the elements and to my surprise, nothing protects him; he is fully exposed; I am the one safe on the other side. I finally exhale; there's something familiar about him. Something that makes me feel safe.

Suddenly, he looks sharply to his right, then lets go of the glass and runs. His abruptness wakes me from my stupor, and I instantly duck into the bushes at my feet, where the ends of the branches scratch my arms. There's no way I'm dreaming. Through the branches I see Order members in pursuit. Only, they haven't seen the person who was standing next to the dome. They are in pursuit of the other, the partner, the one who stayed back. It's not too late for him to run, but he hangs back, as his friend escapes.

The partner holds his hands high in the air as the Order surrounds him. For a moment I can't see what's happening as the six armed guards block my view; I've lost the connection. My head floods with questions. Where will they take him? Why is he here? But none are so big as—how is he alive? The group breaks apart, carrying the stranger in the center, hands behind his back as he's dragged to the main entrance of the dome.

One of the Order points in my direction. My heart skips a beat, and an ache shoots through my chest. *Can they see me?* I cower as low as I can in the bushes, pressing my body against the coarse litter of decayed leaves that cover the ground. The member walks over to the dome, running a finger along the outside before peering through the glass. I hold my breath, so as not to move in the slightest. After a moment, they walk away.

I wait until the group rounds the corner of the dome, out of my sight, before daring to stand up. I brush myself free from debris and turn toward the trees to escape. It won't be safe for me to come back here for a long time, but there's no time to say goodbye as I dodge through the Outer Forest, making my way to the streets of the city, near the entrance of the dome.

I have an overwhelming need to see what will happen to the Outsider. I know it's human nature to be nosy, but have a deeper need to know what happens to him; ultimately I need to know if he was real. For some reason, seeing him inside the dome walls will be proof he exists.

A crowd has already formed around the entrance doors, most likely drawn when the Order rushed outside. It's common to see Order members go outside, on daily excursions to monitor the perimeter. You never know when an infected could show up. At least that's what we've always been told. That, and without protective suits, no one can survive on the outside.

"Nat," a familiar voice yells.

It's Grandmother.

"I thought you were spending this morning with your friends." She states more than asks. Then her voice drops to a whisper, "Did I see you come out of the Outer Forest?"

"I know," I stammer, caught red-handed. I must not have been as careful as I thought. "I'm sorry."

"You're an adult now," she warns, her eyes narrowing. "Try acting like one. Someone else could have seen you."

Someone else did, Grandmother, I want to say. If I told her who, she'd never believe me. She'd call me foolish and silly. Or worse, she'd believe me and report me herself so I would get sent back to the Learning Institute. Not the part the practical education side, either. The other side, from where sometimes screams could be heard while we sat in classes. No—there are things I may want to say to her, but it's time I learned to choose my words carefully. The irony is, she'd be proud of this adult decision.

The lights above the entrance doors to the dome began to blink. Those at the front of the crowd push back in an attempt to avoid any exposure to the outside air. Everyone knows what we've been taught. The outside is dangerous.

"We'll talk about this later," Grandmother says, moving with the crowd as they push past us.

I stretch up on my toes, trying to see. Order members enter the dome to the decontamination area. Each member removes his or her helmet as they stand between the two entrances, one to the outside, and one to the dome. Scans run across their bodies, looking for any indication of radiation. Their shiny, white uniforms reflect the red beams. Suddenly the green lights turn on, and the doors to the inside of the dome slide open. How could he be from the outside and not be contaminated?

The racket of the crowd hushes as the Outsider steps inside. He looks around, smiling at everyone, nodding and saying hello, but no one answers. I push ahead of the others to get a better look, but no one budges, so I give up and push through the back of the crowd, while eager residents move forward. I escape the crowd and run down the street, trying to find a place I can push through to get a closer look. Others see me and catch on; soon I'm running ahead of a new crowd.

We follow the Order past the Apartment District, through the main shopping areas, all the way to the Axis where the crowds have grown as thick as they were at the entrance. Here, the Director and the Delegates keep office as the elected heads of state for this dome and its people—the city of Dome 1618.

As the Outsider disappears into the Axis, people break out into many different discussions. I choose not to participate; I'm more interested in listening to what everyone has to say. Mom always told me, you can get more truths from observing than simply drawing conclusions.

"He must be part of the rebels." I recognize Missus Sharp from the bakery near our apartment talking with a small group of her aged counterparts. "They sneak out, you know. Through some secret passage under the Axis."

"Shush, Muriel." Missus Marx, from the clothing shop across the street, whispers. "You can't keep the peace with talks like that. Everyone will think you're crazy, and before you know it, someone will have to put posters of your face around town."

"No one can go outside the domes," Grandmother speaks up. "They'd be killed by radiation."

The ladies are silent. They know not to challenge Grandmother, who lost both sons to the outside radiation. I, however, do not have the full respect and tact that they do, and forget my recent decision to watch my words.

"Then how did he survive on the outside?" I ask.

Both Missus Sharp and Missus Marx drop their jaws at the same time, but lean in close to hear Grandmother's response.

"He obviously has on protective gear of some sort," she says, flaring her nostrils as she narrows her eyes in my direction. "This is probably a test run; why else would they allow so many innocent people to be exposed?"

"Perhaps they are going to open the Expedition program again," Missus Sharp says, her eyes lighting up.

"That's enough," Grandmother hisses. "Talk like that will get you reported as a rebel."

Grandmother's words are more threatening than they are warning. Poor Missus Sharp's cheeks flush until her ears turn red, before she scurries off after Missus Marx who has already disappeared into the crowd.

I look up at an electronic banner hanging on the side of the Axis. It shows a smiling picture of the Director sitting at a table with the Delegates. Below them, written on the table are the words: *Peace. Love. Order. Dome.* The ridiculous propaganda popped up after our current Director was elected ten years ago, and to my mother's surprise, it performed as it was intended to. The telescreens spread the word and soon people repeated it everywhere in the dome and my mother would grumble about it in the privacy of our apartment.

The dome was never meant to be a permanent residence for its inhabitants. Mom said that was why long ago a Director created a science team for expeditions to test soil and find viable living alternatives outside the dome. Both my parents were selected as expedition scientists, the most sought after position in the Axis. It was truly an honor for them. But sometimes reaching for the best comes with a price. It was radiation outside that killed my parents while they were out on expedition. That same radiation keeps us locked up to this day.

The giant clock on the front of the Axis reads three o'clock. *Oh, no!* My shift starts in thirty minutes, and I still need to change, get signed in, and report to my station. I run home and root through my dresser, trying to find the maintenance worker garb I was given my last day at the Learning Institute. Finally, the beige button-up shirt and black pants appear, right where I left them, pressed and ready.

As I change, I realize something is missing and I feel my chest. *My locket!* My head spins, as my skin tingles, and a cold sweat breaks across my brow. In all the excitement this morning I must have dropped it. But if someone finds it there, I would have no way to deny I broke the rules. Grandmother would be furious, and I would receive a warning, if I'm lucky.

There's no time for me to go back for it; I can't be late for work. Three lates lead to a warning. I'll have to slip out tonight to find it. Even if Grandmother forbids me to return to the clearing, when I tell her about the locket she'll have to let me. She knows the ramifications of my actions as well as I do.

I make it back to the Axis in time to start my first job. As I pass through the front doors I can't help but think of the Outsider again. Where did they take him and will I ever see him again?

CHAPTER 3

The inside of the Axis is crisp, with sleek lines and a simple layout, lacking the wear and tear of the buildings outside. Its cold resemblance to the Learning Institute gives me pause, except here telescreens line the walls from floor to ceiling, displaying the spinning logo of the Director's motto: Three horizontal lines on top of one another, surrounded by an oval. Peace. Love. Order. Dome.

This is the only place in the dome where technology is allowed and used, aside from the screens on the streets. There are other government buildings like the Learning Institute and the Hall of Records that have access to computers, but they're used sparingly. In the Axis, technology is in abundance. It's the central nervous system that keeps the dome operational.

The one thing missing is the presence of blue-collar workers; they're apparent in every other area of the dome, since they reside in the apartment districts, shop in the business districts, and even work behind the Axis in the agricultural district. Inside the Axis, even the secretary at the front desk is refined, with her clean, pressed suit and perfectly placed hair. I suddenly feel self-conscious in my maintenance uniform. Where are the other cleaners?

"Name," she commands, as I approach her desk.

"Natalia Greyes." My voice echoes off the walls.

"Smile for the camera."

Before I can react, a flash blinds my eyes, leaving spots where the secretary once stood. I blink until she comes back into view.

"Approved," the secretary says, pushing a button. A small ID card with my name and picture spits out of a slot facing me on the backside of her desk. "Take the elevator to Basement Level 1. The head of Maintenance is expecting you."

I stand in front of the elevators, watching my hand shake as I press the down button. I've seen pictures of elevators on computers, but have never actually ridden in one. *Ding.* The doors slide apart, and I walk into the rectangular box, where a long line of numbers light up along the opposite wall: 100 all the way down to B2. If the lobby is that spectacular, what did the higher floors look like? I reluctantly press B1.

B1 is lit by long fluorescent lights beaming from the ceiling, shining on the long narrow hall that leads me to the head of Maintenance—a short, curly-haired, round woman. She must be close to seventy, which means she's nearing the end of her time of being beneficial to the dome. On her seventieth birthday she will say goodbye to the dome, and participate in the Last

Banquet, a monthly event where the Director invites those at the end of their time to a ceremony to celebrate their life. Jak, my friend with a passion for politics, has preached on the importance as to why this ceremony was created in the last decade along with other population controls, like reproduction limits, to help sustain the life of those in the dome.

"Okay." The woman offers a warm smile that makes me feel comfortable right away. "I am Mrs. Watson. And you are … " she pauses as I hand over my ID card. "*Natalia Greyes?*" I nod in agreement. "Like the scientists *Greyes?*" Her eyes bulge. I've seen that look before.

"Yes," I murmur. Everyone knows who my parents were; their project was imperative to our survival. Had they succeeded, there would have been no laws on life expectancy or reproduction and people would be living free, outside.

"A shame about what happened," Mrs. Watson says, shaking her head. I can't do anything but nod. "Anyway, our job here is not complicated, but it is timed. Keep on top of things, and you'll be fine. I am giving you floors two, three, and four."

"The Director's office?" I ask, surprised. In all the one hundred upper floors of the Axis, every kid learns the Director's office is located on the second floor. Who wouldn't want to know where the most powerful person in the dome worked?

"No, not the Director's office," she says, her face hardening. "I handle that personally. But the Delegate's offices and other rooms on those floors are fine to enter."

I take my assigned cart and ride the elevator up to Floor 4, where I meet up with three other workers. They're focused on the monotonous work of polishing, washing, and sweeping; there's no time for chitchat. One of the workers points to the office across from her, so I park my cart in front of the door labelled Minister of Agriculture, and mimic her actions, wiping the glass on the wall. It is tedious work.

"No, no." A dark-haired woman on my team *tsks* at me as she looks over my shoulder. "You need to polish in a circular motion." She grabs the rag from my hand and starts to vigorously wipe the glass. I watch her intently, the others not fazed by the interruption.

"I'm sorry," I say as she hands the rag back to me.

She doesn't reply. This job wasn't my first pick. It's going to be a long two weeks until my next assignment.

My coworker continuously corrects my work, hovering over my shoulder like Grandmother would. Every sharp-tongued direction makes me wince, but I keep my mouth shut as we move down to Floor 3, which is a large boardroom. By the time we finish there, she nods in approval, labelling me the window washer, and finally returns to her own cart.

Floor 2 is similar to Floor 4, in that the hallways are lined with offices. I make my way toward the end of the hall, focusing on office door windows. As I reach the end of the corridor, I pause in front of the one door I'm not allowed to enter. *Director* is etched in gold across its glass. No one told me not to clean the outside of the office.

I spray the glass and reach up to polish it with my cloth, but as I press against the window, the door opens. I freeze. *Did I do that?* No, the last person to use it must have been careless. I reach out to click the door shut, but voices come from the office, and a chill sends goosebumps down my arms when I hear the words "—clearing in the Outer Forest."

"We need to send a Horticultural team in tonight, sir," a man's voice comes through the opening. "My team reports that the Outsider was looking at something in the dome. Apparently, there's a clearing there."

"What do we care about a clearing, Samson?" the Director's voice demands. I recognize it from the announcements that come across the monitors throughout each day.

"Well, for one," the man whom the Director called Samson speaks up again, "in the clearing there is an old rotting tree." The Director grunts in disapproval and Samson's voice speeds up. "It was obviously overlooked during cleanup because it is at the outermost ring and faces the exterior of the dome."

"I don't like excuses, Samson," the Director grumbles. "We need all the space we have for healthy trees, to ensure oxygen levels stay premium. An oversight by Horticultural is a detriment to all. What else is there?"

"There's evidence someone has been in the clearing, sir."

My heart slams against my ribs, and a searing pain rips across my chest. Grandmother's warnings flash through my head like a flashback on fast forward.

"Someone was in the Outer Forest? Betker, your department's job is to uphold the law. Are you telling me someone has been sneaking around the Outer Forest and you had no idea?"

Another voice speaks up, dry with an edge of irritation. "Apparently so, sir," Betker replies.

"Does the Outsider know this person?" the Director asks.

"He is not talking yet," Betker says, regaining confidence in his voice. "But my men have their ways. We'll get information out of him."

"I don't like it. Someone hiding in the Outer Forest, and then a stranger found on the outside. It smells awfully like conspiracy to me. Why else would an Outsider risk coming so close to the dome? It's those damn rebels, I know it!"

"He had nothing on him to identify where he came from, sir," Betker says.

"He is secured, correct?"

"Yes," Betker says. "Locked up tight on B2."

"Below the generator!" the Director cries out.

"It's not a concern, sir. He only carried a few personal things on him: a photo, a key, and some food. We, of course, confiscated the food."

"I decide what's of concern around here." I jump as a fist bangs on the desk inside. "I want him moved. Get him off B2 and up to the higher floors where he can be monitored better. Let's find out what he's up to and who his contacts are."

"Yes, sir, right away."

"I want this situation rectified," the Director demands. "And find me the person who was in the Outer Forest."

I grab my bucket and move to another window. A tall man with red hair exits the Director's office, pausing when he notices the door was not closed. I keep my focus on the glass in front of me and hold my breath until he proceeds past me, making his way down the hallway to the elevator.

The Director and the other gentleman never appear, and soon my group finishes Floor 2. I can't wait to get out of this building and back to the clearing. I have to beat the Order and destroy any evidence of my being there.

When we get to B1, the carts are parked and the others hustle out of the office as quickly as they can. I hold back to ask Mrs. Watson one question that is eating at me.

"What else is down here?" I recall Samson mentioning the Outsider was on B2.

"What do you mean?"

"In the elevator I saw buttons for B1, and B2," I explain. "I never thought about what was underneath the Axis before. I'm curious. They didn't teach us about that at the Learning Institute."

"No," Mrs. Watson agrees. "It definitely would not be discussed there. You see, sometimes we pretend terrible things don't exist. "

My eyes widen at her vague reference. She notices and corrects herself. "Ah, don't mind me, Natalia. I'm an old woman spouting off random thoughts. You, too, may be the same way when you are nearing the end of your usefulness in the dome. What was it you asked? Oh yes, under the Axis. Well, on B1 is us of course. The other side of this hallway is the generator. It's what keeps the Axis powered. Without that, everything shuts down, the computers, the banners, even the air purification system."

"And what about B2?" I ask.

"I'm not aware of a B2," she states uncomfortably.

I laugh a little. "There's a button for it in the elevator."

"Of course there is, but listen to me, Natalia," she says in a hushed voice. "You do not want to know about B2. You do not want to visit B2. And you certainly do not ever talk about B2. Understand me? Unspeakable sounds come from down there, horrible things that would haunt your innocent, young, dreams. Just forget about it and pretend it doesn't exist."

"Yes, ma'am," I say, moving toward the door. Panic swells in my chest, sending a painful shudder across my skin.

"Good night, Natalia," she calls out after me.

I wait for the elevator, the fluorescent lights flickering above my head like the stars outside. *What on earth could be happening on B2?*

The elevator dings and the doors slide open. I gasp—the Outsider is standing in the middle of a small group of Order members. His right eye can barely open and is turning a terrible shade of purple, and his body is slumped forward, held up by the Order on either side of him. Our eyes connect and for a moment I see something mischievous spark inside them. A smile plays at the edge of his mouth, making my stomach twist in discomfort. *Does he recognize me from the clearing?*

"You have to wait for this one to come back down Miss … " an Order member peers down at my ID card, " … Greyes." She lifts an eyebrow, as she speaks my last name.

"Okay," I say quietly stepping back from the doors.

"Don't make her wait for me," the Outsider speaks up. "By all means, where are your manners. Shouldn't it be *ladies first?*" He winks at me. "I don't know what passes for etiquette in this dome. It's not as if I'm going anywhere."

The group looks uncomfortable. Someone coughs and another clears his throat.

"We are going up quite a ways, sir," one of the younger Members speaks up from the rear of the elevator. "She looks like she's going home. Only has one floor to go."

"Well, she can't ride with him in here," the Member in the front dictates. He looks back at me, obviously irritated by my unintended interruption.

"Fine. Everyone off."

"And they say chivalry is dead," the Outsider says, winking at me again as he passes by. "Make sure to send it back down for us," he says, leaning toward me. "And don't forget to watch your step, Miss ... Greyes, was it?"

I tear my eyes away from him, my heart racing in my chest as my name rolls off his tongue. I duck into the elevator, still able to smell the earthy odor of the outside on his skin. As I step inside, I see something crumpled up on the floor and cover it with my foot. I slowly turn and press the lobby button on the elevator. As the doors close, his gaze locks with mine again, making a tingle run down my arms into my fingers. I look down at my shoe and move my foot to the side. The crumpled piece of paper stares back at me, but it's not really a piece of paper, it's a photo. I lean over and pick it up as the doors ding and open up.

I stuff the photo in my pocket, hurrying off the elevator and out of the Axis. The secretary barely looks up as I rush past. *What a crazy day!* And I still have to get to the clearing before the Order gets there.

CHAPTER 4

The perimeter of the fence is heavily monitored by Order members. I anxiously time their patrols and watch for an opening at my usual entrance. There, one streetlight's beam ends for a couple feet before the next one begins, allowing me the darkness I need to slip through and enter the forest unseen.

Trees are the perfect cover when an entire city is built to look down. Their leaves have always stretched out like a canopy, hiding me as I ran through them below. But tonight their trunks are just as useful, allowing me to stay hidden as I maneuver around Order members who are strategically placed while the Horticulturalists carry out their assignment.

The moonlight pierces through the trees, brightening as I approach the edge of the dome. My clearing is up ahead, but I can also hear voices. I'm too late.

"I can't believe we got called out for one tree," a man grumbles.

"Had someone been more thorough the first time around," a woman responds, "then we wouldn't be in this mess."

"Sounds like we're out here because the Director flipped out over nothing, as usual."

"It's that Outsider, not this tree that has him on edge."

The buzzing of a saw cuts off the voice then stops.

"It makes you wonder, doesn't it?" the man speaks up.

"What does?"

"How did that Outsider get around without any evidence of radiation sickness?"

"He was wearing protection."

"No, he wasn't. I was in the lobby when they brought him in.

"You don't know everything, plus, who cares? We have more important things to worry about. Like right now, this tree."

"But what if it's safe outside?"

"Then they'll let us know after they talk to him."

The saw starts up again. I creep around the perimeter of the clearing until I reach the bushes that rest against the edge of the dome. I crouch down, until I'm lying on my stomach, and then drag myself along the ground, concealed amongst the bushes.

Ahead I can see something shine in the dirt. I scoot faster, my sounds masked by the saw. When I'm almost within arm's reach, the shape of the locket is visible. How could I have been so stupid? I start to reach out of the bushes when two Order members burst into the clearing. The saw abruptly stops, leaving echoes of its vibrations ringing through the air.

"How are things going?" An Order member close to my age points to the tree.

"Almost done," the woman replies. "Are you here to help us haul out the pieces?"

"Leave them for the morning," the other Order member says, waving his hand dismissively as he turns in my direction. He's older than his partner, but it's not until he turns around and I see his face that my chest tightens and panic courses through my veins; he's the one who peered through the glass when the Outsider was captured.

"Did the Outsider really look inside here?" the other horticulturalist asks.

"Right over here," the older Order member says walking toward me as he puffs out his chest. "After I apprehended him, I noticed something wasn't right with the glass on the dome out there. As I got closer I noticed his handprint; and on the other side was that rotten, old tree. You scientists sure missed this one," He grunts. "All this wasted space could be creating more oxygen."

"We've got a job to get back to," the woman says, irritation at the edge of her words.

"Hold on!" the younger member exclaims. "Well, what do we have here?"

Is it my locket? Or worse, have they spotted me? I freeze, tucked under the bushes, too afraid to breathe. If they catch me, that's it. Everything Grandmother said will come true, only worse because they will think I'm the one conspiring with the Outsider.

"I'll be," the older member says, slapping his partner on the back. "Get my kit out of my pack for me, rookie."

"What did you two find?" the male horticulturalist asks.

"Another handprint," the younger member says as he leans

down and rummages through his bag. He's low enough that if he were to turn his head, he'd see me staring back at him. I don't even dare blink, straining to control every ounce of my body. He grabs a box from the bag and stands up, while I slowly let out an exhale.

"I think we may have found our person of interest," the older member says. He steps toward the bushes, one foot landing on my locket and the other close to my head. So close, I could reach out and grab him. After a few minutes he exclaims, "Got it! This might be our first chance at catching those rebels. Great job, rookie."

"Really?" I can't see the face of the younger member, but I can hear the pride in his voice. I'm not as congratulatory. I know that once they run those prints, I'm screwed.

You two get back to work now, and don't speak a word of this, got it?"

"Yes, sir." The sarcasm drips from the woman's voice.

The sound of the Order members crunching through the woods adds to my panic. How long will it take them to run that print? I know there's a record of my prints in the database, from when I started at the Learning Institute. Everyone's are taken on registration day.

"Do you really think a rebel was in this clearing?" the male horticulturalist asks.

"If they were, they better be careful."

The rev of the saw fills the air as they begin working again.

I reach for my locket, where it's embedded into the dirt, and dig it out with my trembling fingers. *My handprint.* I can't get it out of my head. The ramifications of this are overwhelming. What's going to happen to me now? Is there a way to get out of this? Maybe someone can hack into the system for me. Someone like Jak.

The locket comes loose and I grasp it in my hand as I crawl through the bushes. The saw still roars through the air, as I make my way back to the trees. Once I'm standing again, I dash through the forest, not caring who might hear me. What could be worse than the fate that awaits me now? I'll be sent to the Learning Institute for reformation, or worse, to B2 to live among the screams. I'm not sure which is worse.

By the time I reach the fence, I'm so worked up, I can barely see between my tears. I crawl through the space in the fence and sprint away into the darkness, hiding in the shadows until I'm safe at home. But I know this won't be good enough; no one is safe from his or her actions under the dome.

As I burst into my bedroom, Grandmother is sitting on my bed holding my mother's notebook.

"Where have you been?" she hisses at me. "You missed supper."

"I had to go back to the clearing—"

"You did what!" She jumps up and slaps me with such force I fall back against my bedroom door.

I cradle my cheek as tears run down my face. She has never struck me before, and though I know this time I have gone too far, my tears are not from the sting of her hand as much as my own fear, because this time I know she's right.

"I told you to never, ever, go back there. Do you have any

idea what you are doing?"

"I had to. I dropped my locket earlier and overheard at work they were going to the clearing to cut down a tree. I knew if they found it, they would come after me."

She sits down and throws the notebook on the floor as her hands tremble. She clutches her fingers together in her lap and stares at them as if they're something foreign now. She looks up at my cheek, where I feel the red welt growing. "Oh, Nat," she whispers. "Do you really have no recollection of what happened before? They wouldn't come after you, they would come after us."

"I don't understand," I say. "Why would they come after you?"

"When your parents had their ... unfortunate accident, the Order members came. Do you remember what they did to your grandfather?"

I remember it all too well. It was nine years ago, and I was playing hopscotch on the front sidewalk with other kids. Order Members trampled through our game and entered our building. I had never seen them before, in their crisp suits, and couldn't help but follow them up to the apartment, all the way to my grandparents' unit.

No one saw me standing there when the men said my parents' expedition went *terribly* wrong. The entire Expedition team had been killed by radiation poisoning. I turned, and ran down the stairs, into the street, but didn't stop there. I passed all the familiar faces and buildings I knew until I no longer recognized anything. I kept running, blinded by the watery world of my tears. And that was when I found the opening to the Outer Forest.

"I ran away, remember."

"Oh, that's right," she nods. "Your grandfather got up to run after you, but the Order wouldn't let us leave. We were detained, and there were so many questions—accusations that turned to threats. You know how Grandfather can be. So stubborn. He turned the tables and started accusing the Director and the Order, until finally they took him away."

All I remember was holding Grandfather's hand at the funeral. Was he gone before that? He was silent for such a long time afterward, but wasn't that from the grief?

"What did they accuse you of?"

"They thought your parents were involved in something untoward. They never explained it to us, but it couldn't have been good. Your mother, always scribbling in that notebook. She had too many questions. Thankfully, they cleared your parents in time for a funeral, even if there were no bodies to bury."

"No bodies." My voice comes out in a whisper. "But that's not what happens in radiation poisoning, is it?"

She shakes her head. "It was the radiation that poisoned them, but something much worse killed them. By the time the members got their distress call, it was too late; they found the entire Expedition team had been attacked. Their bodies were ripped apart."

"By what?" I stammer, unable to digest this secret that has been kept from me half my life.

"After the Order identified who was who, we only had pieces to bury," Grandmother says, distant, as if she's returned to the moment she lost her two children. Both my father, and Uncle

Alec, died that day with my mother. Everyone important to me.

"What was it?" I plead. "Wild animals? The infected?"

"All of the families were sworn to secrecy," she says, ignoring me. "No need to interrupt the peace of the dome when the threat was outside it. They assured us the responsible party was taken care of."

"But what was it?"

"We were never told," She snaps her head in my direction, coming back to the present. "The expeditions were shut down and life moved on. That's how you survive, by looking forward. Aren't you listening, Natalia? You don't ask questions—they bring trouble."

The bed groans as she stands up to leave. She pauses, staring at the floor where my mother's notebook is sprawled open. "And get rid of that. Nothing good comes from digging up the past."

"I will not. It's all I have left."

"You never listen," she turns to me, her eyes flashing with anger. "You'll end up taking us down with you. I won't have it. You leave me no choice."

She slams my bedroom door shut behind her, and I hear the click of the lock slide across the outside. The lock she installed shortly after my parents were killed when I used to sneak out at night and go to our old apartment. The lock she used to trap me, like the dome traps her. *No!* She can't lock me in here. I need to go see Jak. I run to the door, and try the handle, but it resists against my hands. I bang on the door, but I know it's pointless. Grandmother's paranoia has no reasoning.

With my back against the wall, I slide down and slump to the floor. My head is spinning with too many questions to handle. Has my entire life been a lie? If my parents weren't killed by radiation, what killed them? I reach in my pocket and pull out the locket, flipping it open to see the photo of my parents. *What killed you? What tore you apart?* To die in such a terrible way—I can't bear the thought.

One thing I know, it could not have been an infected. Someone would have spotted them out there by now. Although, when no one is allowed in the Outer Forest, how can people see what dangers are outside the dome?

I close the locket, and reach for the notebook, but notice the photo I found in the elevator fell onto the floor next to it. It's a photo of a girl, with pigtails and a large grin plastered across her face; she might be three years old. I flip it over onto its back and see the initials N.G. My initials. I flip the photo back over and hold it up to the one on my nightstand. The similarities are undisputable.

How did the Outsider get a photo of me? Did someone give it to him, or worse, did he steal it from my parents? Was he the one who killed them? I fall to my bed; I don't know what to think. Questions roll around inside my head until I'm so overwhelmed the room begins to spin and I succumb to exhaustion.

CHAPTER 5

After a fitful night dreaming of the Order banging down our door, I wasn't sure if I'd ever see my friends again. But the sunlight of morning woke me to not only an unlocked bedroom door, but also a tiny shred of hope that everything that happened yesterday had just been a dream. A terrible, screwed up, dream.

"I can't believe I missed your birthday!" Xara exclaims.

"Yesterday was crazy. I started my contribution—and—stuff."

Her dark ringlets jump around her face as she squeals. "You're eighteen now!"

"Happy birthday, Nat," Jak says in his quiet voice, standing next to her. Though we've all been friends since we started school, Jak is often left in the shadows of Xara's enthusiasm.

"Did you get anything good?" Xara asks. "Or is that too much to ask of your grandmother?" She doesn't hide her eye roll. Xara has put up with me and my frustration with Grandmother for nearly a decade. But she's never complained; the sign of a true friend.

I hold out the locket from my neck and can't help but let a smile spread across my lips when Xara's mouth drops. But I'm not going to open it and show her the photo inside. It's a final secret between my parents and me; something I will never have again.

"Wow, Nat," Xara leans in, "that's gorgeous. Real jewelry. You're so lucky. All my mom gave me was a book about etiquette."

"Maybe she's trying to tell you something," Jak pipes up. Xara punches him in the arm as he hides his face.

"What did you get?" she asks Jak.

"A tie," he beams. "Perfect for working as a Delegate one day."

"You wish." Xara snorts. "You're a business district boy. You'll end up in a bank, at best."

It's true. Jak is from a more privileged area than Xara and me, but she doesn't have to be so single minded. She knows that anyone can try for positions above their district. At eighteen, you get to leave the Learning Institute and go out into the real world where you have up to two years to figure out how you would like to contribute to the dome by trying out a variety of different jobs until you find your fit.

"Did you hear they found someone on the outside?" she says, her brown eyes wide with excitement. "Seriously. They brought him inside—I heard his skin was melting off from radiation exposure."

"No, I don't think that's right—"

"And I heard that the Order took him to the Axis so he could die with dignity."

I recall the Outsider's black eye. He looked pretty alive to me.

"I was asking where he came from, because no one seemed to be worried about that. Mom said in the olden days, people who didn't want to follow the rules of a dome were cast out."

"You think he's from the olden days?" I ask, holding a laugh in. If Xara only knew I'd seen the Outsider up close, she'd never stop talking about him.

"Of course not," she rolls her eyes again. "Don't you get it? He's from another dome. Maybe they still cast their rule-breakers to the outside still. Isn't it freaky? We could be housing a murderer for all we know?"

"But I thought you said his skin was melting off?" I tease.

"You can't believe everything you hear," she laughs.

"All that matters is he was contained," Jak says, seriously. "The Order looks out for us."

I shift uncomfortably. The Order sure did a number to the Outsider, maybe he was a criminal.

"So, what's the plan?" Xara changes the subject.

"I thought we could visit the museum?" Jak offers. "I hear they have an excellent exhibit on—"

"Ugh, Jak, no," Xara scrunches up her nose. "Nat is eighteen now, we can use her to do something fun."

"But it's an exhibit on the Order." Jak's light blue eyes light up. "There's even a piece on the Director and the Delegates."

Jak has always been somewhat obsessed with the Director. Since he was a child, he's dreamed about becoming a Delegate and assisting in the management of our dome.

"I've got it!" Xara squeals, ignoring Jak. "Let's go to a movie, a grown-up one!"

"Yes!" I shout back. An older couple across the street stops and looks at us. Xara and I giggle quietly, then link arms with Jak, and make our way to the theater.

I've never been allowed into the adult side of the theater. Only cartoons and family shows are available to those seventeen and under. All romance and adventure are saved for eighteen and above. Mom once told me there used to be scary movies, but they were removed because they didn't contribute to the dome's motto for peace.

Along the path to the theater, posters of a woman's face are stuck to a few light posts with the word *Missing* printed below. Posters like this used to pop up often when I was a child, but the Order fined those who put them up. Missing posters don't contribute to peace in the dome—they strum up feelings of suspicion and mistrust. But everyone knows no one can really go missing in the dome. If someone disappears, it means they want to start a new life.

Beyond the row of posters, the theater comes into view. I've always appreciated the style of the movie theater building. Its old architecture resembles photos of the old world, and the elaborate carvings on the pillars at the entrance have always captivated me. But everything seems different now that I'm older, and can enter the other side of the theater. It's as if the mystery has finally peeled away, and all that's left is carved stone.

I scan my ID badge at the door and it clicks open, allowing

Xara and Jak to sneak in behind me. It's not long before they're eighteen, so we may as well all enjoy the perks together. We grab our snacks then sneak down the dark aisle, taking our seats together in a middle row. Friends forever. Nothing can come between us.

The screen lights up, showing the original logo of the dome spinning in the center. This is the last place the old logo can be found: a circle enclosing two hands holding a heart. The true presentation of the motto: Peace. Love. Order. *Dome* was only added by our current Director, as a way to remind everyone of why we do what we do: everything for the dome. The words scroll across the bottom of the screen as the Director appears, sitting at a table with the Delegates. His message begins.

> *"I want to take a moment from my busy schedule to thank the people of Dome 1618 for another excellent year. As we carry on with the job given to us by our forefathers, it reminds me how lucky we are to have a dome that understands the importance of all aspects to our motto. We all must keep these words sacred if we are to survive into the future. Peace, love, and order to you all."*

The screen goes black and I slump back into my seat, ready for the show. But half an hour later I'm bored by the slow build to romance, and the main character's selfless commitment to the people of his society. I almost choke on my drink; I've heard this rhetoric in all the children's movies, but on a more immature level. What on earth made me think that movies would be better now that I'm eighteen?

I reach for popcorn and awkwardly brush against Jak's fingers. I start to laugh and then see his face redden, so I quickly withdraw my hand to the arm of my seat. Xara shushes me at the same time and I feel ridiculous. Being eighteen makes me feel less like an adult and more like a child. I shift in my seat, wondering if there is some way I can sneak out.

Jak reaches over and covers my hand with his, sending tingles up my arm. My fingers separate, allowing his to intertwine, and it feels warm and safe. I've always thought of him as a brother, nothing more. Why not? He's the quiet one of our trio, always watching and listening, never fighting for the spotlight. Yet, he's good at everything he does, and everyone loves him. I guess it wouldn't hurt to stay a little longer, but why does this feel so awkward?

Jak's scent drifts over, a mix of soap and ink, remnants of his parents' print shop in the business district where he spends his time after school. It's such a different smell from yesterday, when the Outsider leaned in close to me. His bronzed skin and dark hair are the complete opposite of Jak's blonde hair and pale skin. Jak is confident, but the Outsider has something more, a self-assurance that was borderline arrogant. But he wasn't like that toward me, only the Order, even after they gave him a beating. Is he brave or just plain stupid? My stomach flutters as a smile crosses my lips. Whatever he is, it's exciting to have something new happen inside the dome.

I shift in my seat again, this time moving my hand out from under Jak's hold, unable to stop thinking about the Outsider. Xara nudges me and give me a surprised look as she mouths the word, *Ohmigosh!* She finds the oddest words and phrases and throws them around like everyone knows what she's talking about. Her mother is the Curator at the Hall of Records and is always making Xara study books from the past. That's where Xara hopes to work one day. I picture her sitting at her desk telling people what *buzzkills* they all are.

I know she's thinking about Jak and me, but my cheeks are flushed from thinking about the Outsider. When the movie finally ends and we get up to leave, Jak grabs my hand again. But it's not the same feeling as before. I feel a sudden urge to be alone.

"We can go to your museum now," Xara says, then, turning, she notices our hands interlocked, "unless you two wanted to go alone?"

I could kill Xara right now. Jak's face reddens and I'm pretty sure I can see sweat break out above his upper lip. I abruptly let go of his hand for the second time in the last hour.

"Sorry," I say. "I have to get ready for work." It's half-true.

"What?" Xara asks, her lips trying to hold back a smirk as she looks between Jak and me. "Are you sure you have to go?"

"Those toilets won't scrub themselves." I force a laugh, hoping no one notices. Jak offers a smile, making his dimples appear. My face heats, and for a second I wish I'd never let go of his hand. I wave to my friends and leave. How unexpected my afternoon has become.

CHAPTER 6

Work drags on for two weeks. Every day I get home grumpier than I was the day before, and tonight is no different. I haven't actually scrubbed any toilets—not sure who's job that is—but I swear, if I have to keep polishing windows, I'm going to lose my mind. I've been promoted, up to the Order offices on Floors 5 & 6, but it's still the same duty.

One thing I've done since moving up was try to find the Outsider again, but that quickly came to a dead-end. I thought they might have him holed up in one of their offices, but no such luck. I mentioned it to Xara a couple of times, but she looked at me like I was crazy for dwelling on it. If only I could tell her about the photo.

I attribute another aspect of my grumpiness to the fact I can't return to my clearing. That was my one sacred place, and now it's been taken from me. I only made it back once, and found every piece of my hollow tree had been hauled away, and the clearing was now home to rows of saplings, ready to grow into great trees and provide oxygen inside the dome. It's totally unfair.

But the horror of what could happen if that handprint is traced to me still haunts me at night. Grandmother hasn't mentioned it again, and the Order hasn't come banging our door down; but honestly, how long can it take to run fingerprints? I've tried asking Jak, but without giving him all the background information on what happened with the Outsider, I can't seem to come up with a reason that doesn't make me look guilty of something. I know I'm in the system—every resident is when they start at the Learning Institute—eventually my name has to show up.

In an attempt to pretend everything is normal, I've spent a lot of time in my bedroom pretending to be busy, or sleeping. Mostly, I read Mom's notebook.

My friends have gotten busier since I've withdrawn. Xara was accepted into a permanent position at the Hall of Records last week. I am a little jealous, I'll admit; she's known her place in the dome all along. Jak took an administrative position at the Axis a couple of days after we held hands at the movies; he claims he's already working on a special project. I'm the last one left; I have nowhere to go.

I drop my head to my hands, as I sit on the edge of my bed. If my parents were still alive, would I have become a scientist like them? Would they be disappointed if they could see me now, the daughter of the Greyes scientists, unable to decide what she wants to do with her life? The sound of a knock snaps me from my self-pity.

"Come in."

Grandfather enters with two cups of tea. "I thought you could use this." He smiles. "You seem a little off lately."

I look up into his eyes as I sit up in bed. Even my curtains are drawn, to hide the depressing view of the Outer Forest. I want to tell him everything from the beginning, about the two Outsiders and the handprint. I want to tell him about working at the Axis and B2, and how I know he spent time down there. I want to tell him I know about what really happened to Mom and Dad and pour my heart out to the one who has sacrificed more than the rest of us. Instead, I look down at the tea, now resting between my hands and I say, "I'm fine."

"You know something, Nat," he says, sitting on the foot of my bed that creaks under his weight. His thin white hair is carefully combed off his face, so his round eyes are left unconcealed. "Eighteen is a hard age. It marks so many changes. You leave the comforts of school and enter the work force. Your friends move on in different directions as they figure out their lives, and you might wonder if you'll grow apart. Some people take the entire two years they're allowed, to try to find what will be their permanent contribution to the dome. It's a time of uncertainty, a time when you can easily be influenced." He rests his hand on mine.

I look back up into his eyes, which are surrounded by lines that reveal his age. I do not want to lie to the man who has raised me for half of my life, but telling him the truth might break him. "I promise I won't screw up anymore, Grandfather. I've caused enough trouble."

His eyebrows push together as he shakes his head. "What do you know of trouble at your age?"

"Grandmother told me about what happened to you after Mom and Dad died."

"Your parents were heroes. People forget that when they're scared."

"I know. People still recognize the name. Everyone thought they symbolized the chance for an Outer colony."

Grandfather sighs. "My little Nat, there's so much you don't know. So much I'd like to tell you, but you're still a kid. That colony was the most important thing to your parents. They would have never left that day had they known they wouldn't return ... " his voice breaks.

Tears flood my eyes. I lose control.

"I need to tell you something," I confess. "I used to hide in the Outer Forest. But they found my clearing, and I can't go back." I look back down into my tea.

"I know you have your secrets," he says, winking. "We all do."

"I stopped because I thought they caught me. I swear, Grandfather, I only went there to see the outside. It reminds me of Mom and Dad."

"If the Order suspected you, they would have come and asked all of us about it," Grandfather says. "It doesn't sound like you have anything to worry about."

He stands from my bed, and walks to my window, opening the curtains. The curve of the dome appears above us. "Your mother's favorite things were the stars that shone through the dome. Did you know that?"

I nod. Her grandmother had told her tales of how the skies were once blanketed in stars, before the clouds of the Cleansing War. Only in the last few decades have the clouds begun to part, revealing the hidden skies behind them. At night, their glitter peeks out in clusters through the thick, black dust settled on the outside of the top of our dome. I can only imagine what a sky blanketed in stars would look like.

Grandfather notices the tiny photo on my nightstand. "Where on earth did you get this?" I jump from bed, in an attempt to stop him, but he picks it up before I can reach him. He flips it over to the other side, reading the back, and his hand begins to tremble.

"You don't understand." Panic makes my mouth so dry, I feel like I have to force each syllable out. "I saw the Outsider before they did. There were two of them. One came over to me from the outside of the dome—I think he wanted to tell me something. But he ran when the Order came. The other one had this photo of me. How is that possible?"

"I don't know," his voice comes out barely louder than a whisper. Then silence. I shift from one foot to the next, wishing he would stop staring at the photo and just say something to me. Anything.

"Could you go out for a bit? I need to speak with Grandmother." I don't move. This was not what I expected. He looks up at me, his eyes glossy and pleading. "Will you do this, please? For me?"

My words spill out quickly. "I'm sorry. I swear I didn't mean to lie about the other Outsider. I should have told you sooner. I should have reported it to the Order."

"No," he advises, giving me a reassuring smile. "You did the right thing. Go on. Now." There's a strain in his voice at the end of his sentence.

I'm not going to make him ask me again. I grab my notebook, and leave our apartment building. Grandfather knows something, I'm sure of it. The other thing I'm sure of is that Grandmother will be livid with me.

After a few blocks, my feet stop moving, and I look up. They've taken me to a familiar place—Jak's home. It's late, but his bedroom light is on. When I had to get farther from home than down the hall to Xara's apartment, Jak's place was my only option. Though his mother never approved of her only child hanging with two girls from the apartment districts, she looked the other way because of our parent's positions in the dome. For me it was the ultimate escape. Where better than the townhouses of the business district to make me feel like I was in another world?

Jak answers my knock. Surprise crosses his smooth forehead and blue eyes, but his thin lips break into a smile. "Nat, what are you doing here?"

"Are you free? I needed to get away."

"I was working on some algorithms for work, but that can wait. Are you okay?"

I nod and follow him inside, up to his bedroom; a place where we three friends spent many an afternoon reading books, playing games, and hanging out. It feels good to be back inside the Manning house. Jak's parent's bedroom door is already closed, so it's just Jak and me. All alone.

"I can't remember the last time you were here." Jak laughs. He walks over to his desk and closes a notebook filled with numbers and calculations. I sit on his bed and lie back against his pillows. His desk creaks against its old joints, as he leans on it. Not even the business district gets new furniture.

"Jak, what is the worst thing you've ever done?"

"I don't understand."

Of course he doesn't. Jak was born to serve the dome. He'd never be caught skulking in the Outer Forest, hauling around forbidden objects, like his dead mother's work notes, or interacting with Outsiders. Not Jak. He was squeaky clean.

I sigh. "Why do you want to be a Delegate?"

He crosses his arms against his chest. "I want to work at the Axis—not as a Member of the Order, of course."

"Yeah, but *why?*"

"To make the dome a better place. Hopefully I get to work somewhere in Policies one day."

"You've always known." I lean on my side, watching him stand at his desk. "Not me. I still have no idea."

"You just need something that excites you." His cheeks flush.

"Nothing excites me."

"I haven't told anyone," he says, unfolding his arms and running a hand through his short blonde hair, as a flash of enthusiasm grows in his eyes. "I get to start working tomorrow in the Director's office. They say it's a two-week trial, but if everything goes well, it's permanent. Guess what my title would be? Assistant to the Director!"

"Jak, that's awesome!" I sit up and he joins me on the bed. Our fingers touch, and electricity runs up my arm again. I look at Jak's face. He's my oldest friend. The one I learned to ride bikes with. The one I ran races against. Jak. He has always been there for me, visiting every day after my parents died to make sure I was okay. My Jak. Why have I never seen him in this light, until now?

I lean forward, and feel Jak's soft lips push against mine. His familiarity is a comfort. His mouth moves faster as he pushes his tongue past my parted lips. It feels awkward, but nice, and for the moment, I forget everything that is happening outside this room. For the moment, I'm carefree.

The kiss ends as softly as it began. I lean back and smile, and Jak smiles back.

"I've wanted to do that since we were twelve," he says.

"You did!" I feel my cheeks get hot. "Why didn't you, then?"

"We were barely teenagers," he says, looking away as he wrings his hands together. "You weren't interested in boys or kissing. At least I didn't think you were until you snuck off at lunch one day at school, and kissed James Poole behind the locker rooms."

"James Poole!" I burst into laughter, quickly covering my mouth so not to wake his parents. "Xara dared me to kiss him because I was the only girl in our grade that hadn't. She bet me a chocolate I wouldn't do it. You know me. I hate to lose."

Jak's face is red when he looks back at me. "I was so mad at James that I knocked him over on our way to class." He reaches over and grabs my hand, covering it with his palm.

"All because I kissed him?"

He nods. "In that moment I realized I didn't want anyone else to kiss you."

I laugh, but it comes out strained. The uncomfortable feeling I got in the movie theater starts to creep back under my skin, and I try to pull my hand from Jak's grip. "We were kids."

His gaze bears down on me as his grip tightens. "That's when I realized I was—in love with you." He doesn't take his eyes off mine, as if the answer he wants lies somewhere deep within me. He is dead serious.

"In love?"

"Yes," he whispers. "I love you, Nat."

A cold sweat breaks across my skin. The room feels like it's closing in on me. Trapped. For the first time ever, Jak's room is not a refuge, it's a prison. His hand lets mine go, distracted by my silence, or his own confession. Whatever it is it allows me the chance to slip my hand out from under his, and rub it along my pant leg.

"I don't know what to say," I stammer. I look away, not wanting to see his face anymore. Uneasiness bubbles into my stomach.

"You don't have to say anything." His shoulders slump forward, and I feel pity for my quiet friend. I have only seconds to save this friendship.

"Jak," I put my hand on his shoulder, "I just learned your feelings for me, which will take me time to process, but I came here to tell you something else. Something more important."

"More important than me confessing my love?" The hurt is plain in his voice. You must have had some idea at the movies?"

he asks. His eyes search mine looking for the answer he wants to hear.

My voice cracks. I'm overwhelmed by his intensity; it's too much.

"I'm in trouble. I need your help," I blurt out. Tears spring to my eyes.

His brows raise and then push together, and he grabs my hand again, but this time he's gentle "Tell me what's wrong. Let me help."

What am I going to tell him? Confess how I've broken the rules all these years? Jak, who believes in the dome like no one else I know. Jak, who's about to start working alongside the Director, the most powerful person in the dome? Jak, who loves the only person in this place who cares the least for the rules?

I stare at his face, so trusting and innocent. He's never suffered loss. But the question is, can I trust him? I'm not sure, or am I just being paranoid? But he's still Jak. Maybe even more *mine* than he was before I came tonight. I don't know where to start, so I have no choice but to go to the beginning.

I tell Jak everything from my clearing in the dome, to the encounters I had with the one Outsider. But I leave out the second Outsider, my Grandfather's ordeal with the Order years ago, and the photo I found in the elevator. I'm not ready to give everything up. I end with my Grandmother's slap a fortnight ago, before finally releasing my tears.

Jak's arms surround me, and pull me close, holding me tight as I sob into his chest. The information overload, combined with recent confessions, has turned me into a blubbering fool.

My mother's notebook pokes into my side. I know what I have to do next. It's a sacrifice for my family.

"Can you help me? I need you to dispose of this." I pull out the notebook, and hand it to Jak.

"What?" Jak hesitates. "But that's—"

"Yes," I interrupt, "I know what it is. But I need it destroyed. They'll eventually match me to the handprint. There are things my mother wrote in here; her hopes, dreams, and opinions. I don't want the Order to be able to use it against me, or use it to drag her name through the mud. Please, Jak, do this for me."

"It'll be ok, Nat," Jak runs his hand down my hair. "You have excellent explanations for everything. Yes, you knew you shouldn't be in the Outer Forest, but it's been a sanctuary for you since you were nine. How can they blame a little girl who lost her parents? Should you know better now? Yes, you aren't denying that. But the Outsider? That's not your fault. As for what happened to your parents, that's conjecture. There will always be conspiracy stories in the dome regarding what happened to the Expedition scientists, if you listen in the right places."

"You're right." I take a deep breath. It feels nice to be held like this, as he downplays my worries. He kisses my forehead, as he takes the notebook from my hands. My last real connection to my parents, gone with a kiss.

Jak walks me home, holding my hand in his delicately, as if I could break. We make our way up the street to my grandparents' apartment. The night is perfect, and kissing him at my door, before he leaves me for the night, doesn't seem as overwhelming as it would have a little bit ago. The thought leaves my cheeks warm, and I'm about to imagine what it might feel like, when a block away I see two Order members leaving, with Grandfather between them.

I let go of Jak's hand and scream, "No!", but Jak grabs me from behind, and spins me around into the wall of the building beside us, kissing me with such eagerness it hurts, but there's no passion in it—he's blocking me from the Order. Over his shoulder I see them disappear into their car, and drive away with Grandfather.

"What did you do that for?" I yell, striking my fists against Jak's chest as soon as he lets me go. "You had no right!"

"I'm protecting you from yourself." He grabs my wrists, but I wrestle free. I will not let him restrain me again.

"Go away!" I shout, turning and running into the apartment building. I brace myself between the narrow walls of the stairwell as I take the stairs two at a time. In the hallway I stumble toward the apartment, as my world begins to crumble around me. Grandfather is the last link I have to happiness. I dread a life alone with Grandmother.

The doorway of the apartment is wide open, and inside the chair and table from the kitchen are knocked over. I walk in, cautiously stepping over a spilled vase of fake flowers.

"Grandmother?"

There's no response.

I walk farther into the apartment, and see her standing at the picture window, staring out into the empty street, where Grandfather was taken. A cluster of stars shine in the distance, forming a halo around her silhouette.

"He's gone, Nat," Grandmother says quietly. "He's gone, and I don't think he'll ever return."

I walk up behind her and reach out to give her comfort. But when I see her reflection in the glass, it's not sadness that lies upon her face. It's hate. I drop my hand and take a step back. "What happened?"

"I warned you. I warned you to stay out of the Outer Forest. I warned you to follow the rules. None of this would have happened if you had listened to me."

I thought of my earlier conversation with Jak, and a pang of guilt cramped in my gut. None of this was his fault, but I took it out on him. But he was right; it wasn't my fault, either. I hadn't asked for any of this. I didn't invite the Outsider in. So what if I went to the Outer Forest? Was that really worth imprisonment?

"They wouldn't take Grandfather away because I was in the Outer Forest. It doesn't make any sense."

"Nat." Her voice is sharp and she turns toward me. I brace myself for another slap, but she only narrows her eyes. "This has nothing to do with you. Grandfather called the Order, to try to convince them that he had something to do with the Outsider—so he could protect you. But they already knew it was you, and now they've taken my husband away for treason."

"All because he lied about the picture?"

"You stupid girl. If you hadn't been in that clearing *he* never would have seen you."

"The Outsider?"

"Your uncle—the Order found his handprint on the outside of the glass, opposite yours. He's alive. Alec is back."

"Uncle Alec?" I stammer, trying to find the words to form a question, but all I can hear is, *Alec is back.* "How? You said he died with Mom and Dad."

"Apparently not." Grandmother steps away from the window. Her face comes into view, revealing where tears have trailed down her wrinkles to her pursed lips. "I assume that's where this came from." She tosses the small photo at me, then retreats to her bedroom door where she disappears, slamming the door behind her.

I stare at the photo, crumpled up on the floor. How could something so small have caused so much trouble? I know one thing that Grandmother doesn't. The person they have in the Axis, the Outsider, is not the same person who left the handprint on the dome. My Uncle Alec is somewhere outside still. Somewhere, alive.

CHAPTER 7

When I was growing up, there wasn't enough room to mourn for both my parents, and my uncle at the same time, so I pushed Alec into a small corner of my memories. He was only ten years older than me, so I was more of an inconvenience to him than a niece, and I followed him around everywhere he went. But, he did take time to show me things he found. He was an apprentice geologist and passionate about rocks.

"Look here, Nat." Uncle Alec would demand my direct attention. "This is a river rock. Feel it. Its roundness was formed by the water, long before the Cleansing Wars. It represents how one element can be changed by another, showing there's magic in the world all around us. Your parents brought it back for me from one of their expeditions. One day I will get to go with them."

And he eventually did. Like Jak, he knew the field he wanted to work in before he was eighteen. Because of his passion, he was allowed to start directly in geology when he left the Learning Institute. For that entire year, he brought more and more rocks back to study from the outside. It's funny. I can hardly remember his face. But I can picture almost every rock he had in his collection.

But now, as I wake up, my memory haunts me with his face. Not the one from my childhood, but the one on the other side of the dome wall. My uncle is alive.

We should be celebrating, but instead, the apartment feels like the shroud of death envelops us. Grandmother hides in her room, and Grandfather has been sent to the Axis—most likely to B2, the floor that haunts people with the sound of screams. I'd spent the last weeks worrying about myself, and now the only other person who cared is gone. What's next? As if to answer my thoughts, the doorbell buzzes.

The sound persists, but Grandmother's footsteps don't move toward it. I leave my room, pausing by her bedroom, and peek inside. The curtains are drawn, blocking out whatever light is on the other side. She lies, still as a corpse, and I hold back from checking her pulse. She's fine, just unable to accept what might lie ahead. Sympathy washes over me; I know what it's like to have so many questions. Hers are so deep it's harder to quell them. I close her door and answer the main one.

But as soon as I open it, I wish I hadn't. A Member of the Order stares at me, eyeing me up from head to toe. "Natalia Greyes?"

My stomach lurches, and my pulse races. "Yes." Visions of handcuffs, cells on B2, and swollen eyes overtake my mind.

"You are instructed to report to the Order, Axis, Floor 16," she commands.

It's as if I'm watching myself in slow-motion, from up above. My mouth hangs open, and I freeze, standing there like a child, unable to react.

"Immediately, Miss Greyes." The member raises an eyebrow. "Get dressed and gather your things, please. You will not be returning to the apartment district."

But Floor 16 is not B2. It's far above even the Order offices.

"Do I need my uniform," I ask with an ounce of hope that she might shed some light on where I'm going.

She shakes her head.

I bite the inside of my cheek. "How am I supposed to know what to pack?"

"We have an appointment to keep. Don't make me ask again."

I turn away, shuffling to my room. Every step intensifies the questions bouncing around in my head, the biggest being, *what is going to happen to me?* I grab an overnight bag from my closet, and stuff it with a change of clothes and some personal items. I take the two photos from my nightstand, the one with my parents and the one of me alone; seems fitting, seeing as it caused this mess. With everything stuffed in my bag, I slip my locket into my pocket.

I return to the hallway, pausing one last time by Grandmother's bedroom door, where I place my palm against its smooth surface. *If only you didn't hate me the moment I came to live here, reminding you of everything you lost. If only you loved me enough to come out here and stop this.* My hand drops from her door, and I turn to face my condemnation. I will not show this stranger any fear.

"Let's go," I say, holding my chin up as I step outside the apartment, and close the door behind me.

We arrive at the Axis in speedy fashion. Members are the only ones allowed an electric vehicle. It helps them to carry out their business with the swift hand of justice. As we enter the large lobby, the secretary glances from behind her desk. In a flash, her eyebrows furrow, but she looks away, focusing back on her work as we approach. The member passes her a sheet.

"Insert your old card, please," the secretary says, after a quick scan of the paper. I reach into my bag, and pull out the card that is still attached to my work shirt. The member grabs it from me, and sticks it in the same slot it was spit out of only a few weeks ago. I watch as it's sucked back in, eliminating the last trace of my existence, here in the dome. Within seconds a new card pops out. This one has my photo like the one that disappeared, only, underneath it reads—*Natalia Greyes, Science Division, Floor 16*.

"Science Division?" I stare at the card as the member hands it to me. "I'm confused." The secretary's brow inches up, and then she looks back at her desk before the member can see.

"Let's go," the Member commands.

I follow her to the elevators, still confused. *Where am I going? Are they going to interrogate me upstairs?* Inside the elevator, she presses the button for Floor 16, and the elevator begins its quick ascent. B2 shines at the bottom, and I can't help but think of Grandfather.

"Will I get to see my grandfather?"

She blatantly ignores me, staring straight ahead through her perfectly trimmed bangs. Her lips are pursed between her pale round cheeks, but at their edges are smile lines. She looks tired, not mean—maybe I can appeal to her lighter side. "Listen," I say, clearing my voice. "I think I deserve to know what's going on here before you start torturing me for information.

She bursts out laughing. "Torture? What do you think goes on in the Science Division?"

My face instantly gets hot. *What am I missing?* The elevator dings, and the doors pop open. Her nametag flashes as she walks past me onto Floor 16. *Rowenna London, Science Officer, Floor 16.*

"I don't understand." I chase after her, trying to keep up to her brisk pace. "You're wearing a symbol of the Order." I point to the arm of her jacket. "How can you be a part of the Science Division?"

"I watch over the Science Division. My job is to make sure everything runs smooth, stays on target, and follows the best interests of the dome."

"So you're the watchdog?" I eye her suspiciously. "Making sure nothing gets out of place? What am I supposed to be then? Your prisoner?"

"I will be keeping an eye on you." Rowenna stops, crossing her arms against her chest and looking me up and down. "This is your room. Once you're settled, you can join us on Floor 18. You'll soon learn that the Axis is a combination of living quarters and work areas for all employees. The Science Division takes up Floors 16-36."

"You aren't going to lock me in here?"

Rowenna laughs again, filled with a girlish tone, though she has to be in her mid-twenties. I walk into my new bedroom, a small, dorm-like rectangle with a dresser, bed, and desk connected in that order on either side of the room. "I still don't understand why I'm here."

Her face grows serious, eliminating all evidence of humor. "Honestly, I don't either. You didn't complete an entrance exam. You haven't completed any work terms."

"I didn't ask for this."

"Well, you'd better get used to it." She leans against my door frame. "Someone obviously wants you here. This is your permanent assignment now. You're here for life." She smiles as she steps back and the door slides shut, cutting me off from everything.

I turn back toward my room. *Permanent assignment?* How did that happen? I open my bag and dump the contents on my bed, flopping beside them. I wish I'd packed more than one change of clothes. I lean back onto my pillow and laugh out loud. Instead of being a prisoner on B2, I'm condemned to the Science Division.

The door to my room opens, and I'm greeted by another new face. This one has long, curly, blond hair and a smile plastered on her face like she just found a long, lost friend. She's a couple years older than me, and advances with slender fingers outstretched. "Hi, I'm Tassie Greenwood. Looks like we're roommates." Her smile reveals a flash of white teeth, highlighted by light-pink lip gloss, and her fingernails shimmer with a layer of pearl-pink polish. Every part of her is a reflection of the luxuries not allowed in the dome—at least, not outside the Axis.

"Nice to meet you." I force a smile. "I'm Nat."

"Is that all you brought?" Tassie points to my bag.

"Yes." I grab my clothes, and stuff them back in the bag. "I thought I was coming for one night. I didn't realize this was permanent. They didn't really give me any notice."

"Oh, you look like a little deer in the headlights." Tassie grabs my hands and pulls me up. "Come with me. I'll help you get sorted out. The odd one like you comes in. You must be a legacy, summoned to the big tower because of your parents."

I raise my eyebrows. I've never heard of legacies before.

"What area do your parents work in? Wait! Let me guess, Research and Development?"

"No. My parents are—dead." The words come out like heavy weights. I don't remember the last time I had to say those words. It's old news to everyone back home. I let go of her hands, and cross my arms, pulling them tight to my chest.

"I'm so sorry." Tassie pats my shoulder. "They must have been scientists, though. Why else would you be here without any notice?"

I nod. "They were." But that's all I say. For the first time since I can remember, one person won't look at me like the poor orphan of the Greyes scientists. Today, I want as little attention as possible.

"Let's get you some clothes." Tassie's girlish voice breaks apart the tension in the air. She grabs my hands again, and pulls me out into the hallway.

"So," she begins her tour, "every fifteen floors is a cafeteria.

Our division starts on Floor 16, so we have to use the cafeteria on Floor 30. Don't tell anyone, but sometimes I like to sneak down to the cafeteria on Floor 15. Gives a little variety to my day. Trust me, you get bored of the same fifty people or so to hang out with, day-in, day-out. Especially the boys."

We take the elevator to Floor 30, and it reveals a short hallway. To the north, is the cafeteria, where the clanging of dishes and the buzz of conversation comes through its doors. To the south, is a door labeled Science Division Depot. We go south.

"So, Nat," Tassie smiles, "what Floor are you working on?"

"Floor 18."

"I work on Floors 19 and 20. My area studies the plant life that old expeditions brought back. I'm excited to say that our entire Biological Research department was ecstatic to hear they were reopening Floor 18. It has been nearly a decade since we've seen anything new. One can only do so much with one strain of carrots!"

Her enthusiasm is a nice change, but I still don't know what happens on Floor 18. She talks so much, I understand how Jak must feel when he gets around Xara and me. A pang of guilt hits me at the thought of my best friends. I didn't get the chance to say goodbye to either of them. And if I don't get to apologize to Jak, I'll never forgive myself.

I turn around, and see that Tassie has filled up a cart with outdoor gear, lab gear, casual clothing, personal items, bedding, and tons of other items I never knew existed in the dome. She pushes the cart to the till and dread fills my gut.

"I have no way to pay for all of this."

Tassie shakes her head, letting her curls bounce around her smooth skin, "I have so much to teach you. All we need to do is swipe our ID cards. Everything is free!"

Tassie drops me off at our room, and leaves for work. I make my bed, noticing that these sheets have no tears or repair stitches on them. It takes me forever to put away my new clothes, I've never had this many before. I stand back, staring at the closet; it's bursting at the seams. So many luxuries are offered here in the Axis. What's the catch?

What do I wear to work? I grab a pair of scrubs, similar to Tassie's cotton pants and shirt. Before I leave the room, I look myself over in the mirror. For a moment, it's like my mom is staring back at me. *Am I walking in her shoes?*

Floor 18 looks like Floor 16. A long hallway extends past the elevator in both directions. The sign pointing to the north reads Meeting Room. The sign pointing to the south reads *Lab*. I go south.

I push the handle on the door, but it doesn't budge. A scanner hangs on the wall. I hold up my ID card, and the light on the scanner turns from red to green, and I hear a click. The door opens easily.

Inside the lab everything is bright white, illuminated by the fluorescent lights above. Two long tables run down the center of the room, with scientists working on either side. There are nine of them, including Rowenna. I make ten. Rowenna looks up and waves me over.

"Looks like you made out alright," Rowenna says looking me up and down again. "You managed to find Floor 30?"

"My roommate helped."

"Ah, yes," Rowenna nods, "the always-happy Tassie. She's a good worker. Should be a good roommate. Knows her place well."

"Rowenna—" I begin.

"Call me Roe."

"Roe, how am I supposed to know what to do around here? I have no training. Honestly, I barely paid attention in science classes at the Institute."

"I know, I've seen your transcripts." She sighs. "I'm putting you with Waldorf. He's a good teacher, patient. He'll teach you the basics, which is all you need to know. Trust me."

"But what do we do here?"

"Our role is mainly extraction. Get in and get out. That's it. We're the new Expedition team."

"What? They reopened the division?"

She nods. "You and Evan are new. From what I can tell, it's his outside expertise that sent him here."

"But I've never been—" I pause, about to say *outside*, when I see the Outsider stand up from a table and come toward us. My pulse races as my breath catches in my throat. *He's here, working in the Axis. He's not in a cell.* His hair has been trimmed, revealing more of the soft lines of his face. The faintest shadow of stubble runs along his jawline, meeting in the center, below his lips, which curl up slightly at the edges. I step back as he joins us.

"Nat, this is Evan." She tilts her head, frowning at me. "Have you met before?"

"Briefly." Evan smiles as he holds out his hand to me. I hold back, unsure of whether to touch him or not, but Roe is still watching me carefully. I reach across, and put my hand in his. His skin is warm, but rough. In slow motion, my gaze meets his.

"Nice to meet you again. Sorry, I didn't catch your name."

"It's Nat." I'm barely able to squeak it out. "Remember, we met at the elevator."

"Does Nat stand for something?"

"Natalia. Natalia Greyes."

"Greyes?" Evan says loud enough for everyone to hear. The other scientists look up from their stations, and I wish I had somewhere to run to. I slipped up. *This guy knocks me off my game.*

Roe evidently sees my distress. "Yes, everyone, we have the daughter of the famous *Greyes* on our team. Is that a reason to stop working? I think not. We have an expedition leaving in two days to prepare for. Everyone back to work. Evan, take Nat back to her room. You can fill her in on your roles."

"Yes, ma'am." Evan salutes Roe. A smile plays at the edge of her mouth.

"I think she likes you," I say to Evan once we are alone in the elevator.

"She's a little old for me." He laughs. "Plus, military women aren't really my type."

"You have a type?"

"You think these good looks get wasted on just anyone?" Evan points to himself. "I'll have you know, I like only the brightest. And a little *pretty* never hurt anyone."

I turn away from Evan, wishing we weren't stuck in this

elevator together. I'd met guys like him at the Institute; there was a reason I was one of the last girls to kiss James Poole.

"Come on now," Evan nudges my shoulder with his. "I'm pulling your leg. Where's your sense of humor?"

"I'm surprised you didn't leave yours on B2."

Silence fills the elevator as the doors slide open. He walks into the hallway, his back rigid as he calls out, "Aren't you coming?" His voice is raised. I walk past him to my room, but he follows me inside.

I turn toward him, about to ask him to leave, but he advances toward me. I step back until I bump against the wall. My heart beat feels like it's going to explode from my chest. He leans toward me, and I draw in my breath with a quiet gasp. The earthy smell is gone, replaced by the scent of cologne I've never smelled before. I close my eyes, and savor it as he reaches behind me. With a *click*, Tassie's music pod turns on, blaring some funky pop music. My eyes jump open.

"Eww." Evan shakes his head at the bouncing beats.

"What are you doing in here?" I can barely hear my voice.

"Elevators are about as private as the dorms around here." He gestures toward the ceiling.

I notice the cameras and instantly feel my skin crawl from under my scrubs. I undressed in here. Who the hell was watching?

"How are we supposed to hear each other over the music?" I shout.

Evan grabs my wrists, and pulls me close to his chest, and whispers in my ear. "Trust me, and speak slowly, like this." His breath tickles my neck, and his firm chest presses against mine, through the thin fabric of our lab clothes. He's stronger than I thought. His muscles tense as we sway together to the same rhythm.

I wrap my pale arms around Evan's neck, a stark contrast against his tanned skin which is weather-worn from the outside, touched by a sun I've never been allowed to feel. The pulse in his neck beats through his skin, vibrating close to the bend in my elbow. I want to run my finger over it, to feel the vibration against my own skin. I don't. I bite my lip and look away.

"They want us to help them find areas to examine outside," he whispers. A shudder runs down my back from the sensation of his breath against my bare neck. He pauses and clears his throat. *Does he feel it too?* "They figure my experience, combined with your mother's notebook, will lead them to where the last team left off."

"I don't have my mother's notes any longer."

He hesitates a moment. What does he know of my mother's notes?

"Maybe that's why you didn't end up on B2. They must think you're hiding it all up here." He removes a hand from the small of my back and runs it down my hair. Another shiver runs through me.

"I think they took my grandfather there."

"That, my dear, is not something I'm privy to."

"How did you get out?"

"They tried getting information out of me the old-fashioned way." His body tenses. "But when answers didn't come fast enough, I guess they felt killing me with love would work better." His humor is comforting.

"It looks like they gave you a haircut since I saw you last." I take a deep breath of his cologne again. "And possibly a bath?"

"Though company would have been nice, I did manage the bath on my own."

A nervous laughs sputters out, and I keep my face down, glad we are not face-to-face. Visions of Evan undressing to take a bath flood my head, and my skin heats. I need to change the subject.

"Where did you get that picture?"

"I needed to make sure you knew I was a friend."

"That doesn't explain why you had it." I bite my lip. It's now or never. "So, you didn't kill my parents?"

Evan grabs my shoulders and pulls me away from him, his steel gray eyes narrowing as his face reddens. "Is that what you think?"

"What am I supposed to think? You show up here with a photo of me, one that only my parents would have. They were killed on the outside, and that's where you come from. Then you just expect me to trust you? I don't even know you."

He raises his voice and starts to shake me, anger flashing in his eyes. "Do you know what I did to get here? The crap I put up with? I can't believe you think I had anything to do with your parent's death. It's ridiculous. What was that, nine years ago? I was eleven."

I shrug his hands from my shoulders and shrink away from him, the moment spoiled. Turning around, I shut off Tassie's music. The heat in my face is making me sweat. It was stupid, but Evan just showed me a quick-temper I'm not interested in putting up with.

"Please leave."

"Fine," Evan grumbles from behind me.

I don't turn around until the door slides shut, confirming I'm alone. Then I turn and crawl into my bed, pressing my warm cheeks into the cool cotton as I let out a scream. I'm stuck here, with a bunch of strangers, who expect things from me I can't provide. Now I know the reason I've been brought here. The Order still suspects my mother of something, after all these years. To them, I'm a link to the past, ready to lead them to the evidence they seek. What happens to me when they find out I'm useless?

I role onto my side and run my fingers under the pillow along the smooth sheet. What I wouldn't give for one of my mother's stitches to comfort me. Instead, I curl into a ball and don't move from my bed for the rest of the day. I hear the door slide open and shut, as Tassie comes to get me for lunch, but I decline. At suppertime, when I reject another invitation from her, she brings back Roe. Roe doesn't say a word to me, just watches for a minute, and then leaves. No one bothers me again.

CHAPTER 8

I open my eyes and see Jak sitting on the edge of my bed, half-asleep, propped against the wall of my cubby. His tall frame is hunched to fit at the end of my bed, and his short blonde hair is tousled from its usual perfect placement, crisscrossed as if he's been running his hands through it. I'm not sure I've ever heard Jak talk about being worried, let alone physically show it. His lashes flutter open as I shift in bed.

"Dreaming about me?" he murmurs.

I jolt up and throw my arms around him, pulling him tight against my body. His warm arms slide past my sides until they meet behind me, one resting against the small of my back and the other gently holding the back of my head to his shoulder. A sigh escapes my lips, threatening to wrack my body with sobs.

"Thank goodness!" Tassie squeals. She's sitting on the edge of her bed, watching intently. "I was so worried about you. No one has had a roomie lose it before. I'm going to pay special attention to you from now on, I promise."

I glance up at the camera set deceitfully above us. "There are enough people watching me already. What I need are some friends."

Jak laughs. "You talk like you're in prison."

Tears spring to my eyes, and I push myself away from him to cover my face. Tassie slips out of the room, and Jak slides next to me, holding out his hand, then tucking them back at his sides as if he can't decide how to handle me.

I wipe the tears from my face, before reaching back toward him. His hand feels warm in mine, and I instantly melt against his side.

"I'm so sorry for what I said to you, before, the night they took Grandfather."

"It's okay." His arms wrap behind me and pull me close once again.

"No, it's not," I say, pulling back to see his face. "It was mean and terrible. I thought I'd never see you again, to apologize."

"Easy." He reached up and wipes the last of my tears from my cheeks. "You haven't lost us. We're still here. Xara works a couple blocks away, and you and I both work in the Axis."

"But I can never leave here."

"You're not a prisoner. They just need you on call for expeditions. You're part of a very important team. You get to take up where your mother and father left off."

"How do you know all this?"

"I started working for the Director, remember?"

Right. I'd forgotten Jak was going to finally get to live out his dream. Why did I think he'd forget about me so quick? He'll be down on Floor 2, close to me every day.

"Jak," I decide to change the subject. "Did you destroy my mother's notebook?"

"Yes." His gaze darts away from mine. "I brought it to work yesterday and dealt with it."

"Thank you." I wrap my arms around him again. Now the Order will never be able to point a finger at my mother.

"Nat." His tone changes and he presses his cheek against the top of my head. "I missed you."

"I missed you too."

"I don't want anyone else."

I lean away, absorbing his words, but I can't commit. "Right now, I need to deal with all of this." I wave my hands to the tiny room around us. "Plus, I still have no idea what happened to Grandfather. My entire world has fallen apart. Give me time, please."

He winces as he lets go of me. I know I'm being selfish, but I really can't extend myself any further. I reach for his hand, but he pulls it away and stands, leaving me sitting alone.

"I still love you and Xara, like always." I try to reassure him.

He walks to my desk, absentmindedly running his hand across the top. There's nothing there. I've barely tried to make myself at home in the short amount of time I've been here. I can't tell what he's thinking, his face not meeting mine. But his movements are deliberate and rigid.

"I'd better get back to work." His voice cracks, and he clears his throat. "Duty calls." He pauses at the door, without looking back. "Be careful outside. I don't want anything to happen to you."

"Thank you, Jak. I love you."

"Not in the way I need you to," he mumbles from the hallway.

I throw myself back on my bed and cover my face with my hands. When did life get so complicated? If Jak really loves me, then he should understand I need time to adapt to all this change. Seeing him come when I needed someone means so much to me, but I'm not ready for something serious, and I'm not sure I want that with Jak. Shouldn't I feel more than platonic love?

I touch my ear where Evan whispered yesterday. Evan makes me feel different than Jak does. There's more of a mystery there, but at the same time he frustrates me. Jak is secure, and predictable. I've known him since we were little kids. Evan is unpredictable and showed me just how explosive he can become.

The door to my room slides open, and Evan walks in. My face instantly flushes. Can he tell I was just thinking about him?

"Is that your boyfriend?" Evan thumbs over his shoulder.

"I don't recall inviting you in."

"Come on, kid." He flops onto my bed. "Let's go get some breakfast."

I scramble for my blanket and pull it up to my neck. "I just woke up. Can I have some privacy, please?"

"I'll save you a spot in the cafeteria." Evan steps into the hallway, then turns, poking his head back in. "Lighten up, kid."

"I'm not a kid," I yell after him as the door closes, then I turn and scream into my pillow.

I dress at my own pace, and as far from the camera that I'm able; Evan is not going to govern how I run my morning. By the time I'm finished, I hope he's gone, but when I finally slip through the door of the cafeteria, he waves me over. *Darn.*

I ignore him and get myself some eggs and fruit from the buffet. Outside the Axis, these are a luxury, but here they're in abundance. I wonder what the people in the districts would do if they knew of all the extravagances the Axis has inside its tower walls. While I'm stuck here, I'm going to take advantage of it all.

I pause at the end of the buffet, considering my seating options. The room is filled with white square tables, pushed together to make rows. All the occupants are scientists, evident by their white lab coats and scrubs. They're outlined by the dim light pouring in from the tinted windows that run all along the walls, revealing the dome and the gray skies on the outside. Not even the sun pokes through today.

My runners squeak on the vinyl floor, louder than they should, and people quiet as I pass by. Everyone's gazes burn into my back. *Why are they staring at me?* I dart to the empty seat across from Evan, and keep my head down, wishing I had remained in my bedroom.

"We're discussing locations for our expeditions." Evan explains. "What are your thoughts?"

Two other scientists from our division are sitting with him. One is an older woman—maybe thirty—with red hair that matches her lipstick, and a thick black line outlining her eyes. The other is a man, though I can't pin down his age, gray hair along his flat forehead, outlining his face. It matches the moustache under his nose. Whereas her clothes are smoothly pressed, his are wrinkled, matching his wild hair.

All three of them lean toward me, as if I have the answer they've been waiting for. I ignore them for a moment and break open the shell of my hardboiled egg, but I have to eventually give an answer. Mom's notebook mentioned taking her children somewhere, away from the colony. I can't remember exactly where, but water flowed there.

"Is there water somewhere near, a creek, or river or something like that?" I keep my voice quiet.

"I followed one here." Evan says. I look up from my egg, but he's looking at the others.

"I know where that is, but they will not allow us to go that far," the male scientist says. "Perhaps once we have a few trips under our belt?"

Discouraged, I return my focus to peeling the shell from my egg. I don't know why they asked. What do I know about the outside?

"I agree," the other scientist nods her head. Her voice comes out as steely as her blue eyes. "Roe's already decided we're going to the meadow. It's not too far, and we can stay in the view of the dome."

I jerk my head up. A meadow? Mom mentioned that somewhere in her pages, but what was it about? In some ways I wish I still had her notebook.

The woman extends her hand to me. "I'm Cardinal. Gloria Cardinal. This is Karl Waldorf."

I shake her hand. "I'm—"

"We know." Cardinal cuts me off before grabbing her food tray and standing. "See you back in the lab."

Waldorf scrambles to gather his things. "We'll be working together this afternoon, Greyes." He offers a reassuring smile and then disappears out the door.

"How's your food?" Evan asks. "You haven't stopped playing with your egg." A smile plays at the edge of his lips, making the sides of his eyes wrinkle. He leans back in his chair, relaxing his broad shoulders, as he taps a finger on the table. A scar runs across the back of his hand, slightly lighter than his bronzed skin.

"What happened there?" I point.

His finger stops tapping and his round eyes narrow as he holds his hand out, examining his hand as if noticing the mark for the first time. His lower lip sticks out for a second, before his gaze returns to mine. "Just being a kid, doing stupid things kids do."

"Is that why you call me kid? Because you think I do stupid things?"

He purses his lips together in a frown, drawing the skin tight along his chiseled cheeks. He opens his mouth, about to say something, and then shakes his head. "I can't help it if you're younger than me."

"Only by two years!"

"Don't worry about it, Greyes," Evan says.

"Greyes?" I say raising an eyebrow. "You sound like the others now."

"That's the idea, isn't it?" He looks around the room, scanning the other scientists. The frown returns to his face and his hands ball into fists on the table. Though his eyes reveal nothing, I know he's dropped his façade and for that moment shown me a glimmer of his true self. He turns back to me, his face softening but his voice trails off, without emotion. "Put us all together in this tower, and mold us into one functioning unit for the dome. Keep the Order in order and all that. I've heard it before."

"You have?"

He stares into my eyes as he leans forward. The entire room disappears around me as I focus on what he's about to say. "Don't you like being called *Greyes*? I thought it suited you better than *kid*?" A flash in his eyes shows he's returned to his old self, but he completely ignores my question.

I can't help but smile. "I like *Nat* the best. What do I call you, then?"

"I like it when you call me *Evan*," he whispers. "It rolls off your lips just right."

A tiny gasp escapes my mouth, but I quickly close my lips, suddenly aware he's staring at them. Under my thin shirt my heart races and my stomach flip-flops in unison. My cheeks get hot, and I cover them with my hands, as a tingle runs under my skin.

He leans back in his seat and bites his lower lip, still watching me, waiting for something. Does he want me to answer? What would I say—I wonder what his lips would feel like against mine? My face heats up even more—I can't believe I thought that. I grab my tray and stand up, holding it between us in defense.

"Let's go to the lab,"

"Oh, Greyes," Evan says, getting up. "You are too easy."

We ride the elevator in silence. There's an electric hum between us, or maybe I just feel that way. I need to know more about him. From the corner of my eye, I stare at his face. The corner of his jaw clenches and releases. For a brief moment, I picture myself grasping the side of his face while my lips press against his, my fingers sliding through his hair and twining into his locks. Sweat breaks across my skin, spreading down my neck. I shake the thought from my head and clear my throat.

"Where did you come from?"

"The outside. You know that. You saw me."

Another tiny gasp escapes my lips. So he saw me, too. He knows what no one else does, that I was in the clearing.

I know our ride will end quickly. The elevators at the Axis are nothing if not efficient. "Please, I want to know. Where is your home?"

"I came from a place very much like this one," Evan shrugs.

"Another dome?"

"You could say that." His jaw clenches again, but this time it doesn't let go.

His answers are vague, but the elevator doors open, interrupting my questions. Evan walks out, leaving me alone. Another dome ... I knew there were others. I don't understand why he would have left his.

When I walk into the lab, Waldorf waves me over. "Did Roe tell you I would show you the ropes before we leave tomorrow?" he asks kindly.

"She sure did." I glance around the lab. Steel tables are arranged in rows, and pairs of scientists work on both sides.

Some sit at monitors, probably looking up old reports. Others are cleaning tools. Where Waldorf stands, he has some files open, ready to show me what we're supposed to do.

"Great." Waldorf smiles. "Our department handles retrievals. We go into areas where people once lived and retrieve items that are of use."

"There are still cities out there?"

Waldorf squints from behind his glasses. "Sort of. Most places were annihilated in the war. We have to map out sites, where there once were cities, and then we dig until we find something. Sometimes you can see the outlines of old foundations, but most things of use are hidden in the earth."

I look at the open file on the table, where photos of objects lie inside. Some items are familiar, like pots and pans, pieces of jewelry, and old coins; others are photos of things I've never seen before, odd shapes and items I can't see would be of any use; sculptures of faces, paintings of people dressed in weird clothes, and jewelry like my locket.

"These are all kept in the Hall of Records. Of course, we learn from each item, building off old technology to benefit the residents of our dome."

My hand pauses over the photo of a locket like the one in my bag, back in my room.

"I remember that one." Waldorf smiles fondly. "Your mother found it. She wanted it cleaned up before your birthday. I brought it back with an early shipment."

"That was the last expedition, wasn't it?"

"Yes." Waldorf looks away. "I knew your parents well."

"Aren't you afraid to go back out again? Afraid of the radiation and whatever it was that killed everyone?"

Waldorf's eyes grow wide, revealing the red veins that cover his whites. He grabs my arm, squeezing it tight as he leans toward me. His breath makes my nose scrunch up as he spits out his words. "It was radiation that killed the team. Nothing more." I raise my eyebrows and nod in agreement as he continues. "We used every precaution we could back then. There is nothing to be afraid of. Do you understand?"

I nod, and he finally lets go of me, his eyes softening. I rub my arm, trying to soothe the sting he left behind.

"How did you get away?" I lean back in case he reaches for me again.

"I brought back a shipment, right here to this floor."

"My parents worked in this exact lab?"

"Right at this table with me."

I run my hands across the smooth stainless steel surface, feeling its cool metal against my warm hands. My parents were here. This is where they spent their time when they were away from me.

"Like I said, don't worry about the radiation. We'll be wearing suits tomorrow as a precaution, and we'll take a Geiger counter with us. They've never allowed us to use one before, but since the arrival of the Outsider, it can't be denied there's a possibility that the radiation may not be as dangerous as it once was. Maybe one day soon we'll all be able to leave the dome and colonize on the outside."

"Leave the dome?" Those words still sound impossible. Could

that really be in our future?

"That's always been the purpose, hasn't it?" Waldorf's brow shoots up. "Isn't that why we all become scientists?"

I never chose to be a scientist. I never asked to be here. *So why am I here?* If I don't hold the secrets to my mother's notebook, then how much longer will they keep me in this charade? I have one more question for Waldorf before we began my lessons.

"Where exactly are we going tomorrow?"

Waldorf looks uncomfortable. "We're going to the meadow— the place where the last Expedition team fell."

I grab the side of the table, as the room begins to spin around me. We're going to the place where my parents—I can't bear to finish my thought. How can they take me there? How am I supposed to trust these people? Maybe that's the point, I'm not.

I let go of the table and fall to the ground. Waldorf's voice cries out from above me, and the last thing I see is Evan's face above me before everything goes black.

CHAPTER 9

I wake up on the floor in the lab with white lab coats huddled around me. I start to sit up, but a sharp stabbing pain shoots in the back of my head. I reach for the spot and a small bump meets my touch.

"Everyone back," Evan calls out, kneeling next to me where he's cradling my head in his hands. I stare up at his facial expression, serious and commanding. "Give the kid some breathing room."

"I am not a kid," I say through gritted teeth.

"And, she's back." Evan flashes me his mischievous smile.

He places a hand on my back, helping me to a sitting position. I brace myself against his body, holding his arm until I regain my balance. What just happened?

I think back to my conversation with Waldorf. My locket. It was meant for my ninth birthday as a gift from my parents. *How long did Grandmother keep it from me?*

I look over at Roe, recalling the other part of my conversation with Waldorf. "When were you going to tell me?"

"Tell you what?" She looks confused.

"That we're going to the same place my parents were killed."

"I wasn't sure you could handle it." She shrugs. "Obviously I was correct."

"Correct!" I reach toward her, trying to grab her by the front of her lab coat, but Evan holds me back. "How would you like it if it was sprung on you in casual conversation? You've had plenty of time to tell me."

"When, Greyes?" She rolls her eyes. "When I took you from your home? Did you want me to tell you then? Or would it have been better to tell you yesterday, when you were moping in your bed? Tell me, when was the best time?"

"I didn't ask to be here!"

"So you keep saying. Guess what? None of us asked for you, either. Honestly, I don't know why you were put on this team. Do we need you? No. Do I have a choice? Definitely not. So, make the best of this situation, and be glad that I wasn't asked to come and deliver you to B2 with your grandfather."

Roe gets up and everyone stands frozen, watching us.

"My grandfather is there? You knew all along! I asked you about him—you lied to me."

"Keeping it from you isn't lying to you." Roe waves her hand dismissively. She lets out a big sigh and turns to her office. "Be mad at me if you want. I wasn't the one who took him. I don't even know why he was taken."

"You're as bad as the rest of the Order."

Everyone in the room gasps, and Evan's body stiffens against mine.

Roe turns slowly toward me, her eyes narrowed and lips pursed. "I'm here to do my job. I advise you shut up and do the same."

Evan looks up at Roe and then down at me before standing and pulling me up. "I'll take her for a walk so everyone can cool off." He practically pushes me out of the lab to the elevators.

"I don't need your help."

"You need something," Evan says.

"Why do you have to follow me around? Can't you leave me alone?"

"I made someone a promise," he says through gritted teeth. "I keep my word."

"A promise?" I start to laugh. "To who? The Order? What does everyone think they're going to catch me doing? Sneaking into the forest? Well—that's been taken from me. What's left?"

"I promised I would keep an eye on you," Evan pushes me into the open elevator. Inside he presses the button for the top floor: Floor 100. "I also promised to protect you," he adds.

"Who made you promise that? The only one who cares about me is Jak, and he would definitely not ask you for help. Let me guess, Roe needs something from me, and wants you to try to get it?"

"You don't make things easy," Evan warns. "You need to learn to go with the flow for a bit. And no, it has nothing to do with Roe, or the Order."

"Who was it, then? You don't know anyone else here." Then

I pause, remembering him outside the dome—remembering whose handprint had been left out there across from mine. "My Uncle Alec?" I stutter.

Evan doesn't say anything. He makes eye contact with me and points up toward the cameras in the ceiling. I'm right, it was Alec. I have so many questions for Evan; I don't know where to start or how to ask. The elevator door dings at Floor 100.

I exit onto the roof of the Axis. A large fan is connected to the peak of the dome, its most central point, where it recirculates the air around the dome, filtering it into oxygen for the people below. In truth, I'm breathing recycled air from the last four generations. The fan is powered by the generator on B1. Different vents run from it, going over and down the sides of the Axis, delivering carbon dioxide to the agricultural division, and fresh air to all.

Large targets are set up against a cement wall on the far side of the roof, looking oddly out of place. Their surfaces are pierced with a ton of holes. Across from them is a table with different handguns.

"This is the only place I know that's loud enough so they can't hear us," Evan explains. "This is where the Order has target practice."

"What's going on?" I plant both feet shoulder width apart and cross my arms against my chest. "How do you know my uncle? He was supposed to have died with my parents. How is he still alive?"

"Your uncle got into a fight with your parents that night and took off," Evan explains. "I don't know if you remember, but he says your father and he were always at odds over the dome and the Order. Your uncle wanted your father to take all of you and run away. Your father wasn't comfortable with that idea."

"I don't remember any of that," I say, trying to poke holes in Evan's story.

"I was twelve when he came to our dome as an Outsider," Evan explains. "We'd seen Outsiders before and had been taking them in for a number of years. Sometimes people stayed, and some went back to their old domes. Others moved on to see what else was out there. Your uncle had been out in the wild on his own for almost a year when he showed up. My father took him in. Alec stayed and became one of us."

"If he wanted to leave our dome so bad, why would he move into another?"

"Nat." Evan steps toward me. "My people live outside the dome. We colonized years ago." I stare at Evan in disbelief. The Uncle I used to nag and annoy, and had mourned along with my parents, was living comfortably in a colony all this time.

"Then why did he come back? And why did you come with him?"

"You need to understand," Evan says cautiously, watching my facial expressions. My entire body is vibrating as I try to digest this information. "Your uncle couldn't come back. Not after what he saw."

"What's that supposed to mean?"

"Everyone was murdered that night he left. When Alec returned in the morning, he found their bodies torn apart. Your government men were dragging the bodies away. Alec had no choice. He ran."

"Who did it, then? Was it people you know? Your dome lives on the outside."

"Nat," Evan takes a deep breath, "relax. Our dome is a couple weeks away when travelling on foot from yours. There's no way it was one of our people. We help others. We take stragglers in, people who don't fit under their dome's rules any longer. We didn't even know about your dome until your uncle came to us."

"Then how did you get my photo?" I stare into Evan's eyes. They look tired from all of my questions.

"Your uncle told me to give it to you. He hoped it would show you I am a friend and he is alive."

"How am I supposed to believe any of this?" I throw my hands up in the air. "No one around here tells any full-truths. Just a bunch of half-ones. Where did my uncle go, Evan? What happened when you were caught? I saw you; it was like you let them catch you."

"I promised Alec I would get on the inside and find you. You have to understand, he couldn't risk getting caught. I warned him not to go up to the glass, but-but he saw you, and couldn't help himself. If it wasn't for that—"

He stops mid-sentence, staring at me. The silence hangs heavy between us. I can't bear it.

"What, Evan? Say it already." My old feelings of guilt threaten to rise to the surface and explode. My entire life, I have been nothing but a burden. Now I find out I'm the reason things fell apart. "If it wasn't for me you wouldn't have been caught, right? It's always my fault! It's my fault Grandfather is down on B2. It's my fault he's being pressured for information." I begin to cry. "How was I supposed to know?"

Evan grabs me by the wrists and pulls me up against his chest. His heart beats against my hand as I stretch out my fingers, touching his chest. "Listen, you silly girl," Evan says firmly. "It's not your fault I'm here—that was always the plan. We came here to get you out. Do you understand? Alec is like family to me. I am here for you."

The reality of Evan's words sinks in and I melt against him. Alec came to save me because my mother wanted me out of the dome. But she's gone. Where would I go now? Why would I risk my life outside? I tilt my head up and look into his face. His dark eyes look down at me through thick lashes, and the smell of his cologne surrounds me. His lip twitches, as if he wants to tell me more, but instead his arms hold me tight. Those lips—I think about how they would feel against mine again and a shiver runs through me. Evan loosens his grip.

"Did I hurt you?" The concern in his eyes causes twinges in my chest.

"No," I murmur. I bite my lower lip. I have one more question. "Why did they let you leave B2?"

"The same reason they brought you here. They want information from us."

"Why didn't you tell them about Alec? I mean, they already knew from the handprint."

"They know he's out there, but they still might try to pin the murders on him. That's exactly what we want to avoid. He has questions—the biggest being, what killed your parents? If he gets caught, they'll lock him up, or worse. The Order can't let the people see he's alive."

"Everyone thinks the scientists were killed by radiation," I explain. "The Order would have more explaining to do if he did show up."

"That's why we need to find answers, quick."

I take a deep breath, dealing with information overload again. But this time I feel stronger. I have a purpose. I push back from Evan and he lets go.

"What are we are supposed to do?"

"Keep your enemies close. Keep your eyes open."

I laugh. "Only weeks ago I was washing windows. This week I'm under suspicion of being a threat to the dome."

"Power always fears what it can't control, Greyes."

He reaches over and moves a strand of hair from my face. His fingertips graze my skin, leaving behind a tingling sensation.

I feel safer now, knowing he is being used, just like me. At least I'm not alone anymore.

"What now?" I ask.

"I'm going to teach you how to defend yourself."

We walk over to the table and Evan picks up a handgun. He points it at the target across from us and fires. Even with the roaring fan, the noise of the gunshot surprises me, making me jump.

"Ever held one of these?" He waves the pistol in the air and I shake my head. "Come over here. It's your turn."

The gun is heavier than it looks. I run my fingers across its smooth, cold exterior. Carefully, I lift the weapon and aim it at the target. When I pull the trigger, the handgun recoils so hard I almost drop it.

"Whoa." Evan grabs the gun. "Let me help you."

He puts the gun back in my hands and stands behind me, lifting my arms up with his hands. His warm body presses against mine and I find myself focusing more on his touch than the instructions he's giving.

"Greyes, are you listening to me?" Evan laughs, his warm breath tickling my ear.

I squirm against him as I giggle. Who could pay attention? "What did you say?"

"I said hold it tight this time and brace yourself against the kickback."

"Okay. Evan?"

"Yes, Greyes?"

"Call me Nat."

CHAPTER 10

After target practice, I return to the lab for a long afternoon sitting next to Waldorf, learning how to properly photograph and catalogue artifacts late into the evening. He even shows me his expedition scarf, a ratty, knitted one he claims to have worn on all expeditions. The next morning, he's got it wrapped around his neck, ready to venture to the outside. I'm grateful to get out into the field, away from the monotony of the lab.

In the garage, the protection suits line the wall, facing the rear of the dome, toward the farmers' fields. The electric trucks used to haul food back to the Axis for cleaning and distribution, sit ready, waiting for us to load our gear.

I don the shiny white suit, made of a soft material that squeaks as it pulls against my skin. I feel like I've strapped pillows to my body. How could the former Expedition team have gotten any work done in these getups? I can barely bend over, let alone work and collect samples.

Evan stands beside me, holding his suit up. "This is really ridiculous, you know."

"Don't forget your helmets," Roe calls out. "What are you waiting for, Outsider?

Evan opens his mouth, I'm sure with a smart remark, but I turn to him and repeat his own words. "Go with the flow, remember? Look, even Waldorf is wearing one, scarf and all."

"It's absurd," Evan says, almost falling over as he steps into the suit and tries to pull it up his legs. "Everyone saw me come in from outside. It's no secret, the radiation is gone."

"It's better no one sees you," I remind him. "They'll have forgotten about you by now, or at least have been distracted by the telescreens, focused on some new reason to contribute to the dome.. In fact, last I heard you died from radiation poisoning." I pull my helmet over my head and tap the top. "Better safe than sorry."

"I don't have to like it." He sulks.

"I'll let you sit by me in the truck." I smile from behind my visor. He can't see my cheeks redden from the other side. "Most people around here would be honored to sit by a Greyes."

A smile replaces his frown. "You don't fool me with that charming little front, Greyes." Evan reaches out and pinches my side. I squeal in surprise. "I know the real you."

"What's that?" I step closer.

"If I had to sum it up in two words," he pauses, tapping a finger on his chin, "I'd say feisty and defiant." He throws his helmet on before I can see his face and jumps into the back of the truck. I climb up and sit beside him.

"His voice drops. "But if I had to be honest, I'd say independent and beautiful."

My face explodes with heat from behind my visor. Beautiful? I'm sure he's just trying to push my buttons, but it's nice to know I have an ally. Someone I can trust. I need to have a goal to get me through every day. Evan is the best way to see my uncle again and confirm the truth of what happened to my parents.

The convoy starts up, engines rumbling in the old trucks as we make our way to the main gates. People gather along the side of the road to watch. This is the first time an expedition has left the dome in a long time.

I remember when my parents left on expeditions. People always lined up at the gates to watch the team leave. The trips were a sign of hope. A chance for freedom. I didn't realize that back then. Do people have that same hope as they watch us leave? Are they really that unhappy here? Maybe Grandmother's fear of the Order is right. It's possible there's a lot my generation doesn't understand about how the dome has changed in the last decade.

Both sets of gates slide open, and suddenly we are free. I lean back and stare straight up at the sky. Everything out here is brighter, even though we're shrouded by dark clouds above, the sun still breaks through, lighting up the world. I glance at Evan, who's taken off his helmet. His eyes are closed as he holds his chin up high. He has lived outside the dome for most of his life. Being stuck inside ours the last few weeks must have felt like a prison, whether or not he was on B2 in the end.

"Take it off, Greyes." Evan opens one eye. "I dare you."

"Just a little farther, and we'll be out of sight," Roe yells from the driver's seat.

I ignore him and wait for the all-clear. But he's restless beside me, poking, and shifting, and distracting me from the scenery.

"Always such a good girl, aren't you?" he teases.

I flip up my visor and flash him a grin. He closes his eye, and a smirk plays at the edge of his mouth.

After a few more minutes Roe yells from the front seat again. "How are the readings coming along, Cardinal?"

"It's clear. I can't believe it! Absolutely clear!"

"You heard her!" Roe yells. "All clear!"

Whoops and hollers come from all around me as I pry the helmet from my head, feeling the cool breeze on my face. I remember my favorite excerpt from my mother's notebook: *One day I'm getting Nat outside of this place to somewhere she can breathe fresh air like humankind was meant to. The sun will shine on her face. The wind will blow in her hair.* I tilt my head back and take a deep breath, closing my eyes as my hair whips about my face.

"How does it feel?" Evan's voice is close to my ear. I open my eyes and see he's moved toward me, out of everyone's view. He reaches up and moves a strand of hair from my eyes, sending shivers down the inside of my suit.

"Amazing," I whisper. "I see why my mother loved it out here. I see why she liked to write about it."

"Did she write more than one notebook?" Evan asks.

I shake my head. "I'm the only one who'll ever remember her dreams. No one can take that from me."

Evan reaches over and squeezes my hand, but doesn't let go.

I intertwine my fingers through his, and look up into his eyes. Butterflies are jumping in my stomach.

"Do you think it will be bad? The site, I mean. Do you think there will be anything left of the horror from that night they died?"

He shakes his head and squeezes my hand again. "It's been almost a decade. If the Order didn't wipe that place clean, I'm sure time and the elements have."

I lean my head back again, letting the wind run free in my hair. But this time I can feel Evan's touch, even with the suits between us.

We travel another twenty minutes before Roe stops. There's nothing here but a small hole carved from the edge of the foothills. No blood. No horror. Just rocks and dirt. What did I expect? Maybe I am a foolish kid.

Roe climbs out of the truck to address us all. "This is our first expedition. You'll notice that we didn't bring much for supplies, just our basic work tools. I want us to catalogue everything we find and take photos. This is a trial run, only. If all is successful, our next expedition will be a full day. Everyone understand?"

"Yes, ma'am."

Evan climbs out of the truck in front of me. "You okay?" he asks as he grabs my hands and helps me down.

"Kind of silly to think there'd be something left behind. It's really a wasteland, isn't it?"

"No." He's still holding onto my hands. "It's not silly at all. Why wouldn't you be curious?"

I look up into Evan's eyes. Maybe he doesn't think I'm so

childish after all. He shifts uncomfortably in his protection suit and I smile. It's nice to see him out of sorts for once. His confidence is sometimes stifling.

Unlike the sandy ground surrounding the dome, the ground here is a darker soil. I push my foot into the dirt and kick some of it up. It's dry and brittle. But there still isn't any sign of life.

"These areas would have once been farmlands," Evan explains. "You can tell by how far the site is from the dome. All the domes were small cities before they were covered. They installed the Axis tower at the same time the dome was erected, and then reinforced most of the buildings inside to withstand time, until people could be moved to the outside again."

"Evan, Greyes," Roe looks at us with the same irritation I'm used to from Grandmother, "go make yourselves useful, would you? This isn't a date. Walk the perimeter and if you see anything, do not approach it. Got it? Report back here instantly if there's a problem."

I eye the firearm at Roe's side. Easy to say, when you're an Order member and allowed to carry protection. I wish I had something more than a camera and clipboard to protect me from whatever could be out there.

"Don't look so spooked." Evan bumps my shoulder as we walk into the foothills.

"Is anything alive out here?"

"Seriously, Greyes? What do you think is out here?"

He laughs and I bite down on the inside of my cheek, wishing he was more sensitive about my lack of knowledge.

"Something obviously killed my parents."

His laugh cuts off short. "I'm sorry, I didn't think of that. I was out here for weeks with Alec. We didn't see anything, well except maybe a mouse, or the odd bird. But other than those, not a single living thing."

"Really?" Mice and birds are alive only in storybooks, when you've been closed in a dome for your entire life. But it's not living things I'm afraid of; it's the childhood stories about the infected, monsters who come to get little children while they lie in their beds. I know one could never get in the dome, but out here, who knows what's survived. That childhood fear still lies somewhere deep inside me.

"Have you ever seen an infected?"

"No. Of course not. They were destroyed long ago in the Cleansing war." His face drops. "Why? Has someone in your dome seen them? Did someone tell you there are still some around?"

"No." I feel foolish again. "I thought—you know, how my parents died and all."

"You thought an infected killed them?" Evan is borderline smug, frowning as if I've just asked the stupidest question he's heard today. "Why would you think that?"

"There's obviously no radiation. What do you think killed them?"

"Sometimes the answer is staring you right in the face. I guess hearing they were torn apart would make you think the most obvious answer would be an infected. But sometimes man is most dangerous to himself."

We reach the top of the hill, which has served as the horizon on the other side of the dome walls my entire life. An entire world I never knew existed spreads out before me. A large meadow stretches out between the hills, filled with tall grass and flowers—real ones. Wildflowers are present in every color imaginable, none of which I have ever seen in my life. In the far distance a thick forest of trees borders the end of the meadow.

I step forward, then look back at Evan to see if he's going to stop me.

"Go on." He laughs. "It's safe, I promise."

I run down the other side of the hill into the meadow with my hands outstretched. The grass reaches my waist, and the flowers grow freely, wherever they please. There's no rhyme or reason out here, no structure. Everything just lives.

I spin around, letting my outstretched fingers caress the tops of the grass, as it tickles my hands. I close my eyes and suddenly, so unexpected, I hear laughter escape my lips. This is true happiness. I don't remember the last time I felt it.

I open my eyes and see Evan watching me from the top of the hill. His smirk has been replaced by an actual smile, so I motion for him to join me. He runs at me with his arms spread out, and I squeal, running deeper into the meadow. It's exhilarating to put all inhibitions aside and be free. Nobody is watching, judging, or reprimanding.

Evan grabs me and spins me in the air. The meadow spins by, faster and faster, until we tumble to the ground, ending up face-to-face, him on his back and me on top of him.

"If you wanted to get me on my back you didn't have to trip me."

His boldness brings me back to reality. I jump off him and brush myself off, as he scrambles to get up.

"Nat," he speaks up, "that was a j—"

"It's okay," I cut him off. The heat emanates from my face, and it's not from running around. "It's time we report back, don't you think?"

"The perimeter is safe." Evan nods. He gives me a little push, breaking the tension, and races me to the top of the hill. I'm glad he can joke around, because I'm not used to not being in control of my feelings.

Back at camp, everyone is already packing up their cameras and small soil samples. Waldorf frowns, as he reaches over and pulls a leaf from my hair. He shoots a look at Evan, before slipping the greenery into a small bag and sealing it up. I quickly run my hands through my locks, to check for other debris.

"Did you find anything out there?" Roe asks.

"No," Evan says, a little too quickly.

"A meadow," I say. "It was beautiful."

I'm grilled about the meadow. What types of flowers were there? Were there any signs of microorganisms? I have no idea how to answer any of their questions, and Evan leans against the truck, letting me take the brunt of it all. I'm starting to think the people on my team are more than just expedition scientists. The one thing they all agree on is that our next visit must include a trip to the meadow.

"Perhaps we could bring someone from Biological Research with us," Roe adds.

"I know one who would be ecstatic," I say, thinking of Tassie.

The drive back is bumpy. Roe advises us to put our helmets back on. It is best to not divulge too much information about the outside world before we run tests, she explains. It makes sense to me. After decontamination, we scan one another with handheld scanners that are able to pick up the infection. Everyone is clear. We enter the dome, park the trucks, and take an elevator ride back to the lab where we unload all the boxes, Roe sends us off for personal time. I look around for Evan, and see him disappear behind the elevator doors. He must have someone to see.

I'm not sure how I feel about Evan hanging around someone else. It's not that I'm possessive over him, or have any right to be, it's just—what if it's a girl? But who would be interested in an Outsider? *Why do I care, anyway?*

CHAPTER 11

I go back to my room and find Tassie lying on her bed reading a book, *Plants, Then and Now*. She's oblivious to my presence concentrating deep in her book, but the second our door slides shut, she tosses the book aside and sits upright on her bed.

"You're back! Tell me everything!"

I tell her about the ride out and how the sun and wind felt. I tell her how the dirt changed from sandy to dark soil, as these are points I know she's professionally interested in. But I save the best for last, the one part I know she'll love the most.

"I wish you could have seen it. A green meadow, filled with wildflowers, as far as the eye could see."

She's on her knees bouncing on her bed, squealing. "What kind of flowers? Did you smell them? Did you notice any other vegetation? Oh my goodness, I'm so jealous!"

I fall back onto my bed, unable to wipe the smile from my

face. My cheeks are still flushed from the fresh air and freedom.

"And, Roe said she might take a Biological Research scientist with us next time—" I don't get to finish my sentence; Tassie is screaming at the top of her lungs.

"WHAAAAAAAT!" she cries out. "Are you serious? I have to go find her right now."

She jumps off her bed and bolts out of our bedroom, nearly knocking Evan over, who's standing in our doorway. He freezes, with Tassie pressed against him for a little longer than necessary.

"Hey, I'm in a hurry," she faintly slaps her palm against his chest with a playful tone in her voice. If it wasn't for the confused look on Evan's face, I'd think he likes it. But he steps back and lets her run past him.

"What was that all about?" He points his thumb after her.

"I told her Roe might take a Bio Scientist on the next expedition."

"Roe is going to kill you." Evan laughs. "Tassie will ask her every day until next week. I don't think that girl understands 'no'. But she'll definitely add something to the scenery."

A twinge of jealousy stabs me in the chest. "I don't care." I wish I could change the subject. Tassie didn't strike me as Evan's type, but what do I really know about him?

"I have a surprise for you," Evan says. "That is, if you're not busy?"

"A surprise? You don't have other plans?"

"Who else would hang out with me? Come on." He flashes me a playful smile, his eyes squinting with a flicker of mischief, then pulls me up from my bed out into the hallway.

"Where are we going?" I ask at the elevator. He slips an ID card into my hand as we step inside and the doors slide shut.

"What's this?" I ask looking at the card. There's no photo or name, it simply reads *B2*. I gasp and shove the card into my pocket out of the view of the cameras. My excitement is replaced by a hot burning sensation in the pit of my stomach.

"You know what it is," Evan whispers. "Go ahead. Try it out."

I look at the keypad on the elevator. There is a slit underneath the B2 button. The sharp outline of the card pushes into my skin as I clutch it tight in my palm. I look back at Evan.

"Don't you want to check on your grandfather?" he asks. "We need to hurry. We only have twenty minutes until the cameras are reset."

"Where did you get this card from?"

"I took it off one of the guards when they moved me off that floor." He shrugs. "Figured it might come in handy."

"Why would you ever want to return there?"

Evan laughs. "Are we going to waste the little time we have chatting with each other?"

I turn back to the keypad. Evan is right. I can grab this opportunity or keep wondering how Grandfather is. Is it so wrong to check on him? It's not like we can break him out or anything. But breaking into B2 is a pretty big act of breaking the rules; am I ready to take my indiscretions to the next level?

"Okay." I reach out, my hand trembling as I put the card in the slot. Nothing happens.

Evan reaches across me and presses the button for B2. The elevator whirs into action.

"Don't be scared," he assures me. "I've been down there before, remember? It's not so bad."

I take a deep breath and exhale. Evan reaches over and intertwines his fingers with mine. I'm too nervous to think about anything but Grandfather. Will he be down there? What if he's hurt? The doors ding and open to B2.

I peer out the doors to the darkened hallway beyond where silence stares back at me. Evan's hand rests against the small of my back, but instead of comfort, it sends a tremor through my body.

I walk down the hallway, guided by Evan. We turn a corner where dim blue lights give off enough illumination for us to find our way, their soft glow making me feel safer that I did a moment ago. I glance at Evan, moving confidently past the cells. He was down here before. He knows what to expect. I've only heard the rumors, but even those seem to be wrong—where are the screams?

"What happened to you down here?" I'm not sure if I really want to know the answer, but the silence is killing my psyche.

"I was kept in an interrogation room. I never made it to a cell."

"Did they—torture you?"

"They tried." His body stiffens, but he doesn't let go of me. "There was nothing I could give them but the truth, but it felt like they were looking for a different kind of truth. Something that would make them feel better about what they were doing, I guess. Eventually they took me to Floor 18."

"I heard the Director talking about you when I was cleaning

near his office. He wanted you moved because you were close to the generator."

Evan laughs, "They asked me a lot about my intentions. Was I here to spy on them? Did I want to destroy the dome? It was all ridiculous. They found me with a backpack of food. What did they think I could do?"

"Did they ask you about my uncle?"

"No." He shakes his head. "But isn't that strange? They kept asking me who I was working with, and I said I came alone. Who do you know inside? No one, I said. I told them all about my dome and how we moved outside, but they didn't care. They were much more concerned about why I came. I couldn't tell them about your uncle; who knows what they would have done to you?"

I remember Evan's face that day on the elevator. It was bruised and he had blood on his clothes from his interrogation. *He took all that, just to protect me?*

"Are we safe down here?"

"They're all upstairs in a meeting,"

"How do you know that?"

"I can't give you all my secrets, Greyes." Evan stops and turns to me with a wink. The door behind him is made of the same gray steel as the floor and ceilings. Everything blends together. A small window on the door reveals only darkness inside.

"I'll look around while you visit," Evan says, stepping back. Before I have a chance to respond, he disappears down the hall.

A slight shimmer of the blue light falls across the floor, into the cell. There I spot Grandfather, sitting on the floor, his head leaning back against the wall. He looks smaller than I remember, or maybe it's the size of the room. *What has it been? Two days?* That's since I arrived. *Only three, then?* Yes, it was the day before I left. Why does my old life seem so long ago?

He lifts his head at the sound of the door opening. We don't make eye contact at first. I'm not even sure he can see me.

"Grandfather?" My whisper breaks the silence.

"Nat?" His voice is rough, broken. He holds his arms out in front of him, clawing at the air, evidently disoriented. "Is that you?"

"Yes, Grandfather." I catch a sob in my throat and run over to help him up. His body feels frail in my arms, and he's too weak to stand. Instead I sit next to him and hold him against me, as tears fill my eyes.

"I can't believe they let you in to see me."

"A friend brought me down."

"Don't get into trouble on my account." He's still watching out for me, even in this state. "I get out tonight. Grandmother is coming to get me."

"You do?" Relief washes over me as tears escape onto my cheeks. "Why did they take you in the first place?"

"Something about Alec." He chuckles in the darkness. "I mean, can you really believe it. They asked if I had contact with him. Do I know his whereabouts? Absolutely absurd. I told them I know exactly where he is, in the ground with my other son and daughter-in-law."

I embrace him, glad he still has some spirit left. I don't dare tell him Alec is alive. I'm not sure he could handle the news in his state, and I can't be there to help him pick up the pieces. Best leave that to Grandmother.

"I've been outside on an expedition."

"You have?" He reaches over and grabs my hand, squeezing it with his cold fingers. "Why, that's fantastic. You've found your calling. What was it like?"

"Don't tell anyone," I whisper. "But the radiation is gone."

"Amazing," he says. "Just amazing. Do you know, someone told me that once before. I think it was your mother."

My mother? That's impossible. He must be delirious.

"Be careful, Nat." He squeezes my hand again. "You're all grown up now, and I won't be around forever. Whatever you do, always be cautious. You only get one life."

I can't make promises when I don't know what's going to happen to me once the Order finds Alec. Will they torture me like they did Evan? Will they lock me up like Grandfather?

"Did they hurt you at all?" I change the subject.

"Nothing I couldn't handle," he says. "I've been down here once before, long ago. I know the drill. They have to ruffle their feathers. Show who's in charge. But I did it—I survived. I still have a few years left in these old bones."

Suddenly, the thought that this may be the last time I see Grandfather for a long time overwhelms me. A sob escapes, and my body shakes next to his. His fingers squeeze mine, and I force myself to gain control. Now is not the time to lose it—I wasn't the one pressed for information.

Evan appears at the door, illuminated by the blue light. It's time to go. But I still have so many questions to ask—one more important than the others.

"If you could ever leave the dome, would you?"

Grandfather looks over at me. "I could never leave your grandmother, and you know her. She's stubborn. She would never leave her home."

"What if she wanted to?"

He pauses a moment, and then lets out a sigh. "I'm proud of you, Nat. Don't ever forget that. No matter where life takes you, know I always wanted the best for you."

"I thought I lost you forever." I wrap my arms around him. "You were the best replacement I could have ever had for a father."

"We have to go," Evan whispers.

"Save yourself. You were not meant for this life."

"I love you." I hug him firmly.

Evan grabs my hand, pulling me away. My fingers stretch toward Grandfather's. As we reach the door, he calls out. "Don't ever come back down here again, Nat, do you hear me? There are strange sounds down here. Screams of pure terror coming from somewhere in the darkness. Promise me. Never come back."

My promise escapes my lips as the door closes. Evan pulls me back down the hallway to the elevator. I don't notice where we are going. I bury my face in his chest and mourn the loss of my old life.

CHAPTER 12

Evan pulls me out of the elevator onto the roof, and holds me tight. I bury my head into his chest, drowning in my grief, as he runs his hand through my hair. Did Grandfather know he may never see me again? Was he giving me permission to leave the dome?

After a few minutes, Evan takes my face between his hands and wipes my tears from my cheeks with his thumbs. His eyebrows are drawn together as he clings to me.

"Are you ready for your surprise?"

"I thought that was my surprise?"

"That was something that had to be done," Evan says, turning my head. "This is something just because."

A small blanket with a basket in its center is laid out in the far corner next to the railing. Evan pulls me to spot, and I follow to the ledge, grasping the cool metal of the safety rail with my palms as I lean over and peer down. My breath catches in my throat. It's almost as exhilarating as being outside. The patchwork of crops spreads all the way to the edge of the dome, on this side of the Axis. The workers are barely noticeable, tiny dots moving about below us. Far in the distance is the Outer Forest, my sanctuary, reaching up with its one hundred year old trees, hiding us from the outside.

Evan reaches down to the blanket and picks up a flower. "I brought a piece of the meadow back for you."

He passes the flower to me and our fingers touch, sending electricity through my body. The sensation lingers after he lets go, but I can't tear my eyes away from this single flower. He could have been caught. Why did he do this? I look up at him, to search for an answer on his face, but he's turned away, back to the picnic.

"I got a little bit of everything they're serving at supper tonight." I raise an eyebrow, still too stunned to speak. "I've got a friend." His voice comes out fast, and he rubs the back of his neck. Is he nervous? I've never seen him act like this before.

"You've got a lot of friends for a guy who just got here." I sit across from him, in front of the food.

He shrugs. "People like me. What can I do?" His gaze meets mine for a second, and then turns away as he laughs at his own joke and slides over next to me.

"Where did you go when I was talking to Grandfather?" I ask as I bite into a piece of an orange. The sweet juices run down my chin, tickling my skin as I try to catch them with my hand.

Evan stares as I make a mess of myself. He blinks and looks

away, his cheeks red. "Those screams your grandfather mentioned. I heard them too. They happened the night I was there. They're bloodcurdling, to say the least. When you were talking to him, I checked for other prisoners that might have been getting tortured. I couldn't find anyone else. I don't understand. If he heard them, too, then where are they coming from?"

I shudder at the thought of even more people being tortured in our dome. "Maybe it's the sounds of the generator?" I offer. "It's only one floor above."

"Maybe." Evan frowns. "The one in our dome sure doesn't sound like that."

"You still have your Axis? Tell me about your dome."

Evan leans on his elbow, stretching his legs along the edge of the blanket. The muscles in his biceps flex under his weight. "It's pretty much like this place. They were all designed for the same efficiency and effectiveness. I don't think the government had much time to be creative, after the virus broke out. We still use our dome, if you can believe it. The farms were kept inside, to protect them from the elements. But the majority of people chose to rebuild their housing on the outside, where all districts are equal. There are two settlements, on opposite sides of the dome, and between them we've built a factory, hospital, and other public buildings to help promote more development."

"That's not similar at all."

"Change takes time. When it comes down to it, we're all the same people, living in different areas."

"Did your dome have a B2?"

"It did." His eyes go distant, as he plays with a piece of the blanket. "There are still troublemakers. But, back home they're dealt with in the open, for everyone to see."

"Grandfather gets out tonight. I had been sure he was going to disappear, like the others. Is that what you think happened to all those missing people? They took a little stand against the Order and were locked up on B2?"

"It's easy to get away with bullying the innocent when you have a B2," Evan says. "But that still doesn't account for where those screams are coming from."

I look away, tears filling my eyes.

"What's wrong?" Evan asks, sitting up. "I didn't mean to upset you."

"It's not that. It's hard, knowing I may never see him again. What if he has to participate in the Last Banquet, and I don't get to see him again?"

"Your dome still does that?" Evan's face is lined with disgust. "With any luck we'll prove the outside is safe, and no one will be forced to end their life again."

Live outside? Now I see why the option was so appealing to Mom. Move to the outside and save so many lives. "I wish I wasn't alone to deal with it all."

Evan's brows push together. "You're not alone. I'm here." He looks down and fidgets with the blanket again. "I don't want to lie to you, Nat, but I need to tell you something. You can't tell anyone. I want you to—trust me—so I'm going to trust you and tell you why I'm really here. I'm not only here to protect you, I'm here to investigate your dome."

"Investigate?" I swallow a lump that has formed in the back

of my throat. "Why?"

"This is Alec's idea," Evan explains. "Your mother stumbled across something—something your dome is hiding."

"Mom did? What?"

"Yes." He nods. "Alec saw her the night before she was killed. She told him she hid some clues in her notebook, and they led to evidence she buried on the outside of the dome. Evidence that uncovers something terrible is going on here."

"What is it?"

"She didn't say. All she told Alec was she wanted him to know in case anything happened to her. She wouldn't share it with him at camp that night. That's why Alec got mad and left."

"You think the Order killed them because of some evidence my mom had?"

Evan nods. "Alec believes that notebook holds the secret."

"So he was really coming for the notebook, not for me." I clutch my stomach as dread begins to swell inside my gut.

"Of course not," Evan says.

"Is that why you're hanging around me?" Sweat breaks out on my skin. "Are you hoping I have some clue locked in my head to help you out?"

"No." His eyes squeeze shut as if he wants to hide.

I sound ridiculous. But am I? Everyone wants something from me. Grandmother wants me to get out of her life. The Order members want me close, so they can keep an eye on me. My uncle wants my mother's notebook. And then there's Evan—I thought he was here to watch out for me, but he's also committed to my uncle—what does he really want? I get up and look back, over the ledge, down to the workers in the fields. Everything is easy for them; they don't have to wonder about what's outside the dome, or why their parents were killed.

Evan comes up behind me. I have no words for him, stuck in my own frustration, but I still turn toward him. He reaches forward and tucks my hair behind my ear, then cups my face, resting his thumbs on my cheeks.

"I'm not here to find out anything about your mother's notebook."

His eyes look directly into mine. All I want to do is look away, but I don't. I'm trapped up here, with him. There's nowhere to run. I want to be suspicious. I want to be furious. But my emotions betray me as my racing pulse makes my heart flutter in my chest.

His deep voice lowers, to a whisper. "I'm here because I want to be. I planned this picnic because I wanted to see you smile like you did in the meadow. You should smile more."

I used to smile all the time. Did that change in the last few weeks? I look from Evan's eyes, past his nose, to his lips, and back up again. His fingers meet mine on the ledge, the sensation so strong it feels like they're on fire. He leans in, as if to whisper something more, but tilts his head towards my face. I close my eyes as his lips brush against mine, softly moving with a gentle urgency.

My body melts against his, and I wrap my arms around his neck. His arms guide me closer against his body, while his thumb moves from my cheek, down my neck, sending small shocks of electricity through my body to the ends of my limbs. A tiny gasp escapes my lips. This is so different from kissing Jak.

My third kiss ever—each with a different boy, and each so different from the one before it. The first is barely worth a mention, so long ago it's practically forgotten. The second was with sweet and loyal Jak—my best friend since childhood—the one who loves me. And now I'm kissing Evan with more passion than the others, and he's nothing but a stranger. What's wrong with me? My chest tightens as a twinge of guilt builds. I pull away from Evan and step back.

He snaps out of the trance as well, staring at me as if he can't believe what happened. He looks away, biting his lower lip, and then shakes his head. I instantly regret stopping, but I'm frozen in place, too awestruck to move.

"I never should have done that." He turns back to the picnic. "I don't know why I did. I made a promise to Alec to watch out for you, not to take advantage of you." He busies himself with gathering our things, packing them away as if it could erase any memory of what just occurred between us. Or should I say, what didn't occur, because I've got an ache in my gut that's quickly filling with the fear that I'll never get to kiss him again.

Get a hold of yourself, Nat.

Is that all I was—a mistake? The last thing I need is another person who feels responsible for me. It's the same pressure I've felt since my grandparents took me in, the same feeling I have around the other scientists. Frankly, I'm sick of it all. I can't believe I got so caught up in the moment with Evan, and still want more. I'm nothing more than an obligation to him.

I walk to the table, grab one of the guns, and empty it into the target across from me. This is a good stress release. But it doesn't fill the void that's growing inside me. I throw the gun back on the table and walk toward the elevators.

Evan follows me, but doesn't say another word. The elevator ride feels like forever. I just want to be alone. But as the doors slide open, Jak is standing in the hallway, outside my room. His eyes narrow as he sees Evan standing next to me. I step out and the doors slide shut behind me, taking Evan away.

"Where were you two?" Jak turns his narrowed stare on me.

"We were at supper." My nerves jump under my skin. He doesn't need all the details.

"I don't like that guy," Jak warns me. "You shouldn't hang out together so much."

Can he tell I kissed Evan? My hand shoots up to my lips, swollen from the kiss that never should have happened.

"What does everyone want from me?" I throw my hands in the air. "I'm on the same team as him. There's nothing I can do."

"I'm not sure what his intentions are." Jak reddens. "I mean, come on, Nat, do you even know where he comes from? Why he came to our dome?"

"He came here to let us know it's safe to be outside," I sputter. "Has *your* Director shared that news with you yet? We took off our gear, when we were outside, Jak. There's no radiation."

"I see all the reports before they go to the Director." He narrows his eyes again. "That's my job. And, what do you care if I trust him or not? You barely know the guy."

My mouth drops open—I'm trapped again, but this time with words. I can't think of an argument to defend myself, my mind is racing so fast, so I throw my hands up in exasperation.

"Don't tell me you like him." Jak's tone is cruel, but his eyes show the truth. He's hurt.

My stomach tightens and my mouth goes dry—I need to get out of this hallway. "He's a colleague. Nothing more." I push past Jak and walk into my room.

He follows me inside.

"I'm sorry," his voice softens. "I saw you two together and I felt a little jealous."

"There's nothing between us." This isn't a lie. Evan made that clear.

The corners of his eyes lift. "I'm happy to hear that. Now I want to tell you why I came to see you. I know you feel cooped up inside the Axis, stuck with the same people every day, so I'm inviting you to a night with the Director and the Delegates next week."

I stare at him, blinking rapidly as he continues. "I know we'll still be here in the Axis, but it's a special night for me. I find out if I get to stay as Assistant Director permanently."

I force a smile on my face. "That's great news."

"So, do you forgive me, then, for being so presumptuous about you and Evan? I'd love it if you would be my date?" His eyes dance with excitement.

"Of course I will." I nod. "It's your dream come true."

"You're my dream come true." He reaches to grab my hand, but I step back, making him flinch.

"Sorry." *No, I'm not.* I shake my head. "It's been a long day. I'm exhausted. I need to get to bed."

He nods but his mouth contorts, trying to hold a smile. He turns to leave, but hesitates at the door. "You know how much you mean to me, right?" His back stiffens as his voice comes out flat.

"I do." My body tenses, waiting for Jak's reaction. His broad shoulders finally relax and his blond hair stays in place as he nods. His six-foot frame fills the doorway as he walks out of my room. My heart feels like it's going to explode from my chest.

"Good night, Nat." His voice softens.

The door slides shut behind him and I collapse on my bed. Jak is an added pressure I can't handle. I have to find a way to make him understand I'm not ready for something serious. All I need right now is a good friend. Thankfully, my mind is gracious and allows me to fall sleep at once.

CHAPTER 13

The next morning I go to the cafeteria for breakfast and eye up Sophia, the cafeteria lady. She's the same age as Grandmother, but nicer. Every morning she tries to get me to eat something she's cooked.

"The fruit girl returns," she says, as I pass by with my tray. "Want to try some eggs or bacon today?" I shake my head. "You're going to put me out of business with all this fruit you eat. Look at you, you're too skinny. You need to put some meat on your bones, for that boyfriend of yours."

"Boyfriend?" I almost drop my tray. "You're wrong. Evan and I are just friends."

"Mm-hmm." Her brows push together. "Well, whatever he is, I haven't seen your friend yet. He usually beats you here."

I leave the line and make my way to the tables. Is Sophie one of Evan's secret friends? She seems to have a particular interest in him. I put the thought out of my mind when I see Roe's table has an empty spot, but I hesitate when I see Tassie's bouncing curls across from her.

"C'mon, Roe," Tassie pleads. "I've been reading about the plant life outside. I have some great ideas on what samples to gather."

Roe spots me hanging back and glowers at me. "I hear I have you to thank for this." She motions to Tassie.

"Sorry." I sit in the empty seat, looking around the room, avoiding Roe's frown.

"Looking for your buddy?" Roe asks. "You won't find him. I sent him on a mission before breakfast, but he should be back before lunch."

I pick at my fruit, but I can't seem to find an appetite. The distaste for wasting it is the only reason I force down a few bites. I wish Evan was here. After our departure yesterday, I want to see if things will return to normal. Finally I give up on my food, and leave Tassie pestering Roe.

Inside the lab, Waldorf is half-visible, ducked inside a large box. I slip onto a stool next to him, just as he pulls out a gadget. He jumps when he sees me, and almost knocks his glasses off.

"What's that?" I look around him and notice the box is marked *Hall of Records*.

"Our expedition made me think of some items we found long ago. Some were useful, while others were more frivolous, like this decorative item. He holds up a funny shaped glass object. No room for items that don't have a purpose, in a dome with limited space."

"What is this object's purpose, then?"

"As far as I can tell, it exists simply for its beauty."

"Imagine living in a world that can just enjoy beauty. Wouldn't it be nice to move outside the dome? Then things like this could be everywhere."

"You sound like your mother when you talk like that. *We could build houses over here,* she would say. *Waldorf, you could have a little reading hut over here.* Those were the best days. Lots of excitement back then."

His watery eyes blink, and I look away. Was he close to my parents? They had never talked about their co-workers. They would leave their day life behind in the Axis when they came home at night, or I was just too young to pay attention.

I fumble with the object, a small, circular piece of glass with a black line pointing from its center to one side. It has a familiarity, but I have no idea why.

"There was a piece that attached to it, but I can't find it in here." Waldorf bangs his hands on the top of the box. "It must have been packed separately. I hope it wasn't lost after all these years."

"It reminds me of something."

"It might. It was one of your mother's favorites. I believe she took it home to study."

That's right; it's part of a set. Memories of Mom working at her desk flood my thoughts. A triangular-shaped stand is missing—the circle used to sit inside it. I used to look through it, and objects looked larger—Mom used it to examine her maps and artifacts. A magnifying glass. But I don't remember the black line being on it before. I scratch it with my fingernail and a small section scrapes away. Who would have drawn it there? Plus it seemed silly, without its handle.

Maybe I could use this as an excuse to see Xara?

"Cara Douglass works at the Hall of Records. She might be able to help find the other piece."

Waldorf smiles, lost again in his memories. "Her husband, Jon, was quite the joke teller. He could always lighten up a serious situation."

"His daughter, Xara, got that from him. Could I get permission to go there? I grew up with her daughter Xara, who works there now. We could all look."

"That is a splendid idea." Waldorf's face beams with excitement. "We have to get through some red tape for an outing. Let me see if I can find a way to make it official business." He gives me a wink. I like Waldorf. He's sincere.

"Thank you, thank you!" Tassie's voice enters the lab. She's hot on Roe's heels. "You are not going to regret this, I swear. I am fully prepared. I even have a pre-made list of samples to collect. Ooh, I am so excited!"

Before I can congratulate her, Evan comes through the door behind them. We make eye contact, but I quickly break it and turn back to Waldorf. My heart beats faster.

"Did everyone miss me?" Evan calls out.

"Oh, Evan!" Tassie squeals. "I get to come on your next expedition." I turn and catch her hugging him, from the corner of my eye. "Promise me, please, that you'll take me to the meadow you and Nat saw?" She blinks her long lashes up at him.

"Sure will." Evan smiles, then turns and catches me staring at their embrace. I jerk my attention back to Waldorf, instantly feeling my skin crawl as I shift in my seat.

Tassie squeals one last time and leaves the lab. Evan and Roe go into her office, leaving the door open. I glance over my shoulder again. He's hands over a long tube that he brought with him. She opens the end, and pulls large papers out, unrolling them across her desk. Where did she send Evan? Why would she trust an Outsider with special duties?

"Nat, did you hear me?" Waldorf nudges me.

"Hmm?" I turn back to him. "I'm sorry, I was distracted."

"You are so like your mother," Waldorf tries to smile but his red eyes give him away. "I heard you used to have a little notebook, like she always did. That's where she kept all her secrets." He leans in close. "There are no secrets from the Order, you know."

I eye Waldorf, carefully shifting in my seat to put a little more distance between us. Is he warning me, or advising me? His lips turn from serious back to their soft smile.

"That's why she kept the notebook," he whispers, looking around the room. "To keep an informal record—offline— something that couldn't be tampered with in the system."

"What was she keeping a record of?" I whisper back.

"Mostly her thoughts," Waldorf says. "She met often with other departments and would come up with some of the most interesting conclusions. She was absolutely brilliant. A scientist through and through. Back then, all the departments were allowed to mingle. That's how she fell for your father."

"Really?" I've never heard this story.

"Yes. He was a Microbiologist—the elite of the Axis scientists."

"Why would he leave that department?"

"He was always in love with her," Waldorf explains. "Who could blame him? From the moment they met at the Learning Institute, he chased after her, but she was much too focused on her career."

"How did he win her over?"

"I have no idea," Waldorf sighs. "Chemistry, perhaps. All I know is, one day she fell in love, he transferred to our division, and she was never the same again."

"You say that like it's a bad thing."

"A beautiful mind is a terrible thing to waste." He stares at the glass object in my hands. "Your mother's focus shifted and her potential was affected. Love has that effect on people. Your father was an unnecessary distraction."

I don't appreciate hearing Waldorf talk about my dad like this. It sounds like he was jealous. "Did you know my father well?"

"We grew up in the same neighborhood. The dome is small enough that everyone knows each other in one way or another, don't they?"

"That's true."

"Speaking of friends," he packs up the rest of the box, "I am going to go put in a request for you to visit the Hall of Records right now. I'm sure it won't be a problem." I reach out to hand him the magnifier. "Keep it for good luck." He winks at me and walks out of the lab.

I turn back, but Evan and Roe are no longer in her office. The papers they were looking at are lying in the open for anyone to see. I slowly walk over to her door to see what the big deal is.

Large survey maps are spread out on Roe's desk. Each is a different point of view from the dome. I step inside and shuffle through them. There's nothing remarkable about these. They must be preparing for the next expedition. I'm about to drop the pile, when I notice some writing on the bottom map. My breath catches in my throat; it's my mother's writing.

On impulse, I grab the bottom map, fold it up, and hide it in the back of my pants. I slip out of the lab, no one paying attention to me as Waldorf has already left. I go straight to my room, not daring to pull out the map until I'm alone.

Thankfully, Tassie is still gone. The second our bedroom door slides shut, I stand over my bed, blocking the view of the camera, and carefully lay out the map, setting the glass object on the corner to hold the paper in place. Smoothing the paper out, I run my fingers over my mother's words. She must have used this map while planning one of her expeditions. She could have visited these places, mapping out where to go. The word *Meadow* jumps out at me. It's the meadow I found with Evan.

When I used to walk to school from my grandparents' apartment, or to the Douglass' to pick up Xara, I would think about how my mother had once walked in the same steps. But those paths were well trodden, and her steps would have been covered up by hundreds of other residents making the same trips every day.

But on the outside, well, that was different; the outside was untouched. The cleansing bombs wiped out all sign of previous footprints. The next to walk that ground were my mother and her crew. Seeing the word *Meadow*, reminds me she once walked there. I had been as close to walking with her as I would be ever again. Tears well up in my eyes. My biggest regret is having her notebook destroyed. Not because of the secrets that Waldorf says it holds—I read through it thousands of times over the last ten years and no trade secrets had jumped out at me from its pages. I regret it because that was the last real connection I had with my parents. It was the last piece of them, and I foolishly got rid of it for fear of what would happen if it was found.

I wipe my eyes. I'm tired of crying, and tired of regrets. There is nothing I can do about the past. I need to be strong. I look back down at the map, reading the other words my mother wrote, *Forest* and *River*. I trace my fingers between the three words. My mother's words. My mother's steps. My mother's—notebook. My finger freezes on the word *River*. My mother's notebook talks about the meadow, the forest, and the river. That was where she wanted to take me one day. She mapped these out and connected them, like they are on this map. What does it mean?

Something rustles at the door and I jump. My body freezes as I listen, my hand hovering over the map. The sound stops and I quickly fold up the map, and stuff it into my pocket, as the door slides open.

"Oh my goodness," Tassie says as she walks in. "What a morning. I can't wait to come on an expedition …" Her voice drifts off as I sit on my bed, feeling the sharp folded corners of the map bite into my skin. All I can think about is that triangle. I need to figure out its meaning and remember why it was so important that my mother wrote about it in her notebook.

CHAPTER 14

I spend the rest of my day pondering over the mystery of my mother's map with no avail. It's not until the next morning, when I roll out of bed and find a white envelope lying on the floor inside our door, that a spark of hope burns in my chest. I grab the smooth, white paper, with my name typed neatly across its front, and tear it open to see what's inside.

Miss Natalia Greyes—

Permission has been granted for you to visit the Hall of Records. An assigned Delegate chaperone will pick you up at 0900 hours sharp, at your dorm room. You are granted this visit for Expedition Division purposes only, and will be required to return to the Axis no later than 1100 hours.

The Order

The request barely gives me enough time to get to the Hall of Records, visit with Xara, and get back here, but it's better than nothing. Plus, with the uncomfortable developments in my friendship with Jak, I really needed to see Xara so she can put everything into perspective.

I ride up to the cafeteria and find Evan sitting at a table with Roe and Waldorf. Sitting across from them, I wonder whether they noticed a map was missing. But I'm too excited to see Xara to let anything bother me this morning, whether it's stolen maps, kisses, or Evan's swift rejection of the latter.

"What are you all smiles about?" he asks.

"I get to go see an old friend this morning." I stab a piece of bacon, which Sophie excitedly handed over just a moment ago; I'm celebrating.

"Excellent!" Waldorf exclaims from the seat next to me. "I look forward to your full report when you return."

"What's going on?" Evan looks back and forth between Waldorf and me. His smile is gone, replaced with a small frown.

"You aren't the only one who's given important duties." I point my fork at him.

"Miss Greyes is going to the Hall of Records to find an artifact that may aid us in an upcoming expedition," Waldorf advises. I smirk at Evan.

"What would that be, exactly?" Roe's brow arcs.

"Something of my mother's," I respond with a mouth full of bacon.

"It's a missing piece of a large object," Waldorf explains. "A compass of sorts."

"Interesting that this just happened to come up." Evan glares at me from under his furrowed brows.

"Evan," Roe warns, "it's obviously something that will be useful. Good job, Greyes."

"I'm going with you," Evan states.

"You can't," I say with a mouth full of hash browns. "They're sending a Delegate to chaperone me." Evan's eyes widen and I can't help but enjoy it. It's nice to see him thrown off his game; he's not the only one around here who can get things done. Maybe he can go find Tassie and whine to her about it.

Everyone finishes eating before me, and leaves. I'm not in a rush, as I don't have to report to the lab this morning. As I put away my tray and head for the elevators, Evan surprises me and blocks the doorway with his arm.

"Don't you think it's weird that Waldorf has something that was once your mother's? And now the Order chooses you to go and get it. I don't like this situation one bit."

"Relax." I roll my eyes. "You're being paranoid. Waldorf was part of my mother's team; they went on expeditions together. For Pete's sake, they even grew up in the same neighborhood. I asked to go, no one picked me. I want to see my friend Xara, who works in the Hall of Records. No offense, but I once had a life outside this place."

Evan moves his arm and follows me into the elevator where I punch the button for the lobby. Our ride is quick and quiet. As the doors open he bursts out, "I had a life before this place too, you know."

Jak stands in the corridor, looking quizzically at Evan before smiling at me. "Didn't we all?" He holds his hand out to me, and I take it and step off the elevator.

"What are you doing here?" Evan asks, not leaving my side.

"I'm Nat's chaperone," Jak flashes Evan a smile, before turning to me. "It'll be like old days, just you and me."

"And Xara," I remind him.

"Of course," Evan groans. "It all makes sense now. You two have fun." He slams his hand against the buttons of the elevator, and the doors slide shut.

Jak doesn't let go of my hand as we walk through the lobby. The secretary at the desk smiles at me as we walk past. It's the same girl I've seen every time. I wonder if she remembers me?

Outside, Jak has a car waiting for us.

"You get to drive this?"

"Absolutely," Jak says. "The Director is training me to be a Delegate. He likes my vision for the dome. He said I'm an asset to his team."

"Wow." He holds my door open and I climb into the car. "It's everything you ever wanted."

"Not everything." He slams my door, making my insides jump. This might not be as nice as I thought.

"So they're calling you a Delegate now?" I ask as he climbs into his seat. "I thought your ceremony has to happen first?"

"That's just a formality. I'm already working as an official Delegate."

"That's exciting. I'm happy for you." I reach over and rest my hand on his arm.

He shakes it off. "Nat, this is business. Let's keep our personal issues out of it."

I withdraw into my seat, and stare out the window. I didn't expect this cold reception from Jak. Is he fed up with being just friends? If I don't have him at the Axis, who am I left with—a bunch of people using me to get information?

After a quiet ten minute drive, the large stone exterior of the Hall of Records looms before us. It reaches up into the sky three stories and has two wings that shoot off in opposite directions. It was the oldest building in the dome, dating long before the Cleansing Wars, kept to remind us we can always learn from the past.

I immediately spot Xara waving from the steps. Did she get a note this morning, too? My heart jumps in my chest, rejoicing in happiness to see an ally. Jak's barely stopped the car, before I'm stumbling out the door toward my friend. Xara squeals in excitement, and the two of us run into each other's arms.

"I can't believe it's really you!" she says. "When I heard you were taken to the Axis, I didn't know if I'd ever see you again."

"I'm so glad to see you." I have tears in my eyes. "We have so much to talk about."

"Hi, Xara," Jak calls from behind us, still by the car

"It's like it used to be," Xara says, letting go of me and waving to Jak. "Come on, let's go inside. I'll show you where I work."

A woman walking by grabs me by the arm. "Did I hear you're from the Axis?" Her eyes look wild and desperate. Her hair is strewn around her face and her clothes are crumpled, as if she's been sleeping in them.

"Yes." I try to pull away.

"My daughter," she says, pushing a poster against my chest. "She went missing three weeks ago. Have you seen her there?"

I shake my head. "I'm sorry, I don't know—"

"Please look at her face," the woman pleads, widening her bloodshot eyes. "Have you seen her?"

I grab the poster with my other hand. A beautiful girl in her twenties stares back at me. She has long blond hair, blue eyes, and an infectious smile stretches across her lips. I might have seen her in the business district before, maybe at the bank with Grandmother. "I'm sorry, ma'am—" I start to explain.

"Let go of her," Jak yells, grabbing the woman by her shoulders and pulling her off me.

"But they have my daughter," the older woman screams. "They took my baby."

He drags the woman to the street and leaves her there. I start to run after them, but Xara grabs me and holds me back. "No, Nat," she whispers. "Don't."

I look up at Xara's face as she shakes her head at me. Turning back, Jak is climbing the stairs toward us. His face is angry as he holds a rip together on his sleeve. The woman lies below, sobbing in the middle of the street.

"Someone needs to help her—"

Jak twists his face in my direction and growls, "Get inside now, before there's a scene." Xara pulls me behind her into the building and I shove the poster into my pocket.

The entrance of the Hall of Records is a narrow room with a staircase in the center. Two research rooms flank either side. The Archivists work on this floor, protecting valuable books and documents from our past. On the other side of the room is the library, filled with books from the pre-war days. The Learning Institute would bring us children here for field trips. We were allowed to take one book home with us a month. I always took ones categorized as *fiction*, even though the Institute tried to sway us toward historical or science texts. I much preferred stories about other places, rather than ones that felt like additional lessons. But last I heard, those were destroyed to make room for policy documents.

Instead of entering the library, Xara takes us up the stairs. Here are the Archivists' offices, along with Xara's mother's; as the Curator, Mrs. Douglass oversees the whole building. Her authority is only surpassed by Dean Carleton, an Order member, whose office sits alone on the third floor.

Xara takes us to her cubicle, which is decorated in pink, like her bedroom. For a moment a fluttery feeling of homesickness weighs me down. But I push it away, reminding myself that was never really my home, not after my parents were killed. Our old apartment has been taken over by another family, and no longer holds any comfort for me.

She pushes a large cardboard box aside, and jumps up on the desk. I sit in her chair, and Jak leans against the opening to her cubicle.

"So, what do you guys want to do?" she asks. "I was thinking I could show you what you came to see, then take you to the basement and show you some really cool stuff. Maybe we could all go for lunch after?"

"This is a short, work-related visit," Jak states, crossing his arms.

The excitement drops from Xara's face, and she looks like she's about to get mad at Jak, so I jump in. No need to ruffle Jak's feather's any more than necessary. I'm still not sure what's going on with him. "They're only allowing me two hours. I'm sorry."

Xara looks from Jak, to me, and back again, then lets go of whatever disappointment she was feeling and nods. It's an amazing trait she learned from her mother—the ability to read people.

"Well then, let's not waste the time we have." She slides off the desk and pulls the box forward. It's sealed with tape stamped with the symbol of the Order. I stand up to watch her open it, and am caught unaware by the names scrawled across the top.

"Kaitlin and Jonathan Greyes," I say out loud, running my fingers over their names. It sounds strange hearing their first names—I'm so used to hearing them simply called the Greyes Scientists. It's much easier to distance myself from their absence when they aren't personified by names.

Xara puts her hand on my shoulder, and suddenly I'm embarrassed. It's been almost a decade, but I've thought about my parents more these last few weeks than I have the past year.

"Natalia," Xara's mother's warm voice is heard. "Natalia Greyes, is that you, honey?"

Mrs. Douglass's tall and slender physique enters the cubicle. "Come here and give me a hug! What a treat this is." Her embrace is warm and genuine, and reminds me what unconditional love feels like.

She lets me go and looks me over. "Are they feeding you properly? You're looking a little thin. Jak, I'm counting on you to make sure she's taken care of?" She grabs Jak and pulls him into a hug before he can resist.

"Look at you, all grown up now!" Mrs. Douglass pats Jak on the back. "Don't forget about us little people, now that you're going to be a bigwig over there! In fact, I need you to come with me to my office. I have something important for the Director."

"I'm supposed to stay with Nat."

"Nonsense!" Mrs. Douglass exclaims. "She's a big girl. She can take care of herself. This is the Hall of Records, nothing will happen to her here. Come on." She pulls him by the arm, forcefully removing Jak from the cubicle. "We'll only be a few minutes."

"I hope your mom never changes."

"She misses you." Xara grabs my hand and squeezes it. "We both do." She holds tight and I feel a piece of paper transfer from her hand to mine. I am about to ask her what it is but she purses her lips and shakes her head just enough to show it's meant for later.

"So! Let's see what your department is so *gung-ho* to get their hands on."

"*Gung-ho?*" I ask confused.

Xara starts laughing, "It means enthusiastic. If you only knew how long I have been waiting to use that one. I read about it in an old mid-twentieth century article. I like the sound of it."

"I hope you never change, either."

"I like *me* too much." She winks.

We open the box and a wave of nostalgia washes over me. All the items are things Mom brought home from expeditions and kept in her office. Did they each have a purpose or were they purely decorative? I can't remember. I wish I'd paid more attention.

I dig deep, searching for the triangular artifact I remember from my childhood. My fingers brush across its smooth surface and I begin to pull it out from the bottom. I'm about to tell Xara when an unfamiliar voice slithers in from outside her cubicle. "Good afternoon, ladies." I bury the artifact, catching a glimpse of the numbers *6.1.0* on its tag.

I hear Xara let out a small gasp and stutter, "Hello, sir!"

I stand up straight and come face-to-face with Order member Dean Carleton, keeper of the past. He frowns at both of us, his long bushy eyebrows gathering together. His mouth droops down the corners, pulling the tip of his crooked nose with them. He walks with his arms tucked behind his back, revealing his expensively tailored dark suit.

"Where might your escort be, *Miss Greyes?*" He enunciates my name with an edge of irritation.

"He left with the Curator to get something for the Director, sir," Xara says.

"Was I talking to you, Miss Douglass?" Dean Carleton raises his eyebrows, and the tip of his nose lifts in unison. "Young people don't know proper manners anymore."

"Sorry, sir." Xara's gaze drops to the floor.

"That's better," Dean Carleton says. He turns to me and I stare straight back at him. I will not let him intimidate me. He looks down his nose at me. "Have you found what you came here for, *Miss Greyes?*"

"No, sir." I purse my lips.

"Really?" He lifts only one eyebrow this time. It's so bushy it looks comical, as if it has a mind of its own. "How disappointing. Apparently it's an important piece that was used in the last expedition. You obviously were mistaken to think we had it in our possession," he adds, his eyes narrowing as his stare intensifies. "Or did you have other reasons to want to make this trip?"

"No, sir," I reply, repeating Jak's words. "Purely business. Perhaps if you allowed me to look through all of my parents' things, I might find what I'm looking for."

"I do not believe you were granted that amount of time." A small smile plays at the corners of his mouth. "What a shame that all their things are here, just out of your reach."

"Perhaps you'd let me request some of my mom's personal items?" I ask through gritted teeth.

"I am not in the profession of giving away artifacts," he advises, peering over my shoulder at the open box behind me.

"But, sir," Xara steps out of place, "if they're only trinkets, is that so bad?"

"I thought I told you—" the Dean begins and then changes his mind and steps back. "Personal trinkets, you say? I don't see why not. Put in a written request when you return."

He stares back at me, still carrying a smile at the edge of his mouth, almost daring me to push the issue. I look away and accept that I have won what I wanted. Or did I?

"What brings you down here, Dean Carleton?" Mrs. Douglass' voice comes from the hallway.

"Just checking in on our visitor." The Dean raises his chin. "It appears she lost her chaperone somewhere along the way."

Jak appears, his cheeks red with embarrassment. "Mrs. Douglass needed me to pick up a parcel for the Director."

"And what, may I ask, was this pressing business?"

"Why, my chocolate cake, of course!" Mrs. Douglass laughs. "The Director and I used to be neighbors. He always loved my chocolate cake and makes me promise, every chance I get, to send some over to him."

"You have friends in surprising places," the Dean says, eyeing Mrs. Douglass. He turns his back to us and starts to walk away. "Don't forget, Miss Greyes, you need to get permission if you want some of your mother's things. I would hate for red tape to get in the way of you obtaining what you are looking for."

"What an odd man," Xara whispers, when the Dean is out of earshot. "He always creeps me out. I can't believe he is going to let you have some of your mother's things."

"Yeah, that surprises me too." I watch the Dean turn as he reaches the staircase at the end of the hall. He stares back at me, returning my gaze. A shudder runs up my spine, and I duck back into the cubicle.

"Well," Jak says, "it's time we leave."

"We haven't even been gone an hour."

"You just said what you came for isn't here," Jak says. "I have other business to attend to—important things for the Dome. I'm sure Mrs. Douglass agrees."

She turns to me with pity in her eyes. "Yes, you get that cake back to the Director. I'm sorry you couldn't find what you needed, honey. Another time, maybe?"

"That would be nice," I say, embracing Mrs. Douglass. How can I tell her, there may not be another time, without sounding as crazy as the lady we left out in the street? I look at the desk, longingly, at the box that contains the artifact I want. I can't forget its number—6.1.0.

"Don't forget that request form." Xara hugs me goodbye. "Put it to my attention and I will box the items up."

"You should send Nat a list of the artifacts in this box," Jak advises. "Just in case she missed it."

"What a great idea!" Mrs. Douglass says, ruffling Jak's hair. "Remember. Take care of our girl for us. I'm holding you responsible if anything happens to her."

"Yes, ma'am." Jak nods, clutching the cake. He's still so young an innocent looking, the parcel makes him look like a delivery boy, not a Delegate-in-training.

As we descend the stairs of the Hall of Records, I wonder if I will ever get to see Xara or her mother again. At the bottom of the stairs, Jak holds my door open for me, less as a custom of politeness, and more as a silent command. I hesitate, staring out into the street. There's no sign of the woman, but I still have her poster in my pocket. If her daughter is in the Axis, maybe I can find her, and with her find the proof that Evan needs to get us all out of that place.

CHAPTER 15

Things are very different between Jak and me on the ride home. I've lost all patience with his "grumpy guy" act. I'm not sure if he's still waiting for me to return his "I love you" or if he's mad with how things played out at the Hall of Records. Either way, I don't blame him, but I'd like to clear the air before we get back to the Axis.

"Can we talk?" I break the silence. "You know, like we used to?"

"Things aren't like they used to be, Nat," Jak states through clenched teeth.

"We haven't been here that long," I remind him. "It's only been a few weeks since things started to change."

"I don't want to talk about it."

"Well, I do. And frankly, if you really cared about me, then you would talk to me. Instead, you keep pressuring me for a relationship with you, or else I get nothing. How is that even fair? I haven't had a moment's time to be able to get used to all the changes."

"It's hard for me, too," he squabbles. "Do you know how long I've waited to tell you how I felt? Obviously not. You had no idea I could exist as anything other than a friend. This has been going on much longer than a few weeks for me. It's been years."

"That's not my fault!"

He slams on the brakes in front of the Axis, kicks open his door, and flings mine open. I storm out of the car, all the way to the elevator, half-surprised he's still following me. Inside the elevator I tear into him again. "Think about what you're saying. It's selfish. You get to go home every night, back to the world you've always known, while I have to live with a bunch of strangers."

"You should be happier here," he says. "Everyone knows how much you hated it at your grandparents."

I stumble over my words. "It's not about whether I liked it there or not. Here, everyone knows me as the daughter of the Greyes scientists, and even if I could go back home, Grandmother would never let me. She hates me now. You saw them take Grandfather. Do you have any idea what happened to him down there?"

"Yes." Jak sighs, leaning his head against the back of the elevator. "Yes, I do, Nat. I've kept very close tabs on your grandfather since I got here. Who do you think petitioned the Director to have him released?"

"You did that?" My mouth drops open.

He nods. "I did it all for you, Nat. I was also the one who recommended you for the open spot in the Expedition Division. I thought maybe you could finally feel connected your parents again, and work with the same people they did."

"I don't know what to say. I had no idea."

"Like you, I have had to deal with a lot of change as well. I have been working every waking moment to impress the Director and the Delegates. In the middle of all of that, I still did everything I could to make your life easier. I told you I love you—maybe now, you'll believe me."

I stare at Jak and a wave of pity comes over me. There's a love that I have for him, buried deep inside of me. It's a love that comes from familiarity and comfort. If I ever said I loved him back, I would be lying. I don't have the same love for him as he professes for me. But I can't help myself. His confession draws me to him, from a sense of duty and loyalty."

"You know I love you, Jak—" He sees it as a sign of hope, and leans toward my face with his lips. Before I can think about what is right or wrong, I let him kiss me, a soft, sad kiss.

He pushes against my lips, with a hungry frustration, until the intensity becomes painful. I try to push him back but he's too strong. He grabs my wrist with one hand and I hit him with the other, as the elevator doors open.

"What the—" Evan yells from the corridor. Jak's body is ripped off mine and thrown into the hallway.

"No!" I yell at Evan, surprised by his reaction. "It's partially my fault."

"Stop protecting him," Evan shouts at me. "He was attacking

you in there." His eyes flash with rage.

"Don't lay another hand on me, Outsider." Jak pushes Evan against the wall. "You have no idea what was happening in there. She's not yours. She's mine. She's always been mine."

"She's not an object." Evan spits in Jak's face, pushing him away. Jak throws himself against Evan, and the two of them tumble to the floor.

"Stop it, you two!" I stomp my foot. "I don't belong to anyone. Understand? No one owns me. Not you, or you, or my grandparents. Not even the Order! I belong to myself." I storm past them into my room.

"What's all the commotion?" Tassie asks.

"Boys," I say, throwing myself onto my bed.

"Ah."

Seconds later, the door to our room slides open. It's Evan. He has a small cut on his cheek, but other than that seems okay. He's breathing heavy, and his shirt is torn along the bottom, revealing the skin across his abs.

"I need to talk to you," he says.

"I thought I just made myself clear."

"I'm going to go do some work." Tassie gets up. She stops at the door and looks back at me. "All good?"

"Yes." I appreciate her tact and I wave her out the door. "Fine."

The door slides shut, leaving Evan and I alone. He sits on Tassie's bed, and I sit up on mine, ready to retaliate with whatever lecture he thinks he's about to give me.

"Where's Jak?" I ask, crossing my arms in front of my chest.

"Gone," Evan says. "Or should I say, taken. Some Members must have been alerted. They came off the elevator and escorted him away."

"I hope he's not in trouble."

"Why?" Evan rolls his eyes. "What do you see in that guy? Can't you tell he's trying to advance his career? He's one of them."

"One of whom?" I ask. "Explain this to me, Evan, because I am having a hard time understand who exactly *they* are. I've known Jak pretty much my entire life. He's never done anything to hurt me. Did you know he's the one who got my grandfather released?"

"Yes," Evan says quietly, "but you should to know—"

"Know what, Evan? That Jak is some big bad monster I am supposed to stay away from? Well, he says the same thing about you. Who am I supposed to believe? A guy I've known forever, or a guy I just met."

"You're so frustrating!" Evan slams his hand down on Tassie's pillow.

"I am? How do you think I feel about you? You're so sneaky with the information you give me. Telling me just enough to string me along. How am I supposed to fully trust you?"

"I don't know what it is about you," Evan says, "but you drive me absolutely crazy."

"What do you care? I'm just a job, remember? Leave me alone. You'll be better off."

Evan leans forward and puts one arm on either side of me. Our faces are practically touching and I can tell he is really angry by how he's clenching his jaw. I've hit a button with him this time. But I'm tired of trying not to piss people off.

"You're so innocent, aren't you?" I wince at his words. "Little Miss Greyes. No one can touch her. She doesn't care about anyone. She'll use this person just until she gets what she wants and then move on to the next. All of us are just little pawns to keep her entertained."

"That's not true. I didn't ask you to hang out with me." Doubt gnaws in my gut. How can I be both a burden and a manipulator? Insecurity begins to tear me apart.

"Frankly, I feel bad for Jak. He really thinks you're going to love him back, doesn't he? When are you going to tell him the truth? Or do you still need something from him?"

Tears come to my eyes. I might have been mean, but he's being cruel.

"That's right, Nat." Evan speaks softer. "Other people can be hurtful, too. As for sharing things, you need to understand, it's not safe to tell you everything right now."

"I'm not a child," I say, as tears fall down my face. He lifts a hand and wipes my cheek.

"Then stop acting like one. Stop using your feelings to control your actions. You need to understand, there is a reason I'm here. It's hard to know who we can trust right now. I'm trying to keep you safe."

"I can look out for myself." I avoid his gaze. I wish he'd get out of my space. When he's up close like this, I can smell his cologne, which reminds me of the kiss we had on the roof. But Evan made it clear he wanted nothing to do with me in that way.

"I can't stand being around you sometimes, Greyes." Evan

gets up. He storms out of my bedroom.

"What was that all about?" Tassie says, coming back inside. Did she overhear everything?

"Nothing," I grab my pillow and cover my face. "Absolutely nothing! Evan hates me."

"And what do you want from him?" Tassie asks.

"I don't know." I bury my face in my pillow. "Life was much simpler when I lived outside of the Axis."

"Boys always bring drama." Tassie sighs.

CHAPTER 16

The next week, Tassie joins me every day in the lab to get ready for the next expedition. I'm really bringing her as a buffer, so I don't have to face Evan, but every time I hear them conversing, I wish I'd left her behind. Maybe he's right. Maybe I am a bad person, using the people around me to my benefit. If that's the case, then I wish he'd forget about me, but maybe he already has. We haven't talked since our fight.

Waldorf waves me over as soon as I enter the lab, and Tassie goes to Roe's office to talk about the expedition.

"So," he says rubbing his hands together, "I have it on good authority that today you will be getting the list from the Hall of Records."

"I need to get a requisition form ready, then. Dean Carleton made that very clear. Can you help me with it?"

"They're around here somewhere," he says. "Let me go find

one for you."

"Can I use your network quick? The Curator is supposed to send me a list of artifacts so I write down the right ones."

"Go ahead," he says. "I'm already logged in."

I move into Waldorf's seat at his station. On his monitor, the logo of the Order rotates. I haven't used a network station since my time at the Learning Institute, and there's only one per classroom, so you have to share it with everyone.

Everything you want to know about the Dome is stored on the network. The history area links to the Hall of Records. The Axis area has a lesson about every department inside the tower. The district area talks about the housing sectors, businesses, and shops. Everything is here.

I click on the Resident Center, a special area designated for all the people who live in the dome. Here you can look up everyone in the dome to learn about each other. Everything I could tell someone about myself is listed under my profile. The Order is strict about transparency. Even my messages can be viewed by anyone. I check my name, but there is nothing there. Mrs. Douglass must not have the list completed yet.

I look over and see Waldorf is still busy searching for a requisition form. I absent-mindedly click around the network, entering the image of the Axis, and scroll up through the floors until I reach *Floor 18, Expedition Department.* The computer speaks quietly.

"The Expedition Department: Floor 18. Originally operated as a department of the Axis. Taken under jurisdiction of the Order nine years ago, who closed the program. Recently reopened after the presence of an Outsider displayed the possibility of life outside the dome."

I'm surprised to see the mention of the Outsider in the notes on the Axis. I figured the Order would have tried to hide him from people. I guess it explains why this department is open again.

I click higher up the Axis. Above us are the Botany and Horticulture labs. Above these are the *restricted access* areas: the Genetics lab and the Microbiology labs. The Genetics lab works with the Botany, Horticultural and Agricultural departments to increase food quality and longevity.

The floors above, reaching to the roof, are the Engineering department, that keeps the dome operational, and the Computer labs, which help keep the network running and run the telescreens to promote the messages of the Director.

I click on the Microbiology floors. As children we are all interested in the mysteries of this department, so everyone knows what the link says. I can pretty much recite it as the monitor reads out loud. Now that I know my father worked there, I want to know more.

"The Microbiology labs are where stores of the virus antidote are housed. These floors have the highest security access, for if we were to ever lose the antidote, immune or not, all of mankind would be wiped out. This department also tests us at birth to track those who have the immunity gene and those who do not."

I know all about the virus that originated from monkeys and spread to humans. That's what prompted the annihilation of the monkeys—the intentional genocide of a species. But when it came to mankind, our survival instincts kicked in. Those immune to the virus were sequestered in domed cities, built to withstand the bombs of the Cleansing War. Those who were not immune were killed by the bombs, in an attempt to eradicate any chance of the virus being able to survive. Radiation had covered the world ever since, slowly decaying over time.

I'm about to click on another area when I see a red button pop up at the bottom of the screen. It reads, *Restricted Access granted to Microbiologist Karl Waldorf.* Waldorf is from Microbiology? My finger hovers over the button, about to click on it, when his voice surprises me.

"What have you found?" he asks from the opposite side of the monitor.

I look up at him wide-eyed, wondering if he can see the reflection of the red blinking *Restricted Access* button in my eyes. "Nothing, yet." I force a smile, my finger shaking as it hovers over the button. *Click.* The logo of the Order pops up as the screen loads.

"Look what I found," he says passing me a requisition form over the top of the monitor. "I need your signature." He passes me a pen with his other hand. I place the paper on the monitor and sign my name as the red blinking *Restricted Access* warns me through the paper. I hand the form back to Waldorf over the top of the screen.

"Great! When that list comes through, add the items here." He points to the middle of the form. I nod.

He grabs a chair, and starts to pull it next to me. I click rapidly, trying to get back to my profile.

"What do we have here?" Waldorf asks, leaning in front of me, and taking over the monitor.

"Nothing—I was just looking around—" My throat aches as I try to find words to get me out of this mess. I can hear my heartbeat banging against my ribs, as if it might give out. How much trouble will I be in for trying to access restricted information? I gaze quickly to the doors. I'd be able to outrun Waldorf, but where would I go?

"Looks like I've got a message from Dean Carleton," Waldorf says surprised.

"I must have clicked it accidentally."

"No worries. He's send the list. Looks like he's taking a personal interest in our project. That's good news for us."

"Really." My voice squeaks out.

"Impressing the Delegates means you impress the Director. That's how a person moves up around here. Good job."

I exhale a shaky breath as Waldorf leaves me to transfer item numbers from the list to our form. I end up with enough to fill a box. If Dean Carleton is taking an interest, that means he wants to see the object I'm looking for, which means I need to bury it among a bunch of random objects. I even let Waldorf pick some things that he thinks will be useful for a side project he is working on. I'm happy with this, because if anything, the items Waldorf added do nothing but confuse Dean Carleton even more.

As he looks through my final list, I examine Waldorf. He never mentioned being a Microbiologist before coming here. How does he still have access to their files? I shake my head—Evan's making me overly suspicious. I know everyone I work with had to have jobs before this, in other departments. I laugh out loud at how ridiculous I'm becoming.

"What's so funny?" Waldorf looks up from the list.

"I know nothing about you, aside from the fact that you knew my parents. What did you do after the Expedition program shut down?"

"It was truly a sad day when the Expedition program shut down. Not only because of what happened to our team, but also because it had always been my dream to move outside the dome and be an explorer, like the first adventurers to step foot on this land, centuries ago. Before there was an Expedition program, I was a Geneticist."

"Genetics?" I ask. "They don't talk much about that department at the Learning Institute. Not like Microbiology, everyone talks about that."

"Genetics is an associate department to every other floor," Waldorf explains. "It works alongside all the others, helping them to meet their goals. I don't know why all the glory goes to Microbiology."

"How does Genetics help out?"

"Take the farms, for instance. Yes, there's the Agricultural department out there in the fields with their stations. And inside the Axis we have the Botanists and the Horticulturalists all looking out for our food and plants here in the labs. But who do you think ensures the plant strains we have stay strong? Who do you think created the original strains that could grow in the dome? The Geneticists."

"Interesting. Why don't they put them on a lower floor, closer to the others?"

"Because they do a lot of work with the Microbiologists as well, and everyone knows how important it is to keep the antidote secure."

"What sort of work did you do for the Microbiologists?"

"If I told you that, then I'd have to kill you," Waldorf winks at me through his low spectacles. He's not so bad, and now I know why he has access to Microbiology.

"Alright, everyone," Roe calls out, "pack it up. It's time to get back outside. We're going for an entire day today. Let's not waste it."

The lab explodes with the sound of hoots and hollers of excitement as everyone gathers their things. One thing's missing. Where's Evan? I look around, and Tassie waves to me from Roe's office. I'm glad she'll be out there with me. It won't be easy to avoid him forever.

CHAPTER 17

I catch a glimpse of Evan as we pack up the trucks. We're all dressed in protection suits, helmets included, but I can still find him in the crowd; the way he moves, confident but at the edge of the group, makes him stand out. I wish he'd look in my direction, but he jumps in with Roe, riding shotgun with Waldorf between them. Tassie and I ride in the back of the other truck, with Cardinal driving. Richards, another scientist with whom I have yet to have a conversation, rides shotgun; his wife, Maria, sits in the middle.

"Do you know Mr. and Mrs. Richards from before?" I ask Tassie.

"Yes, they were botanists like me. Cardinal was a geologist, Waldorf a microbiologist, and Roe was with the Order. Well, still is. I guess she's the babysitter."

"A little bit of everything. I guess that's what you want to have when you explore an unknown area."

"What did you do before?" Tassie asks me.

I realize she knows nothing about me prior to our awkward meeting my first day.

"I lived with my grandparents down in the apartment districts. We were only a few blocks from the townhouses. That's where my friend Jak lives."

"It's a shame he's so taken by you," Tassie says. "I think he's hot."

"He's just a friend." I laugh.

"Poor Jak." Tassie giggles. "The boy who never got the girl. I'll make sure to be there to pick up the pieces when you crush him."

We start giggling. It feels so nice to have a friend to laugh over silly things with like Xara and I used to do.

"What about Evan?" She motions her head in his direction. "Does Jak know?"

"There's nothing going on with Evan and me."

"I'm sorry. It's none of my business. I just haven't seen him around you lately. Is everything okay?"

I turn away, and watch the scenery. No, everything is not okay. Evan thinks our dome is hiding something. My once dead uncle, has returned. Add that to both Jak and Evan ignoring me, my future at the Axis is looking more and more like a life-sentence every day.

I reply in the only way Tassie seems to understand. "Boys."

She nods.

Once we reach the hills, I take off my helmet, and let the

wind whip around my hair. Tassie does the same. Her excitement makes up for Evan's absence.

"I love it!" she squeals. "Where was the meadow?"

"Just over that hill." I point as we drive past. The look on Tassie's face falls; I know how much she wanted to see that meadow. Where are we going?

I recall the maps that Roe and Evan had sprawled out on her desk. I have one hidden under my mattress, but I can't recall what was on the other maps. We can't be going too far; we only have the day.

The hills are steep, forcing Tassie and I into the cabs of the trucks. I immediately volunteer to climb in with the Richards so I can avoid Evan, but I notice Evan doesn't hesitate in sliding over to make room for Tassie right next to him. His gaze meets mine. I purse my lips and throw him the nastiest glare I can muster.

Before I can dwell on my jealousy, we reach the top of the hills. It is worth it. At the peak the forest trails down the other side, stretching out farther than I can see. It's surrounded by grasslands, as lush as the meadow, and to the far left something sparkles in the sunlight. My heart jumps—it's the river!

The drive down the hill takes longer, and I resist an overwhelming urge to jump out of the truck and run. Something about the freedom I felt in the meadow still teases the edges of my psyche. But Cardinal would freak at the sight of me jumping out. I stifle a laugh at the thought of her serious façade changing to utter horror.

We pull up next to the river. Its rushing waters remind me of a dark version of the public pool in the dome. Unlike the pool, you can't see the bottom of the river. The water also moves faster here, and the edges are rocky, and slippery, covered in moss. If vegetation is thriving out here again, maybe there is hope for an Outer Colony.

"There's a shallow end down that way if you're interested," Evan says from behind me.

I turn toward him, shrug my shoulders, and turn away to help unload the rest of the truck.

"It might be a little cold for you, Greyes," he shouts after me. "But then again, maybe you'd like that."

Tassie shushes him, but not before I can feel the heat rush to my face. Cold? He hasn't spoken to me all week, and now this? First, he tells me I use people. Now he insinuates in front of everyone that I'm cold. No matter how I try to ignore him, he finds a way to hurt me. I drop what I'm doing, and storm past the truck into the field of wild grass that runs away from the shore.

Tassie catches up to me, which isn't difficult; I'm not really trying to run away. I just want distance from Evan. Why do I still care what he thinks?

We walk in silence along the tall grasses. When I finally look over, I notice she has her backpack with her. At least now I have an excuse to be away from the river. I can help Tassie gather samples.

"You know..." she clears her throat, "he does it to get under your skin. I can tell. Every time you dismiss him, he does something to get your attention. That's all it is."

"You're wrong. He doesn't like me."

"No, Nat. You're wrong. It's the opposite. He does like you."

"What makes you think that?"

"Well," Tassie says taking a deep breath, "he's always keeping tabs on you, wondering where you are, asking questions and stuff. When you're around, he's always watching you, stealing glances when you're not looking. And when you don't respond the way he wants, he reacts. It's totally *Boy likes Girl 101*."

If Tassie knew the real reason Evan pays attention to me is because he promised my uncle he would watch out for me, she'd see things my way. But she doesn't, and I can't tell her. Instead, she's left thinking we need relationship advice. Ugh.

"Sounds more like he's some crazy stalker." I nudge Tassie with my elbow and she stumbles to the side for a moment. She laughs and nudges me back. We break out into a run, chasing one another, leaving thoughts of Evan behind, where they belong.

I have no idea how long we're gone, all I know is that, as more time passes, I feel better. Ahead of us are the sparse beginnings of the forest. The trees are almost as tall as the Outer Forest in the dome. I wonder how long it took them to start growing again after the war? I walk up to one and touch its rough bark; it reminds me of Evan's skin, touched by both the sun and the wind as it grew, unlike those of us—trees included—inside the dome. I lean forward and take a deep inhale of the tree. It smells like outside, earthy and free. Tassie laughs from behind me.

"If you start kissing it, I'm going to have to intervene."

I burst into laughter. I must look ridiculous smelling the trees. She has become a good friend this last bit. I decide to share something personal with her.

"When I was nine, the Order came to my grandparents' home

where I was staying while my parents were on an expedition. The Order came to advise us my parents died while outside the dome."

"Right. Your parents are the Greyes Scientists. They pushed for the Expedition program to start up, you know. You should be proud."

"I didn't know that. There was so much I didn't know. I was only nine. I was devastated when I heard the news. I ran as far as I could and as long as my legs would carry me. When I stopped I found myself at the edges of the Outer Forest in a little clearing. For the last nine years I've visited that clearing nearly every day."

"You never got caught?" Tassie's eyes widen in awe.

"I was lucky. I miss that clearing. These trees, this forest, they're all a reminder of that first taste of freedom I found inside the dome."

"You sound like a true adventurer."

"Like those in the stories they used to let us read when we were kids. Imagine, the entire generation after us will never get to read *fiction*. Why does the Order have to take away everything that's good?"

"Be careful," Tassie smiles, "you're starting to sound like a rebel."

I pull a leaf from the tree and toss it at Tassie. It flutters limp in the air and lands between us.

"Hey, be careful!" she shouts. "That's a perfectly good specimen!"

We spend the next bit collecting samples of grass, bark, moss, and soil, which Tassie tells me also carries vegetation. I am so consumed by finding new things that I don't notice a group of worms attached to the roots of a plant until one reaches out and grazes my wrist.

"Ah!" I scream and drop the plant. "It's alive!"

Tassie runs over and grabs the plant without fear. She holds it between us and shakes the worms from the roots. "Unbelievable! I mean, I knew life had to survive, right? Otherwise how would we have all this?" She waves her arms around. "The worms make the soil rich for the vegetation to grow. And you know the meadow you told me about, well there has to be bees that survived as well, otherwise how would it get pollinated."

"I can't believe it," I say. "I thought nothing lived out here."

"What do you two call me, then?" Evan's voice comes from behind us. We both scream in surprise and Tassie drops the plant. I bend over to pick it up and notice the worms have already half buried themselves back in the soil.

"There are more, you know," Evan explains. "I've seen some other birds, some gophers, and even a rabbit."

"Good for you." I turn away.

"How did they survive?" Tassie ignores me.

Evan shakes his head. "They didn't. Some domes took them in. They've been released over the last decade with the hope of repopulating the world."

"Wow, isn't that cool, Nat?" I don't reply. Tassie clears her throat. "I think I've gotten enough samples. I'm going to head back to the river. You two need to fix whatever it is that's going on." She turns and heads back toward the river.

"I'm coming back with you." I start to follow her.

"Wait." Evan grabs my wrist. "I think Tassie's right. We need to clear the air."

His touch is so faint yet distinct. It sends a flutter to my stomach, which makes me nervous. Nervous, but still angry. I watch Tassie walk away, wishing I could leave with her. When she's out of earshot, I turn toward Evan.

"Why do you have to say terrible things about me?" I ask. "It's one thing to tell me I use people, when it was just you and me. But to call me *cold* in front of everyone, what are you trying to prove? Do you need everyone to know you hate me?"

"Hate you?" Hurt crosses Evan's eyes. "Is that what you think?"

"I get it." I pull my hand out of his. I look longingly toward Tassie but she's already halfway across the field. "People have felt responsible for me ever since my parents died. I'm used to it, okay? I let my childish feelings get in the way and I didn't mean to embarrass you. I understand you're here to do a job, but I don't need you to make me feel like an idiot in the process. I won't get in your way, I promise. Just leave me alone."

I ramble on and on, unable to stop. Evan looks at me with a half-smirk, which makes me more furious. He grabs for my hand, taking a step toward me, and I stumble back until I push up against the rough bark of the tree behind me. I stare at him, waiting for an explanation, fighting the urge to run as my heart beats so fast it burns in my chest. The warmth of his hand holding mine spreads up my arm to my face, stinging my cheeks.

"I don't hate you, Greyes."

"Why did you say those things, then?"

"I do stupid things when I'm confused."

"Why are you confused?"

He stares at me, looking from my eyes down to my lips and up again. He is inches from my face, and I can't stop myself. I lean toward him.

"I can't." He turns away from me, his face scrunching up as if in pain.

I look away. Tears fill my eyes. I step away from the tree, letting go of his hand, severing the last of our connection. Rejection cuts like a knife in my chest.

He steps after me, then stops and throws his hands up in the air. "I want to, but—I'm sorry. It's so hard not to kiss you. I wish—I didn't have to—what I'm trying to say is—" He stumbles over his words but all I hear is *sorry* and *I wish I didn't have to*. Yet again, I've made myself look like a fool. I leave the tree and start walking away.

"Nat, wait."

But it's too late to save my pride. I break into a run. I cannot bear to look at him. My feelings erupt. I feel like a child again, sitting in the movie theater being hushed by my friends, or being stared at by the adults on the street as we giggle and laugh. I can't even read other people's feelings for me. Jak wants me, but I don't want him. Evan doesn't want me, yet I keep pursuing him, and I don't even know if I want that.

When I reach the river, I see I'm a little off in my direction. I can't see the trucks or the rest of the group, but I do see Cardinal a few yards away. I need some time to regain my composure before she sees me like this, a crying mess. She's downstream, wading where the shore slopes up to the bank. It reminds me that

I am out here to work, too. There's no time for foolish feelings or playing around. I wipe my face and make my way over to see what she's doing.

Cardinal holds up some rocks for me to see when I get close. I don't see the importance; they look like plain old rocks to me. "You remind me of my uncle."

"Alec?"

"You knew him?"

"We worked in Geology together."

She doesn't offer anything more, and I don't ask. I've gotten used to Cardinal's flat responses. I kick off my shoes and wade into the water to get a better look. The cool sensation of the river rushes past my bare legs and I struggle to keep my footing on the slippery rocks.

"How can you stand in here like that? It's freezing." My teeth begin to chatter as the cold climbs up my legs.

"Check these out, Greyes." She passes me the slime-covered rocks. "There are algae on these rocks." I shrug. "It shows that life has come back everywhere, outside. She passes me a small jar she holds in her other hand. I peer inside and see tiny little fish swimming in it. "Minnows!" Cardinal exclaims. "Can you believe it? Real, live fish. It's extraordinary."

I can't help but smile, despite my misery. Cardinal was so cold when we first met that I pretty much avoided her every day in the lab. Now I see a side of her I like—a side I can relate to. Everyone shows their true colors when they have a passion.

I hand Cardinal back her prize. "Where's the rest of the group?"

"Follow the river. You'll come across the trucks and a small camp they set up. Waldorf brought out a surprise. You'll hear it before you see it."

I wade out of the water and grab my shoes from the shore and carry them with me. After a few minutes, the trucks come in to view. I also notice something unfamiliar in the air—music. I run toward the camp to see what Waldorf brought.

The first person I see is Evan. Not only did he beat me back to camp, but he has his arms around Tassie, and they're dancing. Jealousy rips through my chest, leaving pain in its wake. It lands in the pit of my stomach where it burns a hole. I freeze, about to turn the other way. But then I'm spotted.

"Look, Greyes," Waldorf exclaims. "I brought this old music player and got it to work. It was quite simple, actually—"

Evan and Tassie are laughing as he spins her around once, and then pulls her close. She lays her head against his chest and anger wildly rears itself inside me. Obviously Evan couldn't kiss me because he has feelings for someone else. If he'd only told me earlier, I wouldn't have looked so stupid. I look back at Waldorf, realizing he is still talking to me.

"—so it's something we could set up for the residents to use. Wouldn't that be great? They could have a large music hall for dances and gatherings." Waldorf beams at me from behind his thick glasses.

I throw my arms around him, grateful for his ideas. I wonder if this excitement was similar to what he experienced while on expeditions with my parents. "That's amazing. People need more joy, and less pressure. You'll be doing a great thing if you can get this approved."

He stands there beaming in all his glory. "You inspired me, searching for your mother's things. I paid a visit at the Hall of Records this week, searching for this item specifically for our trip today."

"You were at the Hall of Records and didn't tell me?"

"Would you like to dance?" Roe interrupts us, holding a hand out to Waldorf. He pushes his glasses back up on his nose, and straightens his scarf before taking her hand. Soon everyone joins in together. Tassie breaks away from the group and pulls me out to dance with her. Even in my jealousy I can't be mad at her. It's not her fault if Evan likes her.

Cardinal returns with her samples, and we break for lunch. Evan tries to sit next to me, but I move when I see him coming, letting him be alone with Tassie. The rest of the afternoon goes well. Waldorf, Roe, and Evan review maps after lunch, and disappear for a few hours, allowing me a break from having to face Evan. I offer to help Cardinal, the Richards, and Tassie, with the rest of their sample collecting. It's monotonous work, but I learn a lot about the plants around us, and their usefulness.

"Take this one," Mr. Richards holds up a pink-flowered plant, "this is a *Hedysarum alpinum*. Its root is very nutritious but its seeds can have a paralytic effect if eaten in large doses. Dangerous, yet beautiful. There's so much we can learn about plants. Why, one could live in the wild with the proper knowledge under his or her belt."

Mrs. Richards smiles and joins the conversation. "My husband, the dreamer. He thinks we should be pioneers, offering to create the first settlement outside the dome."

"This land is untouched." Mr. Richards spreads out his arms. "There's so much the science departments could learn out here in an uncontrolled environment."

We get everything tagged, bagged, and sorted. There are lots of boxes of samples this time. No one will be able to ride in the back of the trucks on the way home.

Roe returns shortly after we are finished, and announces, "Time to pack up camp, everyone. Today was a success. Let's get these treasures back to Floor 18 so we can get them processed. Can someone please help the botanist? She's gathered enough samples for a lifetime."

"Hey." Tassie smiles. "I have an entire department eagerly waiting for my return. We need new challenges."

"Let me help you." I watch as Evan grabs one of Tassie's large boxes.

My body tenses up again. I pack up some of the belongings we brought with us, to keep myself busy. When I'm done, I grab one to carry to the truck.

"Can I help you?" Evan's voice startles me. He reaches for my hand, hidden behind the box.

I step back. "No. I don't need your help. I'm sure you and Tassie can find more things to do together." I walk away feeling a brief moment of self-satisfaction as I put my things in the back of the truck. Then, I notice Evan holding the door open for Tassie to climb in. I immediately regret my reaction. He looks over and catches me staring. I try to force a smile, but he looks away, and climbs in the truck after Tassie. I join Cardinal and the Richards again for the ride back.

After we return and deliver our samples to Floor 18, we are freed to grab a late supper. "Take the evening off, people," Roe calls out. "Go have some fun."

I pass Evan and his stare burns against my back. I push ahead of the others, making sure I get to the elevators before he does. Even if it is for one floor, I don't want to be in a confined space with him. I'm afraid of what stupid thing I might say next.

I get to my room, and find Jak waiting in the hallway for me. He's dressed in an expensive-looking suit, holds a bouquet of flowers, and is smiling, until he sees the confusion on my face. "You forgot," he says, handing me the bouquet.

Suit. Flowers. Oh, no! "Your night!" I cry out. "Jak! I'm sorry. I've been caught up in preparing for this last expedition. Give me twenty minutes to clean up."

"Alright," he grumbles. "I'll be waiting out here for you." I grab the bouquet and go up on my tiptoes, kissing him on the cheek. I toss the flowers on my desk inside my room, and run to the showers to get cleaned up.

When I get out of the showers, Jak is gone and Tassie is in our room. She sees my anxiety. "I forgot about Jak's initiation night," I spout out, as I stand in my towel.

"He'll be right back," she explains. "He ran to get something."

"I completely forgot. What will I wear?"

"Here …" She jumps up and goes to her closet, flipping through her outfits. She grabs a shimmering dress, made of silvery cotton. "It's perfect."

She helps me slip into the dress, which casts reflections around the room from the fluorescent lights above. I stare at myself in the mirror, trying to brush my unruly dark waves.

"Stop," she says, grabbing the brush. "I'll do hair, you do makeup."

"What do you think it will be like?" I ask as she brushes my hair back.

"Have you met the Delegates' wives before?" I shake my head. "They are fancy ladies. I wish I could spend an evening with them."

My stomach turns. I'm far from fancy. What on earth would I talk to them about?

After a few more tugs, she lets me dig into my makeup, but here again, I'm at a loss and she takes over. "Oh, Nat," she smiles. "I have so much to teach you."

She spins me around to face the mirror, and I gawk. I look better than I ever imagined I could. The makeup has blended together the freckles that appeared from the last two outings, making my complexion smooth and perfect. She's also tamed my hair into looking like hers, making my long strands soft and wavy as they cascade around my face. I can't help but smile. I remind myself of my mother. I look much less like a tomboy tonight.

Both Tassie and I turn as our bedroom door opens. Jak and Evan are standing on the other side facing each other. They turn at the same time, and both look shocked at my transformation, and then bump against each other as they step inside.

"I, uh," Evan starts. "I came to see why you two didn't join us for a late supper upstairs."

"Nat has a date tonight." Tassie claps her hands. "It's a Delegate initiation! Congratulations, Jak." She flutters her eyelashes at him. "Nat is *so* lucky."

"It was worth the wait," he says, staring at me. "Let's go; we've missed half the cocktail hour."

I glance at Evan as I walk past. His teeth are clenched and his arms are crossed against his chest. I can see his jaw flexing as he stares at me, but there's no emotion in his eyes. Just a blank stare. My stomach burns in disappointment. Why did I think he was here to see me?

"Enjoy your date, Greyes," he grumbles as the door slides shut.

Jak takes my hand and pulls me down the hallway, constantly looking at me with a sidelong glance. In the elevator, on our way to Floor 3, we turn at the same time and start to laugh.

"Who would have thought we'd both be here, now?" he asks.

"At least one of us got our dream."

"Oh, Nat," Jak says putting his arm around me. "You wouldn't know your dreams if they slapped you in the face." Images of my last night with Grandmother flicker through my head, and a shiver runs through my body, making my skin cold and clammy. Jak drops his arm from around me and shuffles his feet. "I'm sorry. I didn't mean—"

"Let's not wreck tonight with apologies," I say, looking down at my shoes. They match my dress, a luxury I'd never had in my life outside the Axis. "I'm just grateful things can go back to normal."

Maybe Jak is right, I really wouldn't know if I wanted something unless I couldn't have it. The elevator dings. I reach over and squeeze Jak's hand. "Let's do this."

CHAPTER 18

A red carpet extends from the Floor 3 elevator, disappearing into a sea of black and white. I readjust my silvery dress, feeling suddenly out of place. Tassie's dress is much too short for an event like this.

As we walk into the crowd, I recognize faces of those from the business district: shop owners, bankers, and other business people. No one from the apartment district is present. This party is for the upper classes.

Two faces I personally know appear. I have not seen Mr. and Mrs. Manning since before my birthday. Jak weaves us through the crowd in their direction.

"Oh, Natalia." Mrs. Manning smiles at me. "Aren't you an image of loveliness?" She leans forward and kisses the air on each side of my face. I manage to avoid spilling her cocktail. "Jak tells us you are a part of the Expedition program now. Very illustrious.

Taking after your parents, I see?" This is the most attention I have received from Mrs. Manning in all the time Jak and I were friends, growing up.

"Yes, Mother." Jak holds me on display on his arm. "Isn't she beautiful?"

"Lovely choice, darling," Mrs. Manning leans forward and greets Jak the same way she greeted me.

Mr. Manning nods to me and holds his hand out to Jak. "Good job, son. We are very proud."

Is this what it would be like to have parents now? A lot of air-kissing and compliments. Though I would take this any day over living with Grandmother, it's nothing close to the connection I have with Grandfather.

"Thank you, Father." Jak firmly shakes his father's perfectly manicured hand. "I better find the Director, sir. I'd like him to meet Nat before the ceremony begins."

His parents turn toward a group of other shop owners and we make our way through the crowd. We move toward the end of the hallway, where the Director's office is. The door is open. Outside the entrance I notice the familiar faces of the current Delegates. Samson, Carleton, Brandt, and Betker are all standing with their wives, visiting with various Order members. Samson is in charge of all agricultural divisions. Brandt is in charge of all commercial and residential zones. Betker is the head of the Order. And then there is Carleton, head of the Hall of Records. He notices me right away, and his eyes stay glued on me as he pushes past his comrades, into our path.

"Miss Greyes," his long, drawn-out voice addresses me, "how

lovely you look tonight. I had no idea we would be graced with your presence. It is a delight." He holds out his hand, and I take its clammy coldness into mine, and curtsey, letting go as quickly as I can without offending him. He leans in. "I trust you found the items you were looking for?"

"The list has been sent in." I force a smile, as everyone around us watches. The other Delegates close in.

"I will pack it for you personally," Carleton whispers.

Jak pulls me away from the old man. "If I may introduce my date to the rest of you, this is my old friend, Natalia Greyes."

"Oh, my," Brandt pipes in with a jovial voice. "She's not old at all. Be careful how you introduce a woman, Manning."

"We'll teach him the ropes, little lady," Betker says slapping Jak on the back. "Don't you worry."

I smile and nod, wanting to recoil from each of their handshakes. They have a casual machismo that makes me uncomfortable. There's nothing professional about them; I'm an object here for Jak to show off, nothing more to them. I notice their wives hang back, whispering with one another. Staying as separate as they can from the rest of the crowd.

"Did I hear someone wants to see me?" the Director's gruff voice comes from the doorway of his office.

"Yes, sir," Jak straightens up. "I want to introduce you to my date, Nat-er, I mean, Natalia Greyes."

The Director holds out his plump hand and I take it and curtsey as I did with Carleton, but before I can withdraw my hand, he places his other hand on top of mine and pulls me close.

"Why," he says, surprised. "I recognize those eyes. Are you

the daughter of Kaitlin and Jonathan Greyes?"

"Yes, sir."

"I knew it. I'd recognize those eyes anywhere." He stares intently at me. "Your mother came to this office many a time to discuss politics. You see, she never liked the way I ran the science programs. Scientists and politics, the two don't mix well."

"I'm afraid I don't know much about her, sir." I lock my gaze onto his eyes. "I was only nine when the incident happened."

He nods. "I suppose you were. Time does go so fast, doesn't it? That's exactly why we need to preserve and protect the quality of the life we have here in the dome, wouldn't you agree, Miss Greyes?" All the Delegates are nodding in agreement.

"Peace. Love. Order. Dome." I rattle off the motto with the most sincere smile I can find. "Yes, sir, without any of these, where would we be?"

"My thoughts exactly," the Director says, patting the top of my hand. "Good girl you've found here, Manning. I'd hold on to her as tight as possible, if it were me." He breaks into a disgusting laugh. "Let's get started, shall we?"

The group disperses, and the Director begins a long speech. He talks of the ways of the dome and how we need to keep the motto strong, a part of this being a solid foundation for those who keep things running. In this roundabout way, the Director brings Jak into the mix, as an essential part to the foundation of the Delegates and their support to the Director.

"That's why it is my honor to welcome Jak Manning to the new position of Assistant to the Director."

Jak stands, the fluorescent lights catching his blue eyes at just the right angle to make them sparkle. He looks so innocent, among this sea of sharks and crude businesspeople. Will Jak become like them? The Director shakes Jak's hand, awarding him his permanent position, and lifelong dream.

By the time the pomp is over, my stomach is growling. I was left standing with the Delegate wives all this time. The one next to me is married to Brandt. While everyone claps when the ceremony is over, she nudges me in the arm.

"Ladies," she addresses her counterparts, "we need to get this little thing fed. I could hear her poor tummy the entire time the Director was talking."

I clutch my stomach in embarrassment.

"Probably was more interesting than the speech," Betker's wife says. Samson's wife spits out a laugh.

"Oh, Clary." Brandt's wife shakes her head. "You are terrible. Come with us, honey, we know where the good food is kept."

I follow the Delegate wives into the Director's office. Their husbands, along with Jak and the Director, are swallowed up into a crowd from the finance district.

Samson's wife closes the door behind us. "Finally, some peace and quiet." She lights a cigarette. I'm shocked. No one in the dome smokes. "Don't look so surprised, little one." She waves a hand, dismissing me. "There are perks to being married to a Delegate. I'm Catherine, by the way." She holds out a hand and I shake it.

The Delegates live in a gated community, with some of the other professionals in the dome such as doctors, lawyers, and CEOs. Their community is separate from all the districts, running along the edge of the Outer Forest.

"Where did you grow up?" Carleton's wife asks, tilting her head. She's frail and tiny.

"In the apartment district." Their faces drop before I finish. "Right at the edge. That's how I know Jak. His parents' townhouse was only a few blocks away."

"Those Mannings act like they are the peak of the shop district," Clary laughs. "I didn't realize they were so close to the apartments."

"Must be terrible living in such close quarters to one another," Brandt's wife says, her eyes widening with concern.

"We have our own units," I say.

"Oh, Deidre, it's not like they all sleep in one room," Clary says. "Sometimes you're so daft. It's like a mini-house." She pours herself a large drink from the Director's bar.

"Well, that's not so bad, I guess." Clary smiles at me. "Here, eat."

I fill a plate with food, and turn toward them. They all watch me intently. "Aren't you going to eat, too?"

"Oh, darling." Clary shakes her head. "We ate before we came. It's not appropriate for a Delegate's wife to gorge herself at these functions."

"People have expectations of us." Deidre nods. Carleton's wife nods in agreement. I fear if she nods too long, her head may fall off. "You'll find out when you become one of us." Deidre smiles at me.

"That won't be any time soon."

"Oh, I'm sure your boy will ask the question, now that he has a permanent position," Deidre advises.

I almost spit out my food. "We're not dating."

"Really?" Clary says, leaning forward. "Betker told me that Jak is always talking about his plans with you. The Director likes his team to have family ideals. It keeps them properly motivated towards the goals of the Dome."

"We're old friends. We've known each other forever."

"Who's old friends?" the Director says, storming into his office.

"Eek!" Carleton's wife shrieks.

"Oh, Victoria, relax," Clary says. She puts out her arms and the Director comes over and gives her a big hug.

"Aren't you ravishing tonight, Clary." The Director groans as he holds her a little too long and too tight. "I tell you, if I didn't know your husband so well ..." He grunts out a laugh, and lets her go. "I hope you ladies are making our new addition feel welcome."

"Oh yes, of course, sir," Deidre says flutters her eyelashes and plants a kiss on the Director's cheek.

"If I may," the Director addresses the wives, "I'd like a moment alone with Miss Greyes to discuss politics."

"Yes, sir," Deidre says, flashing her bright white teeth. She ushers the wives out of the Director's office, and I notice Catherine look back at me, biting her lip. Clary also shoots me a look, but it's not as concerned. The door closes behind them.

"So," the Director says, walking over to the bar and pours a drink. "What do you think about working here at the Axis?"

"I like it sir, thank you." I try to force another smile, but my cheeks are starting to hurt.

"Don't call me *sir.*" He laughs and hands me the drink. "It's so formal."

"*Director,* then?" I take a sip. The strong bite of the amber fluid burns my taste buds.

"Have you ever tasted whiskey before?"

"No, sir. I mean, Director."

"You do remind me of your mother." He leans in and moves a strand of hair from my face. I force myself not to flinch at his touch.

I step away from him, moving over to his desk where I set down my plate of food. The room feels off-center. It must be nerves. I take another sip of the drink, this time longer, to try to avoid the Director's gaze.

"Did you know her well?"

"Ah yes." He comes over to the desk. "She was a force to be reckoned with. Filled with many great ideas, some of which we still implement today in the Science Division. She also had many political opinions, which I reminded her were best left for the Delegates and me to sort out."

"I don't remember much." I take another long sip.

"Too bad she didn't leave anything behind."

"I had her notebook, but that's gone now." I have no idea why I share this information with the Director. It spills out of my mouth before I can process any thoughts.

The Director smiles. "I have a confession. I have something you might want back." He walks over to the other side of his desk.

"You do?" I take another long sip of my drink. I can't seem to stop drinking it.

He opens a drawer in his desk, and pulls out something familiar, but I barely notice it as the room starts to spin. I grab the edge of the desk in front of me, and try to focus, and the object starts to register in my memory. I look back a second time. It's my mother's notebook.

"How did you get that?"

"Oh, don't be mad," he says. "Young Jak brought it here to shred, but I advised him all documents brought into the Axis must be reviewed by the Order before they can be destroyed. Betker looked it over, and advised there was nothing in it that would compromise Axis, or Order business. Hence, I thought I would keep it, and return it to you myself one day. How lucky it is that you graced me with your presence tonight."

I reach for the notebook, but he pulls it just out of my grasp. I get up and walk around the desk, holding my hand out, but the room spins even worse when I stand. My unsteadiness gets the better of me, and I stumble, nearly falling across his desk.

"Perhaps you should give me that drink, my dear." The Director takes the glass from my hand. "I must have accidentally poured you some of my truth whiskey. I use it on guests I need to get information from. I don't need any information from you, do I?" He grabs my wrist, twisting my arm as he pulls me into his lap.

"No, sir." I try to stand. "I mean, Director."

"Good girl. Now, before I let you leave with this notebook, I will share something with you. Something not many people know. Your mother became a bit of a problem for this office. She stuck her nose into departments she never should have. Am I going to have that same problem with you?"

The little food I ate gurgles in my stomach. Is he threatening me? "No." I grab my mother's notebook.

"Good." He lets go of the notebook and places a hand on my knee. "Now we can be friends. I'd hate for you to affect your boyfriend's future with this office."

"He's not my boyfriend," I say through clenched teeth.

The door to the office opens and Jak walks in. He stops short in the doorway, his mouth dropping open when he sees where I'm sitting. The Director lets go of my leg and loosens his grip on my wrist.

"Manning!" the Director calls out. "Just the person we were talking about. Friendly little gal you brought tonight."

I jump out of the chair, catching the bottom of my dress on something on the inside of his desk. I catch a glimpse of a button as my dress tears on it. I pick up my mother's notebook, and run from the office.

"Thanks for the visit, Miss Greyes," the Director calls after me. "I look forward to the next time we meet." My stomach lurches again, threatening to empty itself into the hallway filled with people. I don't care if Jak follows me, all I know is I need out of this place. Clary smiles smugly at me as I run past. All these people are so selfish and terrible. But right now, I don't care. Right now, I'm clutching my mother's notebook, thinking about the button I saw on the inside of the Director's desk. The button that reads B3.

CHAPTER 19

Jak guides me to the elevators. I don't expect him to and I certainly don't want him to, but I'm in no state to argue. As soon as the doors slide shut, cutting out the music of the party, he reaches out and hits the stop button.

"What the hell is going on with you, Nat? First you want nothing to do with me. Then, you run after this Outsider you know nothing about. And finally, you forget about how important tonight is to me, and end up throwing yourself at the Director. What are you trying to prove?"

"I didn't ask to be here at the Axis. You decided that would be best. I didn't ask to be put on a team with Evan. It just happened. I seem to have very little control about what goes on in my life. Did you know the Delegates expect us to get married? Is this something you were planning on telling me at some point, or did you decide that for me, too?"

He grabs my wrist, and turns me toward him. "That's how they think. I get that you don't feel the same way about me, but you can't blame me for trying. If you hadn't met that damn Outsider, everything would be fine. What do you see in him? He's not even a resident." His grip on my wrist tightens.

"There's nothing going on between Evan and me, trust me. Maybe you're spending too much time with your so-called hero." I wrench my wrist away from his grasp. "I hope you don't graduate to drugging girls, making them sit in your lap at the next party."

"What are you saying?"

"Wake up, Jak." I hit the elevator start button. The upward movement throws me off-balance and I grab the railing. "Your Director is not perfect. He has a bottle of whiskey with a drug in it that he uses to get information out of people. Plus, he had my mother's notebook all this time, even after you told me you destroyed it."

Jak looks down at the notebook and back at me. I fall against the wall, gripping the railing to steady myself. Jak's brows furrow. "I can explain the notebook."

"No need. Your boss already did." The elevator doors open and I step out, supporting myself against the wall. "Go ask him what happened in his office. I'm sure he'll tell you the truth." I roll my eyes as the elevator doors close, and I'm left with a sour taste in my mouth and the surprised look on Jak's face. Or maybe it was disappointment? I don't care. I need to find my room and sleep this off.

I stumble down the hallway, until I locate my door. Thankfully, Tassie's gone. I lie down, but the room spins around even more that way. I try to stand, but stumble off my bed, and crash to the floor. The door slides open, and I hold up my hand. "Leave me alone, Jak."

"Nat!" Evan's voice cries out.

His hands reach under my arms and pull me onto my bed. I collapse against him, inhaling his cologne, and this makes my stomach heave, but I manage to hold everything in.

"Are you okay?" He runs his hands through my hair, moving it off my face. "What happened to your dress?"

"Nothing like being drugged, groped, and lied to, all in one evening."

"I'm going to kill Jak," Evan says, balling his fists. His nostrils flare as he takes a deep breath.

"Jak did the lying part. The rest was all the Director's doing."

"What kinds of people run this place?" Evan sits next to me on the bed. "Do you want me to leave you alone?"

"No." I reach for his hand. "Stay. Please. I'm fine, he just gave me some truth serum."

"What sort of questions did he ask?"

"None, really. He kept asking if I was going to be good or not. He's sick. I ripped my dress on his desk, trying to get away."

"I don't want you alone anymore." Evan shakes his head. "I don't trust them."

My head feels light and fuzzy as the drugs take full effect. I can only smile at Evan. He's right. I shouldn't be alone. I can't argue with that. "Why don't you like me? I mean, I know you don't hate me, but sometimes I think you really like me but then you don't. It's confusing."

"I like you." Evan laughs. "Can't you tell?"

"Not in the same way you like Tassie. I don't blame you. She's very pretty. She thinks you like someone else, but I know it's her, isn't it?"

"Are these the sorts of things you girls talk about?"

"Sometimes." I lean against my cubby, smiling. "Sometimes we talk about plants. Sometimes we talk about boys."

"I do like someone," Evan says. "I tried avoiding her, to make sure I didn't get distracted from my job, but there she is, always sidetracking me. And it's not on purpose. I can't help myself anymore."

"Maybe you love Tassie." I feel a pang of jealousy tighten my chest.

"Oh, Greyes, you goof." Evan squeezes my hand. "I'm talking about you."

I must be hearing things. Or maybe it's the drugs. I rub my temples, trying to massage away my lightheadedness. Is he serious? "But that doesn't make any sense. I practically threw myself at you. I thought—well, you said—"

"I know what I said." He shifts on the bed, getting close. "But no matter how hard I try, there you are, always popping into my thoughts even when I try to ignore you."

Evan leans forward, and kisses the tip of my nose. It's slow but short, and not at all what I expect, or should I say, want. I definitely want something more. He pauses a moment and then leans back, looking back into my eyes. "See, I could never like Tassie or anyone else, now that I've met you."

I lean forward this time, pushing my lips against Evan's. I'm not as gentle as he is. His fingers reach behind me, pulling me closer, until he's pressed against my body. I release my frustration by wrapping my hands behind his neck and running my fingers through his hair. Tassie was right. I have to give her credit. She knows more about boys than I do.

Eventually I stop to catch my breath, and rest my cheek against his chest, listening to a mixture of his breathing and heartbeat as he runs his hands along my bare arm. He smells like the trees in the forest. Free.

"Let me go get you some tea from the cafeteria."

"Mmm. Tea sounds nice."

He shifts from underneath me, and every cell in my body cries out for him to stay, but I let him go. He stands in front of me, his eyes lined with deep concern, but I'm too tired to sit up and put him at ease. I grab my pillow, and put it in his empty place, clutching it close until he returns.

"I'll be right back. Maybe Sophie has something that can counteract this truth drug you got. Not that I want you to stop telling me all your secrets."

I try to throw my shoe at Evan, but he ducks out of my room. As I lie there, everything feels suffocating. This dress is soiled from the Director's touch and Jak's accusing eyes. I slip it off, dropping it to the floor, and manage to slide into sweat pants and a cotton shirt while lying on my bed. I climb back in my bed, and touch my lips, where Evan's kiss still reverberates.

He comes back in about fifteen minutes with a steaming mug. "Sophie says it will wear off on its own within the hour. She's heard of it used before on others. It won't hurt you."

Evan passes me the tea, and as I reach for it he grabs my hand, turning it over to reveal the small bruises left behind by the Director as he held me on his lap. I can't shake these off as easily as the dress. "Who did this?"

"The Director wanted to get his point across." I pull my hand away and hide the marks under my sleeve.

"What point is that?"

"I think my mother double-crossed him. He wanted to make sure I understood that was not acceptable. Maybe that's why I'm here. So he can watch me."

"I'm not leaving you alone anymore."

"I'm fine." I rub my wrist through my shirt as my skin crawls. It's time to change the subject. "There was something I saw in the Director's office."

"Okay ..." Evan sits next to me, and we both lean against the wall at the side of my bed.

"Have you ever heard of B3?"

"B3?" Evan says. "Well, I know there is a B1, where the generator room is, and B2 is detainment."

"Exactly. So what could be on B3?"

"What makes you think there is a B3?"

"I saw a button on the Director's desk that had 'B3' written on it."

"You saw that with your own eyes?"

I nod.

"B3 is a theory your Uncle has. He said your mother told him that the Axis kidnapped people and put them on B3."

"Why would they do that?"

"Your uncle told us about mysterious disappearances that went on in this dome."

I think about the posters out in the dome, showing all the missing people. Their families distraught, trying to find answers, like the woman on the stairs at the Hall of Records. You'd think in a dome of this size you'd eventually run into someone again. "Those people left their families to start new lives."

"So the Order tells you. Your mother thought they were taken against their will."

"What for?"

"She thought it had to do with the Microbiology department. Your uncle said she confronted the Director, and that was when restricted access was put in place on the Microbiology and Genetics levels."

I reach behind me to my desk drawer and pull out the poster from the woman at the Hall of Records, and toss it to Evan. "You're telling me that they're performing tests on people like this? That girl looks almost like me—she's only a couple of years older."

"Those departments do more than house the virus. They create new strains that need testing."

Had my mother uncovered something this big? People would be livid. It would bring down the Director and the Delegates. Even the Order couldn't be trusted anymore. "So that's why the Director wanted my mother's notebook."

"What do you mean?"

"Jak was supposed to destroy it, but the Director made him hand it over first."

"Is there anything in it?"

I shake my head. "I pored over that notebook for the last nine years. There isn't one reference about B3 or her suspicions. Do you think she really had proof?"

"The fact that they're hiding B3 is suspicious enough. You saw the button. I wonder if that's the only way in?"

"What do we do now?"

"I'm going to go to B3."

My head jerks toward him. "You can't go down there. What if it's dangerous?"

Are you worried about what happens to me, Greyes?"

"Waldorf is from the Microbiology department. Maybe he could tell me more of what goes on up there."

"I don't think we should tip anyone off."

"Well, I don't want you to go to B3. What if you got killed?"

Evan reaches over and runs his fingers through the hair at the back of my head, sending shivers along my skin. "That would suck, because I wouldn't get to do this again." He pulls me close, and kisses me again. This time it's less eager, nice and slow. When it's over I stay pressed against him, the heat of his body warming mine, as I drift off to sleep.

CHAPTER 20

My bedroom door slides open, letting the glow of the fluorescents spill into the room. I reach for Evan in the shadows of my cubby, but my bed is empty and cold. Footsteps approach our door, faster and faster, and my heartbeat races to match them. Suddenly they stop and I sit frozen, waiting for the owner to show their face. But no one comes.

I crawl out of bed, my feet silently moving across the cool tiled floor. I reach for my open door frame, just as a girl with long blond hair *swooshes* past the opening, down the hallway toward the elevators.

"Wait!" I try to call out. But no sound leaves my mouth.

I run out of my room, toward the elevator. Its doors slide shut, giving me a glimpse of the girl's face. It's the face of the missing girl, from the poster I received at the Hall of Records.

"Stop!" I scream in my head.

I bang on the elevator doors, until they open, revealing the Director's office. My head spins, and I know this isn't right but I still step inside. The blond girl sits in the Director's lap, wide-eyed and innocent, mouthing words to me I cannot hear. The Director pushes her down on the desk, and slams a fist against the button. A loud grinding noise fills the air, so loud it makes my ears ring. I fall to my knees, clutching my head, and look up just in time to see the blonde girl swallowed into a giant hole in the floor where the Director's desk once sat.

I reach out, screaming 'no', but it's too late. The Director stands, laughing a deep laugh that shakes the room.

He points a finger at me and growls, "You're next, Nat." His body grows larger and larger until his finger is close to my nose. I try to run, but the ground is shaking so bad, I can barely move.

"Nat, wake up."

I slowly open my eyes, and as the dark room comes into focus, I can make out Evan's outline sitting on the edge of my bed. He's gently shaking my shoulder.

"What are you doing?" I am half asleep with memories of the Director's laugh still reverberating in my head.

"Shhh." He holds his finger to his lips. "I have something to show you."

"What time is it?"

"Really early. Come on," he whispers.

I groan and force my muscles to climb out of bed and follow Evan into the hallway. I cautiously glance at the elevator doors, half expecting the blond girl to be standing there. Of course she isn't. I shake her face from my thoughts. I look down and see

I'm still in my comfy clothes and Evan's still wearing his clothes from earlier. Had he stayed with me all this time? We slip into the elevator and he hits the button for Floor 30.

"Stay in the corner of the elevator and keep your face down. That way, they can't tell who you are."

My pulse speeds up, and I breathe a sigh of relief as the doors slide open, revealing the plain box of the elevator. "Who are they?"

"The computer operators," Evan explains. "They monitor all the cameras in the dome as well as the banners. I've got a friend working up there tonight, but we still need to take precautions."

So that's who watches me dress every day—the computer operators. I tuck my chin against my chest. Why would they care if we're going to the cafeteria?

The doors slide open on Floor 30. It's creepy up here in the dark. The light from the stars sneaks through the windows, casting long shadows across the floor from the empty tables and chairs that are usually filled with people. The silence adds to the effect. Evan climbs behind the counter, and motions for me to follow. Where are we going? He walks through the kitchen, and knocks a sequence on a door on the back wall. I catch up and wait behind him.

As the door clicks open, he grabs my hand and entwines his fingers with mine. He pulls me into a room lined with shelves of food from the gardens. I feel like we're sneaking a midnight snack. In the middle of the room is a long table with a number of people sitting at it, prepping food for the day. It takes me a moment before I realize they are people I recognize.

Sophie, the woman who runs the cafeteria, sits at the head of the table. To her right is Mrs. Watson, head of maintenance. I haven't seen her since my last day working on her crew. I didn't know she worked in the kitchen, too.

"Come, sit." Sophie motions to empty seats. "There's lots of work to get done. I'm glad you brought a friend to help."

"Hello, Natalia," Mrs. Watson smiles. "You may not remember, but your mother used to bring you here. Ah, you were just a little one back then."

I shake my head. I have no recollection of being in the Axis before my eighteenth birthday. What would my mother have been doing up here?

Evan sits next to Sophie, and I take the seat beside him. Across from me is the girl who works the front desk in the lobby. "I'm Leta." She extends her hand.

I reach out to shake her hand. "I'm confused. I thought you all worked in other areas."

Sophie laughs. "We're waiting for a couple more before we begin." Evan gives me a reassuring nod. As if on cue, a quiet knock comes from the other side of the door—the pattern matches Evan's. Three short knocks, then a pause, and one more knock. Sophie opens the door, and Mr. & Mrs. Richards walk into the room and sit at the end of the table next to Leta and me.

"Sorry we're late," Mr. Richards explains. "There were complications."

"Were you followed?" Mrs. Watson jerks her head up.

"No. We got delayed in our corridor," Mrs. Richards says.

"Good," Sophie says. "Let's begin."

"Where are the others?" Evan asks.

"Extenuating circumstances," Mrs. Watson replies.

"Status updates, please." Sophie rests her hands on the table, looking around the room.

Leta pipes up across from me. "I have a working copy of a Computer Operator ID card. That gives us two areas now: Detainment and Systems."

"We still need Engineering." Sophie taps her fingers on the table. "That and Genetics, and Microbiology."

"Add the Director's office to that mix," Evan speaks up.

"Really?" Mrs. Watson asks raising her eyebrows. "Why?"

"Nat was in there last night, and got a peek at a button on the side of his desk labelled 'B3'," he explains. "I think we may have our final step."

"How did you get into the Director's office?" Sophie narrows her eyes at me.

Everyone's eyes fall on me. I force a swallow to try to clear the lump in my throat. "I was invited to the Delegate party last night."

Sophie stares at me long and hard, until Mrs. Watson breaks the silence. "That will not be a problem. I clean his office."

"I need a couple of days to make that copy," Leta explains. "That's the next time I'm on nights, so I can make copies in private."

"Don't they still monitor your work at night?" I ask.

"Absolutely," she explains. "That's why it takes me so long to make one copy. I have to wait for the perfect time. At shift change, we reboot the system. I have only thirty seconds to get a copy entered and printed through the old manual system before the computers boot back up."

"We might be able to get you a Microbiology card by then," Evan says. "As for Engineering, let me see if I can sort that out."

"How about the maps?" Mrs. Watson probes. "Do you have the location of Kaitlin's files yet?"

I jerk my head up at the mention of my mother's name.

"Not yet," Evan says. "It's in the works."

"What's this about my mother?"

"She buried some files outside the dome. Alec is unsure where, but they hold the evidence needed to bring down the Director."

"Your mother always told me that if anything happened to her, her notebook would lead us to what we needed." Sophie says, "Do you have it with you?"

"Not here, it's back in my room. What do you mean my mother always told you? I don't understand—how did you know her?"

"She was the one who started these meetings, dearie," Mrs. Watson speaks up. "Kaitlin was investigating the Axis. She was a Geneticist before she was on the Expedition team. In fact, she was demoted to the Expedition program after she made some complaints about things going on in Genetics. She continued to investigate, even after they took away her access."

"She found us along the way," Sophie explained. "We have all lost loved ones who just up and disappeared one day."

"No one can go missing in the dome. Everyone knows people have a choice to move to another part of the dome if they want to start a new life." I find myself repeating the same rhetoric I've heard spouted from the telescreens.

"My son would have never left his young wife and baby," Mrs. Watson explains.

"My husband and I were celebrating our fortieth anniversary," Sophie says.

"My brother was only five," Leta says sadly.

"Our parents wouldn't have left us alone as teenagers," the Richards speak up.

They've all lost people, like I have, only theirs didn't turn up dead. They went missing, ending up on posters plastered around the dome, without any answers. If my mother really did form this group, it was because she truly believed something terrible was happening in our dome.

"Who did my mother lose?" I ask.

"Her parents," Sophie says quietly.

I had always been told my grandparents died shortly after I was born. Why should I be shocked? My parents kept so much from me. But really, what would they have said to a nine-year-old?

"What are you trying to do here, with all these keycards, and secret meetings?"

"Evan hasn't told you?" Sophie asks, narrowing her gaze on him. "He really should have before bringing you into our inner circle."

I look at Evan, but he only stares down at the table in front of him. I look back at Sophie, shaking my head.

"We're carrying on with your mother's wishes." she explains. "By the end of the month, we're bringing down the Axis, and exposing the corrupt offices of the Director and the Delegates."

CHAPTER 21

"Where's your proof?" I ask Evan when we get back to his room. Seeing as Tassie is still sleeping in mine, I thought it would be best to go to his room, as I am determined to get answers.

"All the missing people, to start with. It's a little suspicious, don't you think? And now the fact that B3 exists."

"That's just a theory, Evan."

"Don't forget, your mother was investigating this long before now. If we can find her files, then I can show you. All the proof we need will be there."

"What if there are no files? What if they were found when the scientists were discovered?"

"Don't you get it, Nat?" Evan asks. "There was no radiation poisoning. Your parents and the rest of that group were on to something. That's why they were murdered."

"Murder?" I say slowly, the word foreign as it rolls off my tongue. "No one is ever murdered in the dome. Taken away, sure. But killed in cold-blood—that is unheard of. It seems too evil, even for the Director."

"Believe what you want to believe, but I know there's more going on in this dome than you can accept." The frustration in his voice is unmistakable.

"Don't be short with me." Heat rises to my face with each word that leaves my mouth. "I get it, Evan. Don't forget, you just brought me into your secret circle. There's a lot of information I need to process. I didn't realize you had so much going on here."

"You're always processing information." He throws his hands up in the air.

"That's because no one tells me anything," I yell.

He turns to me, staring with hard gray eyes, but mine fire right back. A smile creeps across his lips, and he steps toward me, close enough I can feel the heat off his body. "You're one of a kind, Greyes." He pulls me into his arms, down to his bed. "I'm under so much pressure to get to the bottom of this. Plus, I have no contact with the outside, so I'm worried about Alec, and I think about home all the time. I wish you could see it; see what a society out in the open can really be like."

It is hard to comprehend what being free would be like. Until I turned eighteen, I thought I was free. I never thought my world was "bad". We have rules, but rules are needed everywhere. But when those rules aren't transparent, and they're made to keep us in the dark, that is "bad". I nuzzle into Evan's neck, warm and soft against my cheek. I open my eyes and see his pulse beating and remember the first time, months ago, on the elevator when we first were alone together.

We lie together, not kissing, just being close. It's a connection that's needed right now, to ground us from all that's going on. The most important thing we need to do is focus on finding my mother's proof. Without that, everything is speculation.

I understand that people need to be in charge of governments, that's the point of elections. But people need to be in charge of their own lives as well, don't they? Was I in charge of mine? I didn't get to choose my contribution, it was assigned to me. My grandparents didn't get to choose the area of the dome they live in; they were restricted to the apartment district by their status. Add in my mother's theories, and the dome seems more like a prison than a home.

Evan nudges my shoulder. I must have fallen asleep, my head resting on his chest, in the crook of his arm. "Hungry?"

"Yes." All this thinking sure works up an appetite.

In the cafeteria, I see my world in a different light. I'm on the outside edges of the conversations, listening in as an observer. I sit here wondering, is this person aware of B3? Whose side is that person on? Does this person know what's really going on in the dome?

Waldorf sits next to me, his glasses sliding to the end of his nose as he leans over. "Our box came! I can't believe it. We just put that request in."

That is odd. Carleton said he was going to pack it personally. He must have run to the Hall straight from the party last night.

The idea of his slimy hands touching my mother's things makes me shiver in disgust.

Roe sits down across from Waldorf. "Late night, Greyes?"

"No, why?" I ask. Paranoia sinks in my stomach.

"Relax." She laughs. "I thought maybe you had a hot date. I saw you getting on the elevator with that Manning boy. You still have curls in your hair and makeup on your face."

I grasp at my hair and face and realize she's right. Tassie walks past our table and lets out a whistle. She leans in beside Roe. "Late night?" She winks.

I roll my eyes. Do I have to be the center of attention?

"Oh no, Nat," Tassie says, fluttering her eyelashes and lowering her voice. "I meant the visitor you had in your room last night when I got back."

"Visitor?" Roe eyes me curiously. "So the party must have gone really well."

"It was nothing," I grumble, wiping my hands on my legs as my palms start to sweat.

"Come on, now, Greyes," Evan laughs from across the table. "You're going to give me a complex."

My face turns red, and I stumble over my words. "Nothing happened."

"What?" Roe's brows shoot up. "You—and Evan?"

I shoot from my seat, knocking my chair over behind me. "We fell asleep talking."

Roe bursts out laughing, and I mumble something about needing to go clean up as I scramble to the elevators. Embarrassment spreads across my face.

I take my time cleaning up before I make my way to the lab. I have never had to deal with a crush before, let alone watch it go public in front of my eyes. I need to stay on task and get back to business. I grab the glass magnifier from my room. If the triangle is really in the box, then we've got our match.

When the elevator doors open, I stand outside the lab, mortified at having to face everyone. With a deep breath, I walk through. Surprisingly, no one looks my way. I zip over to my spot near Waldorf.

He claps his hands at my arrival. "Glad you're back. Take a look at this." He pushes the open box in front of me. "I promise, I haven't touched anything. I wanted you to have the honors."

Waldorf's excitement makes me smile. I start pulling out items, wondering if Carleton realized everything I selected was meant to throw him off. Just because he's creepy doesn't mean he's smart. I hand each object over to Waldorf, who sets them on the table, recalling where they found each and every one of them.

"Your mother found this buried in some rocks in the meadow," he says, or, "Your mother found this in the water near the shore at the river." Each piece was a link to Waldorf's past. By the end his eyes are watery.

He takes off his glasses and wipes his eyes with the back of his hand. "How silly of me. I'm an old softy, I guess. I do miss your mother sometimes." He shuffles away, mumbling to himself, and I leave him to his thoughts.

Finally, I pull out the item I'm looking for.

You can't tell at first that this object matches the glass circle. That's something from my memories alone. Mom told me she found the magnifier in the outskirts of the forest, untouched by the Cleansing War, buried under stones and debris that had piled up over time. The regrowth of the forest uprooted a number of items from their grave, poking them up high enough for her to catch a glimpse. What had been hidden decades ago is now here in my hands. I pull the triangular stand out of the box and place it on the table in front of me.

"Where did your partner go?" Evan steps next to me.

"Memory lane got overwhelming."

"Speaking of sensitive, are you okay? You ran out of the cafeteria pretty fast."

"They put me on the spot."

"They're teasing. Who cares?" He reaches over and grabs my hand.

I pull it away, but instantly wish I hadn't. Public affection isn't promoted in the dome. "Easy for you to say. No one was bugging you." I duck my head back down to my work.

"They sure did when you left." He slides into Waldorf's seat and puts his hand on mine again. I let it stay there this time. "What are you and Waldorf up to over here?"

"He's looking for a missing piece to something he had of my mother's." I slide the triangle over to Evan. "Here it is."

"This was your mother's?" Evan picks up the glass and slides it into the empty space in the center of the triangle. "What does it do?"

"Nothing, really. It used to spin in the center of this stand. See, it's a magnifying glass." I hold the glass up to my eye and show Evan.

"What's this line for?"

"That was never there before," I say. "Someone must have put it there."

"Maybe your mom did?"

"Why would she?"

"No idea. Speaking of your mother's things, I've also been looking for something of hers. Your uncle said there was a map with markings on it showing where she hid the files. All of that was confiscated when the Expedition program was shut down, but when I got the maps from Geology, it wasn't in the pile."

I chew on the edge of my lip. "If I tell you something, do you promise not to be mad?"

He narrows his eyes. "That's a loaded sentence, Greyes."

"I took that map off Roe's desk."

"Nat!" Evan whispers, squeezing my hand playfully.

"I know. But I had no idea what you needed it for. I recognized my mom's drawings and didn't think you'd miss it. I've still got it in my room. Want to see?"

"People are going to talk." His voice comes out playfully.

I hit Evan on the arm, but a tingle flutters across my stomach at the thought of us being alone together. I scoop up my mother's things, and slide off the stool.

"Well, are you coming, or what?"

Evan slips next to me, and wraps an arm around my waist. I almost pull away, worried what everyone will think, but I don't. If this dome is going to change, so am I.

"Wouldn't miss time alone with you, for anything," he whispers.

CHAPTER 22

The map is sprawled across my bed, and Evan stands next to me, studying it. Three seemingly innocent words: River, Forest, and Meadow. To the unknowing eye, they blend in with the other notes Mom wrote all over the map. To us they are markers indicating something she has hidden on the outside; proof that could bring down the entire Order.

"These are the only areas she has actually labelled on the map." Evan points to the words. "Everything else is just field notes. But they still don't actually show us where to look."

"Maybe it's encrypted in the notes?" I point to the side. "*Found carvings in stone along river – need to go back and take tracings.*"

"I don't think she'd be that obvious."

"I'm not sure what else to look for." I shrug.

"What about her notebook?"

Evan sits at my desk where the notebook lies open. We've

been at this for over an hour now, going back and forth between the two. Along with the notes in her diary about her expeditions, the margins are filled with things she had seen of interest: drawings of artifacts, sketches of landscapes, and tracings of different markings.

I set the triangular handle of the magnifying glass on the desk next to the glass, which Evan's been trying to move around the map to see if the line matches up with anything. He has a musky smell to him today. I lean in and look over his shoulder and take a deep breath. He turns his head toward me.

"What do you think?"

"It's nice. But then, you always smell good."

"I think it's time for a break." He sits at my desk and looks up at me through his dark lashes, before wrapping his arms around my waist, pulling me onto his lap. I nuzzle my face in his neck, brushing small kisses along his skin. A small moan escapes Evan's lips, right next to my ear, sending goosebumps tingling down my neck.

"Nat! You're a genius!" Evan pushes me off his lap.

"Wh-what?" I'm off-balance in more ways than one.

"The handle of the magnifying glass." He picks it up. "Look at these symbols! I can't believe we missed it."

The three corners of the triangular handle each have a symbol scratched into the plastic surface. It's hard to notice, unless the light catches it just right. One has three flowing lines stacked on top of each other. Another is the shape of a tree. The last is a flower. They're crude, but obvious.

"So ..." He looks up at me with his mischievous smile. "Look at your mother's notebook. When she talks about the river, she draws three wavy lines in the margin. Same thing for the forest, but there she draws the tree. In the meadow, she draws a flower. Without the magnifying glass, you would never think it's connected!"

"It still doesn't help with the map."

"You put the magnifying glass on the map with those three corners on top of those three words and voila!"

He sets the magnifying glass on the map inside the handle, adjusting both until he matches action with words. I peek over his shoulder at his handiwork.

The black line on the glass sticks out like a sore thumb. Only it's not just a line, it can't be. Against the white paper, placed in its correct position, it crosses with another line on the map, making an X. I suck in my breath. Is it possible? Did he find the spot where my mother's files are hidden?

"I can't believe it," I whisper, excitement building in my chest. "You figured it out!" I squeal as I throw my arms around him.

He stands and spins me around. "We need to call a meeting tonight."

The rest of the day drags on. Roe gets a message that Waldorf has fallen ill and will be taking the rest of the day off. I feel bad for him. Memories of my mother must have deeply affected him.

At night I lie in bed, wondering when Evan will come to get me. I listen to Tassie's heavy breathing for about half an hour, until finally a soft tap comes from outside my door. I lift my mattress, pulling out the map and magnifying glass to take as evidence.

The same people as last time greet us from inside the cafeteria pantry.

"What's so urgent?" Sophie taps her fingers on the table. "I don't like going off schedule. It makes us more vulnerable."

"This is important," Evan says laying the map on the table. "Trust me."

I spread out the map across the weathered table and everyone leans forward, to get a better look.

"You found Kaitlin's map?" Mrs. Watson says. "Very good job."

"It was right under our noses all along." Evan winks at me. "And, check this out." He places the magnifier on the map, lining up the symbols and words. "We did it."

"You found the spot." Mrs. Richards claps her hands.

Sophie picks up the magnifier and looks at Evan and me with a stern glare. "Do you remember where that line crossed now?" Her tone silences everyone.

"Yes." Evan points to the map. "Right here. In the meadow, just before the forest. You can barely see the mark on the map but now that I know it's there—"

Sophie smashes the magnifier on the floor. A gasp escapes my lips. "I can't believe you did that!"

"You should be thanking me. Now, no one else can get their hands on this location." She stands and grabs a broom, sweeping away the glass. I run over and grab the triangle from the debris.

"Waldorf will be suspicious if I don't have this," my voice cracks, as I try to explain. The puzzle my mother left behind has now been destroyed.

"We'd better get going." Evan folds up the map.

A knock comes from the door. Sophie snaps her head up, her

brows drawn together. She thrusts the broom at Evan, then takes a deep breath and adjusts her apron and walks to the door.

"Yes," she says, opening it.

Roe walks into the room. My pulse starts to race as I try to think up an excuse for why I'm here. I quickly glance at Evan. Thankfully the map is folded and hidden back in his pocket.

"I thought you couldn't make it on such short notice," Sophie whispers.

Roe's gaze lands on me before she speaks. "You'd better get out now. I came to warn you. The Order is on their way. Thankfully, I was in the lab when the transmission came through."

The room disperses and everyone nervously waits by the elevators. Sophie stays behind to finish prepping for the day. The Richards leave first, followed by Mrs. Watson and Leta. Roe, Evan, and I wait for the next elevator to arrive. When it does, a Member of the Order is on it.

He salutes her. Roe obviously outranks him.

"Hello, Matthews," Roe says, standing more erect. "I caught these two lovebirds sneaking a late night snack,"

"I didn't realize they called someone else in," he says.

"They didn't." Roe juts out her chin. "The call came across my radio, and it's my area, so I thought I would come to see who it was. This is their second offense. They'll be marked for a citation next time."

"Yes, ma'am," the Member says, ignoring us. Roe dismisses him and the four of us get in the elevator. Evan gets off on Floor 17. I get off on Floor 16. All I can think about is that I never would have guessed Roe was one of the rebels.

CHAPTER 23

The next day Roe calls Evan and me into her office. News has already spread that we were caught together upstairs in the cafeteria after hours. A few people snicker behind our backs. If they knew what we had really been up to, I wonder who'd be snickering, and who'd be appalled.

"We were lucky last night," she says after Evan closes the door. "No more emergency meetings without going through me first. Got it?"

"Got it," Evan agrees.

"The Order has been tightening security since your arrival. I know some time has passed, but there are things happening in the Dome that you don't hear about in the Axis. What did I miss last night?"

"We located Kaitlin's hiding place," Evan explains. "We couldn't have done it without Nat."

"Good." Roe looks at me. "I had concerns when they assigned you to our division. I wasn't sure whether you were a spy, seeing as you have a good friend at the Director's side. I think they were hoping to get something out of you. Thankfully, your little romance has provided an excellent cover."

I shift in my chair. Is that all this is between Evan and me? A cover for him to get his task completed? I hadn't thought of that. He did push me pretty quick off his lap yesterday, when he figured out the map.

"What do you think my mother hid?" I speak up. "I know you say it's proof, but what kind of proof are you hoping for?"

"Your mother had photos of people who had gone missing," Roe explains. "She wouldn't say where she took them, just that there was nothing we could do for them anymore. She buried those photos outside the dome and was going to expose the Director. She was betrayed before she had the chance."

I'm shocked. "By whom?"

"I still don't know," Roe explains. "But I intend to find out before we allow any others into our little group. It used to be much larger; I've only regrouped with the most trustworthy ones out of those who are left."

"What does that mean?" I quickly run through the people that were at the meeting last night. Could one of them have betrayed my mom?

"Over half the group disappeared after your parents were killed."

"Who didn't you include?" I ask, biting the inside of my lip.

"There are three of them. Carter works up in the Computer

Room. We really need him to carry out the next stage of our plan after we retrieve your mother's photos, so I hope we can trust him. Then there's one of the Delegates. I am not ready to disclose his name quite yet. It's too dangerous given his position. If he's the one who betrayed your mother, and he knew we were on to him, then all of us would disappear."

"Who's the third?"

"Waldorf," Roe says staring at me, blank faced.

My muscles tighten. "Waldorf," I manage to whisper. "You must be wrong." My pulse starts racing. "He talks of my mother all the time—they were close. He was close to her."

"It's no news that Waldorf was fond of your mother. A little too fond, if you ask most people. He was practically obsessed. She was too kind to turn him away. Instead, she tried to be friends. But he didn't understand. I think he really thought she might leave your father for him one day."

"Obsessing over someone is different from wanting to hurt them." My voice comes out shaky.

"You know, he was out there that night." Roe leans back in her chair. "He conveniently left before the attack."

I look out the window of Roe's door at where Waldorf is working at his station. He's like a child, harmlessly talking to himself as he records artifacts from our last expedition. Every time he talks about my mother, he gets upset. Is that from loss or regret? I don't know what to think.

"He's the one who told her about the testing. The one who told her how they were trying to come up with a vaccine to cure the infected."

"Infected don't exist anymore," I rattle back.

"Infected. No. The infection. Yes. Thanks to Waldorf, a small group of us know that the infection does in fact still exist. It exists in freezers on restricted floors in the Microbiology Division. And your mother said she would prove that they had hidden a test subject; someone stolen from the streets of the dome."

"Where would they keep all the missing people? They can't hide them here in the Axis." I'm still trying to poke holes in this story. To think something so hideous has been going on all these years is almost too much to accept.

"The screams on B2," Evan says, jumping out of his chair.

"You can sometimes hear them in the basement, yes."

My mouth drops open. I know where the people are. "B3!" I jump up next to Evan. "They're keeping them on B3."

That's exactly what we're thinking." Roe nods. "Up until you found that button, we had no idea where the testing was taking place."

"It means," Evan speaks up, his voice rising, "we need to get a map from Engineering to show us the layout on B3. That's the only way we'll be able to chart a way out once we blow up the generator."

"What?" I step back, almost tripping against my chair. "What will that accomplish?"

"Nat," Roe says firmly. "We need to shut down this dome. We need to shut down the tests and destroy the infected in the process. We can't let them get out. Evan knows the layout of the domes."

"But what about the people?" I ask. "What about the workers

in the Axis? They're innocent."

"We aren't going to go through with anything until, *one*, we evacuate the Axis; and, *two*, confirm there are no survivors on B3."

"What about the residents?" I shake my head, still in shock. "They don't have a choice in any of this."

"They'll finally have a choice." Evan puts a hand on my arm. "They have the choice to stay and rebuild. They have the choice to venture outside. They will have nothing but choices."

I shake his hand off my arm. "If you blow up the generator, you could bring down the Axis. There would be no dome left."

"It's a risk we need to take," he says, resting his gaze on mine.

"You start working on a plan to get that Engineering keycard." Roe redirects her attention to Evan. "I will be working on getting an Expedition booked right away."

I stand there, still shaking my head, unable to accept the last part of their plan. How can they think blowing up the Axis is a good idea? They aren't giving people choices; they're going to force them to make one.

"What should I do?"

"Stay out of trouble," Roe says. "I mean it."

CHAPTER 24

The plan is much more intrusive than I thought it would be. I never imagined we would be planning to bring down the Axis. I thought we would simply be exposing the Director and the Delegates, and bring down the government. I thought we would open the doors to the outside. But, this? No, this plan could get people hurt.

I look at Evan, who followed me out of the lab and is standing at the elevators with me. How could he think I'd be okay with this? How could I trust him? I barely know him. What kind of person would risk the lives of innocents? If their theory is true, it makes us as bad as the Director.

"I know Roe told you to stay out of trouble tonight," Evan nudges my shoulder, "but for my plan to work, I need your help."

"Like you need me for a cover?" I hit the elevator button a little too hard.

"What do you mean?"

"I mean, isn't it rather convenient that as soon as you show some interest in me, you've got better excuses for sneaking around this place? I would have helped you out without being strung along."

"Whoa." He follows me onto the elevator. "That's not what this is at all."

"Really? What is this, then? Because you're still keeping things from me."

He reaches past me and hits Floor 30, then grabs me by the shoulders and presses his lips against mine. I push him off and the elevator doors slide open, offering me an escape.

"See," I say, leaving him behind on the elevator, "this is what I'm talking about."

"What?" Evan asks. "I'm not allowed to kiss you anymore? Do you think I'm going to woo you into blindly following my plan to bring down the dome? No offense, but I don't think anyone can charm you into submission."

"What is it you want from me? Be honest for once, and tell me."

"I want you." Evan grabs my hand. "The rest I can do alone. I think I made it very clear in your room the other night that I really do want you. There were no people around to put on a show for, just me and you. Do you still think I have an ulterior motive?"

I don't answer, unable to stop the doubt from gnawing away at the edges of my thoughts.

"I trust you." Evan puts a finger to my chin and lifts my

face up to his. "Now, you can start to trust me and join me this afternoon, or you can go back to the lab. Your choice."

"Can I hear the plan first?"

"Okay, but hear me out all the way. I am going to the Engineering cafeteria, next. The cafeterias trade specialty dishes, and today is Sophie's turn to trade one with Engineering. We will drop off the food, and get out. That simple."

"But why are you really going?" I sift through his half-truth.

"To get an ID card," Evan says.

I purse my lips and swallow. "Okay, let's do it."

Sophie is waiting for us behind the counter. "Put these on." She shoves an apron at each of us. She leaves us with two trolleys, loaded with boxes. I have no idea what's in them, but they're light.

I follow Evan onto the elevator. "Do I need to be ready to run?"

"Trust me, Greyes." He winks.

We get off the elevator at Floor 90, and I see the layout is the same as ours, 60 floors below. I laugh at myself for thinking way up here might be different. Every floor must be designed with the same efficiencies.

We wheel the trolleys to the cafeteria line and wait for the Head Cook. The cafeteria is pretty empty, aside from a small table of people. Sitting at the head of the table is Matthews, the Order member from last night. He makes eye contact with me for a second, then does a double take and looks back. I can tell he's trying to place me.

"Ah!" The Head Cook for Floor 90 comes out from the back. "You've brought me Sophie's delicious lefsa! I can never get this recipe correct. Tell her, thank you so much. I will send some of my staff down with my delicious mozza balls later."

"Sounds good." Evan shakes the Head Cook's hand.

We turn to go and I keep my head down, hoping to get out of here unscathed.

"Hey," Matthews calls over from his table. "You two. Come here."

Evan stops in front of me and points his thumb to his chest. "Are you talking to me?"

I hold my breath, and slowly turn toward Matthews. I have a bad feeling about this.

"Haven't I seen you two before?" he asks.

"You met us last night," Evan says.

Matthews gets up from his table, blocking our path to the elevators. He crosses his arms in front of his chest and narrows his eyes at us.

"No." Matthews shakes his head. "I'm sure I've seen you somewhere else." He points to Evan. "Hey, you're the Out—"

Before Matthews can finish, Evan knocks him to the ground. I freeze as they tussle—Evan on top of Matthews. A few of the Engineers run over and pull Evan off, and Matthews back to his feet. When they do, I notice Matthews' eye is starting to swell.

"You're going to pay for this!" Matthews screams at Evan.

"It's worth it," Evan says. A hint of vengeance twitches at the sides of his mouth.

The elevator doors open, and other Order members come running out. They grab Evan and me, before commanding the Engineers go back to their lunch tables.

"Damn Outsider." Matthews spits at Evan. "You thought you were so smart, getting yourself out of B2. Well, guess what, you're going straight back there—you and your pretty little girlfriend."

The hair on the back of my neck rises. What was Evan thinking? We're in a completely different section of the dome, away from all of our friends. Will they even know what happened to us, or will we end up like the others—missing?

"It's a citation," Roe says, stepping off the elevator, "not a trip to detainment."

"Ma'am," the Order members say, standing up straight and saluting.

"Ma'am," Matthews interrupts, "he assaulted an Order member."

Roe peers closely at Matthews' face and tilts her head. "Looks like he did a good job of it."

"Ma'am—" Matthews begins with a whine.

"Listen, Matthews," Roe says sternly. "I'm aware of your position, but this isn't a playground for you to air your dirty laundry. I understand you two have a history. You were one of the officers assigned to Evan's original detainment here, correct?"

"Yes, ma'am," Matthews says, smirking at Evan.

"Then I'd say you're square," Roe says curtly.

"Square!" Matthews moans. "He attacked me in public. I have witnesses."

"Let it go, Matthews," Roe says. "He's getting a citation. I don't want another peep out of you two over this. Got it?" She points her finger back and forth between Matthews and Evan.

"Got it." Evan shrugs off the hands of the Order member.

Mine lets go of me.

"Got it," Matthews grumbles.

"Good," Roe says. "Matthews, back to work." She turns toward us. "You two, come with me, and I don't want to see either of you back up on Floor 90 again."

"Yes, ma'am," I agree.

On the elevator, I turn to Evan. "What were you thinking?"

"It was payback," he says without making eye contact.

"I'm not impressed." Roe looks down her nose at him. "I don't have time to babysit and monitor your every move in this dome, do you understand?"

"Are you impressed now?" Evan blocks the camera and flashes us an ID card.

I gasp. "Did that say *Engineering*?"

"I took advantage of the situation," he explains. "When the Engineers ran over to help their Order member, I reached over and pulled this off one of them."

"I am impressed." She nods, offering nothing more than a half-smile. "Now report to Mrs. Watson."

"Then back to the lab?" he asks.

"No. You have some toilets to scrub to pay off that citation." The smile grows across her face.

"What!" Evan exclaims. "Can't you make it go away?"

"I'm too busy for that." She laughs. "Plus, we have to make it look like you were punished. I've got a last-minute expedition to plan. We go out in the morning."

My stomach twists. I didn't know we'd be going out again so soon. Will I find out my mother's secret tomorrow?

CHAPTER 25

The next morning the lab is chaotic with packing. Excitement is thick in the air for another day outside the dome, and everyone keeps bumping into one another as they scramble to make sure nothing is missed.

I don't run around with the rest of them. Roe pulled Evan and I into her office as soon as we arrive, and advised us that we will be assigned to monitor the perimeter, like the first time, giving us the opportunity to look for my mother's files. I'm excited to be alone with Evan, but I can't seem to make my nerves relax. Today is the day I can carry out my mother's wishes.

Evan seems to have his nerves under control; he's upbeat, despite his night of manual labor. He bustles about from person to person, helping each get ready. How long has he been preparing for this opportunity?

As the trucks get ready to roll out, Evan slides in the back, next to me. Having his body close to mine helps me relax.

"I was thinking," He waves his hands around. "We need a shovel and a box. We don't know what we're going to find."

"Won't we look suspicious walking off with a box and shovel?"

Evan nods. "I thought of that, too. There's a lot of time to think when you're scrubbing toilets. I've got a good idea for a cover. Trust me."

"Only if you promise not to tackle anyone out there." I nudge his shoulder.

"Not even you." He glances sideways at me, grabbing my hand.

I lean against the back of the truck. If that was my only concern, I'd be fine. Nervousness trickles through my limbs, making my knee bounce. When we find my mother's proof, what happens when we get back? How much time will I have to convince Evan not to destroy the dome?

We drive past the first site we'd visited, but this time turning to the right. Here, we skirt around the base of the hill instead of driving up it, and park near the other side of the forest.

"Okay, team," Roe says, climbing out of the truck. "I want to focus on collection from the forest floor. Bio wants us to gather some mossier forms of vegetation. Evan and Nat, can you survey the area? Report back by lunch."

"We need a box and a shovel," Evan states.

Waldorf, standing across the truck from us, wrinkles his brows together. My breath catches in my throat, waiting for someone to uncover our plan.

"Tassie asked us to gather some flowers from the meadow,

seeing as she missed it last time," Evan explains. Waldorf shrugs and goes back to unloading, his expedition scarf hanging loose in front of him.

"Of course," Roe says. "But only one box. This isn't a trip to feed everyone's fancies."

Evan grabs a shovel and hands the box to me. We start our trek up the hill. It's rockier on this side, but thankfully, it's not steep.

"What is the land like between here and your dome?" I ask Evan. This is something I've been curious about. More so since I realized he's going to be making the trek back after we destroy the virus in my dome.

"Pretty much like this." Evan gestures around us. "Maybe a little hillier in some parts, a few more trees in others."

"I don't like the desert around the dome," I say. "Maybe it's because that's all I've stared at my entire life. I wish I could see more of this stuff."

Evan holds his hand out to me. "Come with me. You'd love it. The farms we've established around our dome have helped with terraforming the earth. It's full of fields of different crops. Some, we left in the dome of course, to protect them, just in case."

Was leaving a possibility? I'd just come to terms with moving outside the dome. But completely leaving everything I know. It was a lot to think about.

"I'd like to see us develop the outside," I say.

"You will," Evan says. "It takes time. I understand why people are afraid of change. I mean, our dome isn't perfect. There are a lot of things we still do that don't make sense to me. But that's society. It takes time to implement change."

"Look." I reach the top of the hill. "We're here."

In front of us is the large meadow, nestled in its half circle of hills. The forest flanks it, to our right. I look down to see if I can find some marker that matches my mother's map, but all I can see is a meadow.

"This will be harder than I thought," Evan says. "But we only have until lunch before Roe has to send people after us, so let's get looking."

I walk down the hill into the meadow. Evan is far ahead of me. "I don't understand," he shouts back. "It should be in this general area. There's nothing here—what are we supposed to do, start digging?"

Everything around us is tall and wild. What did my mother see? What stood out to her? I try to think about what she saw on the day she died; the day she chose her hiding place. That fateful day nine years ago. Then I realize something that answers my question.

"Evan!" I call out. "Evan, come here!"

He runs over to me. "What's up," he asks, out of breath.

"I think I figured it out. It was my birthday. The day my parents died. Well, my birthday was over a month ago."

"I don't get it." Evan looks confused.

"The flowers." I spread my arms. "They weren't in bloom—my mother would have been able to see more of the ground. Those are terrain maps, right? They would have marked everything on the ground that stood out, rocks, logs, and whatever."

"We need to canvass the area," he says. "Here, hold my hand."

He takes my hand in his and we begin walking around the meadow, making rows as we travel. We cover a good section where we think the "X" might land, but after an hour we take a break.

"I brought you this from the cafeteria." He hands me an apple as we sit in the grass. "I know how much you love your fruit."

"Thanks." I take the bright red fruit and roll it in my hands. "Did you grow up with lots of fruit?"

"Nothing as perfect-looking as yours. We started to grow things organically, without any outside influences. They come out a little spottier and less hardy, but once the dome came down, we had to rely more on nature."

"I didn't get to eat much fruit while I was growing up. We were rationed in the apartment districts. One fruit, per week, per person. Sometimes Jak would sneak me some of his. Where he lived, extra rations came three times a week."

"That's terrible. People who live in better areas get better food more often? Even more reason to bring this place down."

"It really wasn't that bad," I say. "I knew we were different, but didn't think much about the divide. It wasn't until I went to Jak's ceremony that I saw how much more they get."

"Jak was a good friend to you, wasn't he?" Evan asks, fidgeting with his apple.

"He was. He always looked after me. But in the end, he was the one who had them bring me to the Axis."

"Is that such a bad thing?"

It wasn't my choice, that's what makes it bad. After my parents died, I made it my mission to make sure things that happened to me were my choice. Jak took that away from me, when it came to my contribution assignment. I sit in silence, unable to answer Evan's question.

"If he hadn't, we may have never been able to do this." He runs his fingers across mine and leans over, brushing his lips along my neck. I reach up and entwine my fingers in his hair, as his kisses reach my lips, and move over to the opposite side of my neck. A small moan escapes my lips, and I open my eyes. A dark object sits in the grass behind Evan. My heart jumps in excitement and I push him away.

"What happened?" Evan says with disappointment.

"Look! Behind you. I think we found it."

Evan rolls over and looks behind him. "I can't believe it!"

He stands up and grabs the shovel and we run over to an old rotted log, decomposing amongst the grass. I nudge it with my foot and its fragile exterior caves in where I make contact.

"Where should we start digging?" Evan asks.

"I don't think we need to," I say. "I keep thinking about what my mother saw that day. She didn't plan to hide this stuff. It just happened. She probably didn't have a shovel, right? She found the next best thing."

"The log," Evan says, agreeing. He begins to push the log out of the way. Parts of it crumble in his hands, while other pieces are easy to push back. As the log breaks apart, it reveals a metal box.

I drop to my knees and grab the box with both hands. It shakes in my grasp. Evan puts his hands over mine, and I look up at him through blurry eyes as a tear escapes down my cheek.

He wipes it away. "It's okay, Nat. You can do it."

I slowly open the lid, which has rusted over, just as its surface deteriorated on the outside. As the lid lifts, my heart drops into the pit of my stomach.

"It's ... empty," my voice escapes in a whisper. "I can't believe it. Where are the files? Where's the proof?"

I look up at Evan, and he grabs the box from my hands, staring at it in disbelief. "It can't be," he says, shaking his head. "Maybe this is the wrong box?"

My head spins. All this build up for what? Nothing. If we can't prove what my mother found, we can't bring down the Director. Her death was for nothing.

Then I see it. I see the truth. It's standing up on the hilltop watching us. His glasses and long scarf give him away. I jump out of the grass and lose all self-control.

"What did you do?" I scream at the top of my lungs. "What did you do to her?"

Waldorf stares at me from afar. I start running towards him but he disappears down the other side of the hill. Evan catches me before I reach the hilltop.

"Don't stop me." I push Evan away as he tries to reach for me. "It was him. Can't you see? He took everything. He is the traitor."

"Wait!"

"No!" I scream at Evan and break into a run, chasing after Waldorf. He's much older than me, but I have to climb the hill to reach him, so I'm farther away than I'd hoped. I can see him far below, talking to Roe and packing up a vehicle. By the time I get to the bottom of the hill on the other side, Waldorf, Roe, and Mr. Richards are driving away.

Evan comes up behind me and I am about to yell at him again but instead I collapse in to his arms, sobbing. Defeat overtakes me. Mrs. Richards and Cardinal come running out of the forest, and I quickly let go of Evan and wipe my face.

"Where's the other vehicle?" Mrs. Richards asks warily. "And my husband?"

"Waldorf," Evan says.

"Oh dear," Cardinal nods. "I guess we'll find out now if he ever truly believed in the cause."

CHAPTER 26

My dreams haunt me. Uncle Alec stands on the other side of the dome, calling to me for help. Behind him, my parents are ripped apart by the infected. Their screams ring out, piercing my ears. "Run. Run away," I scream. He doesn't listen to me. As the infected reach him, I wake up in a cold sweat.

I try to sit up, but Evan's arm is lying on top of me. He stayed with me last night. I feel safe knowing he's here. But I also feel watched. I'm sure Evan's ulterior motives are to keep me far away from Waldorf, until Roe has a plan. Waldorf—the man everyone thought loved my mother, when in reality he was the reason she was murdered.

The next day, Evan is very quiet. He only responds with one-word answers and is withdrawn at breakfast. In the lab he storms out of Roe's office, knocking some of the maps onto the floor.

"What's wrong?" I kneel to pick up some of the papers.

"You have to ask?"

"It's not my fault," I shoot back.

"I'm sorry," he grumbles. "Everything is stalled, now. What do we do? Your mother's files are gone. I can't get a straight answer from Roe at all. She keeps telling me the matter is being dealt with. What's that supposed to mean?"

"Has Roe ever let you down? She must have a plan, and she'll let you know when the time is right."

"Yeah. Well, it sure would be nice to know when that'll be, as I rot in here." He throws his hands up in the air.

"Rot?" My voice drops. "Is it really so bad here?"

Evan jerks his head up. "I didn't mean that. I'm not myself today. I should go cool off."

"Do you want me to come?"

"No. Stay here and find out what's going on. Whatever happens, make sure you stay out of trouble." He stares at me in silence, and then kisses me on the forehead before walking out of the lab.

Roe motions me into her office.

"What's going on?" I ask as I walk in. "Evan is wound up. Can't you tell us what's happening with Waldorf?"

"I can," she says. "After you talk to Waldorf. I tried rattling his cage all night with Richards, but he's refusing to talk unless he can speak to you first."

"Me?" I spit out a nervous laugh. "You can't be serious?"

"I am. Your mom is the link between you and Waldorf. I think his guilt has finally caught up with him."

"What if I don't want to talk to him? I despise him. There's nothing he can say that will change that." I shake my head.

"If it's our only chance to get your mother's files, will you still ignore his request?"

"He still has them?" She nods and I let out a long sigh. "Fine."

"That's what I thought," she says. "Here." Roe hands me a key card. It reads *Microbiology Division.*

"He gave you this?" I'm shocked.

"Yes," she says. "We've already taken a copy. He promises much more after he talks to you."

"What am I supposed to say to him?"

"I don't care if you say nothing," Roe says. "But, get going before he changes his mind. He might be our only chance to destroy whatever they're hiding in those labs, once and for all. I'm relying on you to tell me whether we can trust him or not."

"I'm not qualified to make that decision."

"Do you think any of us are?" she asks. "Do you think one day we all woke up and decided we were cut out for treason and espionage? No. But one day, thanks to your mother, we woke up and realized that everything here is a farce. There is no *Peace. Love. Order. Dome.* Instead there are these giant lies and the people in power who hide behind them."

"But what if I'm wrong?" I ask.

"Trust your gut," Roe advises. "They were *your* parents. If anyone should hate him, it is you. If you realize you don't, then maybe there's something we can use him for. Get going, Greyes. Now."

I leave Roe's office with ID card in hand. My coworkers' stares burn into my back as I leave the lab. They all know. They all know that Waldorf was the traitor—the one who had my parents killed. And now they know I have to go beg him for the proof. I slam my hand against the elevator button. I'll be damned if I beg for anything.

I walk into the elevator and slip the ID card into the slot under Floor 50's button. Like B2, an ID card is the only way to get through the restricted access. I brace myself as the elevator whisks me up to Floor 50, faster than I can prepare.

I get off the elevator, shaking with each step I take. I need to face Waldorf, but the idea of confronting him scares me. I'm not afraid of him so much as I'm not ready to hear the truth come from his lips. But I don't have a choice. I take a deep breath and push open a glass door that has his name written on it: *Karl Waldorf, Head Microbiologist.*

His dark and puffy eyes widen the minute I enter. I force myself to meet his gaze; he looks exhausted. Where did Roe and Mr. Richards take him last night? He looks as roughed-up as Evan did that day he left B2.

"You came." He scrambles to stand and greet me. Thankfully, Mr. Richards is here with us. He puts a hand on Waldorf's shoulder, pushing him back into his chair.

I make myself swallow, trying to moisten my mouth, which is so dry, I have to force my tongue to move. "You didn't leave me a choice."

"We all have a choice." He plays with some papers on his desk.

"Well?" I cross my arms against my chest, willing myself to stay. "Get on with it, then."

"Can we have some privacy, please?" My back stiffens as Waldorf makes his request to Mr. Richards, who looks at me with concern.

I nod. "It's okay."

"I'll be outside this door, Nat. Call me if there's trouble."

Waldorf's stare doesn't leave me as Mr. Richards walks outside.

"You remind me so much of her." He tilts his head as he examines me. "Your face, your hair, it's really amazing how genetics work. I've always admired that science."

A shudder runs down my back, leaving an icky feeling in its trail. I clear my throat. "I'm not here to talk science."

"Oh?" Waldorf says. "I thought you were. Isn't that what they all want? Kaitlin's proof the virus is being used? But not you. No, you want answers—answers about your parents and that expedition nine years ago. That's why I refused to talk to any of them. Only you. Only your intentions are pure."

Waldorf's glassy eyes stare at me. He seems off from his usual eccentricity. "I think their intention to rid the dome of the virus is pure." I try to convince him.

"See, I told you we'd talk science. Yes, the virus is here. There's an entire floor of it up here in the Microbiology Division. Guess where? Just past this office. Beyond this room are the freezers and labs for this entire floor."

"Is it true you test it on people?"

"Not me, personally. But yes, I oversee the program."

"How? Why?" I can't keep up with the questions pouring into my head.

"How else can we test its potential and prepare for the worst?"

"That doesn't make any sense—they are innocent people."

"We've been developing a vaccine," Waldorf says. "In case there's ever another outbreak. We've been working on it day and night for many decades. There aren't animals to run tests on, like the old days. They're needed for food and sustenance. But people—well they're always in abundance, aren't they? One thing the dome doesn't need is more people."

"It's murder," I stammer. "Why would we need to keep testing the virus, after all these years? All the people who were infected were killed in the Cleansing Wars."

"Here's an interesting fact." Waldorf walks around me in his office. "One they don't teach you at the Learning Institute. Did you know that immunity is not an inheritable trait? That's what spurred your mother into action."

"My mother? What did she know about any of this?"

"She was a brilliant geneticist, before the Expedition program. We had many talks, your mother and I. Many, many talks late into the night. We were nothing more than friends, though I did love her deeply. I would have done anything for her, had she loved me back in the same way, but she did not. She loved your father, fool that he was. He wasn't much of a scientist. Not like her."

"You told her about the testing, didn't you?"

He nods. "I wanted her to see its importance, and bring her with me over to Microbiology. We would both be invaluable to the program with our experience working in Genetics. That was the only reason I followed her to the Expedition program, so that she could see it wasn't safe outside—too many variables. Too much risk."

"If you cared so much about her, then why did you betray her?"

"Betray her?" Waldorf looks surprised. "I never would have. At least not on purpose. It was an accident—a misunderstanding. On that last expedition, she told me her plans to bring down the Director. She had her proof, there in the meadow, and tried to make me understand. But I couldn't let her carry out her plans to destroy the dome. It was too dangerous; the virus would get outside—it would spread. We would have to go through the Cleansing Wars all over again. She insisted. There was no way I could persuade her without help."

"They were killed because of you!" I jump out of my chair. "Stop playing around with words. What did you call me here for?"

"Forgiveness," Waldorf looks away. "I've lived with my guilt all this time, but the moment you stepped through those lab doors, I knew it was my chance for redemption. You were the missing link. Everything she did was to protect you."

"How was I in danger?"

"You are not immune," he explains. "Both she and your father were, but not you. She couldn't stand the idea of you being taken for testing one day."

"What do you mean, not immune? How would you know?"

"Over time, generations have bred the immunity gene out. You can't test a vaccine on the immune; you need people who can be infected, first. Luckily, we have a dome with many people like you, ready to be plucked from the streets. Everyone's immunity is tested when they enter the Learning Institute. There's a log of all of you, kept in the Director's office."

Waldorf slumps to the side as he reaches for a bottle of whiskey on his desk. It's the same one I fell prey to at Jak's initiation party.

"Where did you get that bottle?"

"The Director sent it up for me." Waldorf waves the bottle in the air. "He's coming to see me at the end of the day for a celebratory drink."

"What are you celebrating?" I ask cautiously.

"The end of the rebellion," Waldorf says. "He's going to finish off what he started a decade ago."

I move toward the door. I'm not sure what information Roe was hoping to get from Waldorf, but it's too late. I need to notify everyone. We need to get out of the dome and save ourselves.

"Wait!" Waldorf stands. "I have something for you." He grabs a box from under his desk, and pushes it toward me. "Here's the immunity serum. I finished it after your mother's death. It was the least I could do for her. You need to take it. All of you do. Then get it to Evan's dome and have it replicated."

"Why are you giving me this, if you're going to rat us out to the Director?" I ask.

"I said he's coming to see me shortly." Waldorf turns away. "But I don't plan on being able to give him any information. He used this drink on me once before, nine years ago. I couldn't help myself when I heard the words come out of my mouth, revealing your mother's plans."

"It wasn't your fault," I say, shocked, as the words leave my mouth.

"I went back." He stares at the ceiling, though I know he's lost in his memories. "I was on the rescue mission they sent. They said there was no communication from the team, but I knew better. I knew the moment the Director stole that information from me, that I'd never see my friends again. It was terrible—the horror. We found them torn to pieces—attacked by the test subjects your mother sought to protect. The infected lie dead as well, killed by the hands of the Order members who brought them."

"Why didn't you say something?" My chin trembles as the words come out disconnected.

"What could I do?" he asks. "Look what happened to your mother when she took a stand. I wasn't half as brave as her. I went to the meadow and took her files, then hid them all this time until I found someone as brave as her who could stand up to the Director again. I worked very hard at destroying the virus from within the Microbiology labs over the years. But it is impossible—we don't have the capability to do it here. The immunity program must be stopped and the virus has to be locked away, forever."

Waldorf hands me a microchip. "My work is all on here. Pass this on to other scientists in Evan's dome. Perhaps they can finish what I could not."

I hesitate before taking the microchip from Waldorf. He looks sad and pathetic, yet I still cannot forgive him. I snatch it from his grasp. "Because of your cowardice and weakness, my parents are dead." My words make him wince, and I continue, wanting him to hurt more. "All the rest is just you trying for absolution. I do not forgive you. Maybe you can find some way to do it yourself."

Waldorf holds up a vial. "The guilt has killed me on the inside. I can't live with it any longer. This is my only salvation." He tosses the vial back, drinking every last drop, then throws it against the wall. "Now, get out of here and lock that door. Get out of here and don't ever come back."

I run blindly from the room, clutching the box in my arms. The vial Waldorf drank from does not match the one holding the immunity serum.

"What's wrong?" Mr. Richards asks.

"Lock the door! Waldorf infected himself."

CHAPTER 27

We leave the office secure, and I go straight down to Roe's office. Her mouth drops as I burst in—I probably look like I'm crazy. I throw the box onto her desk and stand there, unsure where to start.

"What happened?" She stares at the box.

I look out her office door, and see Mr. Richards warning his wife and the others.

"Waldorf's gone."

"What! We had a deal. He gave us his ID card. That coward!"

"He was there," I explain. "He confessed to everything. But it really wasn't his fault; the Director used this truth serum and drugged Waldorf to get the information out of him. They've got the virus up there, Roe. And it's not dormant. Waldorf confirmed it's unsecured in the freezers behind his office."

"Okay," Roe says, "I don't understand. Where is Waldorf now?"

"He infected himself, right in front of me; he drank the virus. The Director's coming to visit him. I think Waldorf hopes to kill him."

"Damn it!" Roe bangs a fist on her desk. "Damn Waldorf. Now we can't access those freezers. We can't destroy the virus, and now the Director will find him, forcing our hand. We need to find a way to get our message out to people, and destroy the Axis."

"He says this is the immunity serum," I push the box toward her. "Everyone needs to take it."

"How can we trust him, after all he's done?"

"He was filled with remorse," I say, but I see her point. "He said it was for his own absolution."

Roe shakes her head. "I don't know, Nat. What if it's the virus? I can't risk my team. We'll just have to hope no one gets infected during this upheaval."

"Roe, there isn't any time for this. I reach in the box and pull out a vial, slipping it into an injection needle from the box. I have no idea what I'm doing, but there isn't time to worry about it. I'm the weakest link in this crew, now that my mother's proof has been found. I lift the needle and plunge it into my arm.

"No!" Roe cries out.

The vaccine burns as it enters my body. I watch the vial as a cloud of my blood mixes with the serum. Blood that is not immune to the virus. In seconds the vial drains into my body, and I pull the needle out, dropping it on Roe's desk.

She watches me, with her hands held in the air between us, as she backs herself to the door. "I'm fine, Roe. Look at me."

"I'm just making sure," she says. "Cardinal! Bring me one of the scanners."

I turn to look out the doorway and see the others, standing frozen, watching us. Cardinal rushes toward Roe, and hands her an infection scanner. Roe turns it on, pointing it toward me. The lights run up and down my body, but nothing beeps. I'm not infected.

I breathe out a sigh of relief. It's over. "See." I hold up my hands in peace.

"Maybe more time needs to pass. I'll try again in twenty minutes."

"There isn't time, Roe." I look to Mr. Richards, pleading.

"She's right," he says. "Once the Director sees Waldorf, it will only be a matter of time before he comes down here to investigate the rest of the team."

I turn and pull more vials from the box. Something pokes out from the bottom. I tug on the corner, and out comes a photo.

My heart drops. It's a photo of the infected. But it's not the same photo you see in history class. It's a photo showing *Dome 1618* painted on the wall behind the infected. I hand the photo to Roe and empty the rest of the box. The bottom is lined with over twenty photos. It's my mother's proof.

"I'm going to give the rest of the lab a choice to take the serum, or not," Roe explains. "Then I will go get Sophie, Leta, and Mrs. Watson, and explain our predicament. It looks like it's time to put our plan in action. Thanks for being the guinea pig."

We walk back into the lab. "Where's Evan?" I look around.

"I guess he hasn't come back from cooling down yet."

"I'll find him." I run out of the lab to the elevators and go down to Floor 17 to Evan's room. His room is empty. It looks messed up a bit. Was he really that mad? I run down to my room, to check if he stopped in while I was gone to visit Waldorf, but only Tassie is in there.

"Have you seen Evan?"

"Sure did," Tassie rolls her eyes. "Man, was he in quite a state. He came down here looking for you, grumbling how nothing was working out, and I thought he was talking about you two so I told him to do something about it. He snapped at me and asked if all girls were so opinionated. Then he stormed out and said he would get the job done himself. I tell you, that was a mood and a half."

"Where was he going?"

"No idea," Tassie says. "Downstairs somewhere, was all I could make out."

Prickly goosebumps break out all over my skin and the room starts to spin. I can't believe it. He's going to look for the proof we already have. I need to stop him. I turn and run out of the room.

I bang on the buttons in the elevator, panicking that I won't get to Evan in time. What will happen if he goes to B3? I need to stop him.

Finally the elevator whirs into action, descending to Floor 2. The doors slide open, revealing an empty hallway. There's no sign of Evan.

The Director's door opens, and I jump into the room next to me. It's a filing room filled with rows of shelving. I peek outside and see the Director leave his office with Jak. They turn down a side hallway and disappear. I am about to leave the filing room when Samson's wife, Catherine, speaks up from behind me.

"Natalia?" Her brows furrow as she shakes her head. "What are you doing in here?"

"Oh, I was getting some things for Roe." I make up an excuse.

"What does Roe need from the Director's files?" Catherine asks me, walking to the doorway and peering into the hallway behind me. Her voice lowers to a whisper. "Do you know how much trouble you could get into if you were caught down here?"

"Let me go, Catherine." I change my tone, holding my hands in the air. "I haven't taken anything. Pretend you never saw me."

"That's not what I'm concerned about." She rolls her eyes as she peers out the doorway again. "What are you doing down here? Samson and I haven't been able to make the last few meetings. Are things ready to start moving along?"

I'm not sure whether or not to believe her, but I need Catherine to get out of my way and let me go look for Evan. Maybe she can even be of some help.

"I need you to go find Samson and take him to Roe's office right now. It's urgent. Once you're gone, I'm leaving this room."

"Is something wrong?" she asks. "I think he's going upstairs with the Director."

"Catherine, you two must go see Roe. Now. Do not take anyone else with you, do you understand?" I want to warn her about Waldorf, and tell her to save her husband, but I can't risk him tipping off the Director. With any luck, Waldorf will take out the most crooked man inside the dome, and offer the rest of us the distraction we need.

Catherine stares at me for a moment, looking genuinely confused, but rushes out of the filing room. I can only hope she's trustworthy. I peek out and watch her get on the elevator. When the doors close, I sneak back into the hallway and into the Director's office.

His office is just as I remember it. The bar with the truth serum sits along the left wall, and to my right is a row of bookcases. I scurry to the large mahogany desk and sit in the Director's chair. I don't dare turn the light on and draw attention.

The Director's voice comes from the hallway. Damn! I hurry and feel for the button, finally locating its circular dimple in the wood. As I press my finger against it, a grinding noise comes from the row of bookshelves. Two slide open, revealing an elevator.

I run toward the elevator as the Director's office door opens. Inside there's one button without any label. It's now or never. As my finger releases the button, Jak and the Director walk into the office and turn on the lights. Their heads turn toward me at the same time. Anger crosses the Director's face; nothing but shock spreads across Jak's. For that split second, relief washes over me. Jak knows nothing about B3.

The elevator doors click shut, and I descend to the unknown. I have no idea what to expect when those doors open. All I care about is finding Evan.

The elevators open to a dark hallway. Fluorescent lights flicker along the ceiling as if to replicate the stars that peer through the darkened clouds outside. The screams Mrs. Watson described are ringing out from the empty hallways that stretch in front of me. I hesitate from fear, then timidly take a step into the unknown.

I make my way down the hallway and approach a large steel door with a small glass window. I crawl up and peek inside. Empty. Down the hallway, I continue looking in rooms, getting braver as each is as vacant as its predecessor.

When I glance into the window on the last door, two hands bang against the glass from the other side. My heart jumps, and adrenaline shoots through my limbs. The hands leave streaks of blood across the glass. I force myself to take a closer look.

Through the glass a woman clutches her face with her fingers, pulling at skin that droops from her face. Her hair has fallen out, and a chunk hangs limp from her scalp. My stomach lurches at the sight of one of her eyes, hanging limp from its socket. I tear myself away from the window. She's infected.

The end of the hallway splits into two directions, and I follow it to the right. Here, the same cell doors line the walls, but instead of opening to tiny rooms, each houses a lab on its other side. Next to each door, a large glass window displays operating tables and surgical equipment. What did they do to people down here?

The end of the hallway starts to curve to the left and footsteps approach from the other side. I open the door closest to me, and slip inside, letting the heavy steel close behind me.

The lights in the room blink on. They must be motion-activated. A groan comes from behind me and I quickly spin around, only to see an infected tied down to an operating table. Thankfully, it has not seen me yet.

A shadowy figure walks past the window. Did the Director follow me? I peer over the ledge and see Evan walking down the corridor. I forget about the infected and knock on the window to get his attention. He jumps and turns to me, his eyes widening at the sight of me.

The infected on the table starts to shriek as it desperately fights against its restraints. Its blood-red eyes focus on me. One of its arms gets free and it starts clawing in my direction. I run toward the door and push against it. The door doesn't budge. I try again. Nothing. I turn back and see that the monster has both arms free. It tries to stand up but falls from the bed, releasing one of its legs. There is only one restraint holding it back from attacking me.

"Evan!" I scream as I bang my hands against the door. "Help me!"

He's already on the other side and pushes the door open. I fall into the hallway, and he pulls the door shut as the infected lunges at the door. The door clicks shut and we both freeze, standing in the middle of the hallway.

"What are you doing down here?" His eyes practically jump out of his skull as he glares at me.

"I should ask you the same question."

"You could have been killed."

"You could get infected."

"No, Nat." He shakes his head. "I can't. I'm immune. But you aren't."

"How did you know?"

"Alec."

"I am now," I advise him. "Waldorf gave us an immunity serum."

The infected hurtles itself at the window, and Evan grabs my arm, pulling me with him out of sight. As soon as we're away, the banging stops. It seems our very presence is what sets it off.

"Everything is in motion upstairs," I explain. "Waldorf had my mother's files."

"I guess I don't need these, then," Evan says holding up a tiny camera. "Around the curve there's an entire pen of them."

"All those poor innocent people?" I shake my head. "Why do they need so many?"

"It's as if they're building up a defense," Evan says.

"Or an army," the Director's voice comes from behind us. I spin around and find Jak, the Director, and several Order members on either side of them. I turn to run.

"Don't." Evan grabs my hand. "There's nowhere to go."

"Listen to your *boyfriend*," the Director says.

Order members come up behind us, from the other end of the hallway. Evan grips my hand tightly as we stand trapped between a throng of infected and their creators. I look over at Jak. Just how innocent was he in all of this?

"We know what's going on down here." I hold my ground.

"You're smart, like your mother," the Director says. "Unfortunately, it didn't get her very far in life. You, however, will be given a second chance."

"I don't need any favors from you."

"It's not your favor," the Director says smugly. "It's for Manning. The poor boy is head over heels for you. The best I could promise him is to send you to the Learning Institute for reprogramming."

"No." I shake my head. "I won't go there."

"You will, or you'll die," the Director warns. "Peace. Love. Order. Dome. Is that such a bad life?"

"You're nothing but a liar."

"Careful, Miss Greyes." He raises his hand in the air. "I'll even sweeten the deal for you. Evan will be sent home where he can spread the word that Dome 1618 is not to be opposed. It is a force to be reckoned with. Attack us again and we'll release the infected on your people."

"I'd love that opportunity." Evan curls his lip into a snarl.

"Jak," I plead. "You aren't like this. Listen to him. He would hurt innocent people."

"War is war." Jak holds his chin in the air.

"Look around you, Jak," I continue. "This floor is for testing. Who do you think the test subjects are? Volunteers?"

He looks around at the empty rooms, then back at me.

"It's the people who have been listed as missing. They've been kidnapped and brought down here. People like me, who aren't immune to the virus."

Jak looks around, unsure of himself. As if on cue, the infected in the lab room throws itself against the window beside them. Jak jumps, and I can see doubt cross his face.

"Please, Jak." I try one last time. "Please. I know you're not like this. I know you care."

"Enough!" the Director commands. "Take them away."

CHAPTER 28

Once back in the Director's office, Evan is dragged to the elevators by the Order members. I'm left alone with the Director and Jak.

"You will take her there now," the Director insists, banging his fist on his desk. "Let them know it's an emergency entry. I can't come; I need to go see Waldorf and finalize the list of these rebels." He leans in close to my face, and the stench of his breath makes my nose scrunch. "Your mother's work will finally be brought to an end."

I spit in his face, and his eyes widen for only a second. "They'll come for you. If not us, Evan's dome will, one day. You will pay for all of this."

A smirk spreads across his lips as he wipes my saliva off with his handkerchief. "I have no doubt they will be coming. Not only will it solidify my point that the outside is dangerous, but it will also give me a chance to show the people why we need to utilize the virus. How can they deny the importance of our work when it saves them in a war against the Outsiders?"

"You can't be foolish enough to release the virus back into the world. Don't you understand? That was the point of the domes. To protect people."

"Sometimes people need to be protected from themselves," the Director says, tossing his handkerchief into the garbage can. "Manning, take her away now."

I'm hauled out of the Axis by an Order member Jak calls over to help. The member is Matthews. He smirks as soon as he lays eyes on me.

"Take her down to my car," Jak says. "I have to grab some paperwork from my office."

"I'll take good care of her," Matthews says, pushing me in front of him, toward the elevator.

As the doors slide shut, Matthews corners me. "Where's your buddy?"

I stare over his shoulder at the doors, keeping my head high.

Matthews punches the door and I clench my eyes shut. "Where is he?"

"They're sending him home." I open my eyes as a sneer crosses my lips. "I guess you won't get your revenge after all."

"Impossible," he says. "I saw them take him upstairs. Where are they keeping him?"

I shake my head. Upstairs? Maybe they are letting Evan gather his things to go home. A quiver ripples in my stomach. Will I ever see him again, and if I do, will I remember who he is?

I barely stay on my feet as Matthews pushes me through the lobby. Leta's counterpart stands from her desk, like a deer in headlights. Poor thing. Axis not all you thought it'd be?

When we reach the car, Matthews pins me against its side. "You think you're special, working with that Outsider, don't you? Well, look at you now." He presses his finger against my chest. "You aren't so smug, are you? You're just a little rat, from the apartment sector—"

"Get off her, now." Jak's voice cuts through the air like a knife. Matthews steps back, and I cross my arms as I catch my breath, feeling the pain left behind from the force of Matthews touch.

"Sorry, sir," he explains. "I was reminding our girl who she's dealing with."

Jak eyes the member, and steps in close toward him. "And who would you be?"

"Officer Matthews, sir."

"I won't forget that." Jak's jaw tightens. "And she's *my* girl. Got it?" Matthews nods. "Dismissed." Jak waves his hand in the air and Matthews scurries back into the Axis.

"Thank you—"

"Don't." Jak shakes his head, not looking at me. He hasn't looked at me since I left B3. He opens the car door for me, almost slamming it closed against my leg as I get in the vehicle.

"Why would you do this?" I ask, when he gets in on the other side.

"You aren't thinking straight, Nat," Jak says.

"How could you do this to me?" I ask with tears filling my eyes. "I thought you were my—"

"Friend?" Jak scoffs. "Of course I am. I always will be, right? Nothing more than a friend." Jak's voice breaks, giving away his true feelings. He still loves me, buried beneath his hate and all that propaganda he's been fed.

"Don't do this, Jak. Don't let him control you like this. Remember your dreams to make this a better place? You could still do that. You aren't like them."

"Leave me alone, Nat." Jak scowls at me. I can see the pain stretched across his face. He pulls the car over at the side of the road. I try to wipe away my tears, but I'm drowning in them. My heart flops against my chest as pain rips through it. I start to sob, unable to catch my breath. I've been best friends with Jak since childhood. He was there for everything. I knew he'd be hurt. I knew he'd be angry. But I never expected him to betray me like this.

Jak gets out and opens my door. He grabs me by the hand and pulls me out of the car. I can't stop him. I can't resist any longer; I'm defeated. "Maybe you'll like the new Nat better," I cry.

"Open your eyes, Nat," Jak says, shaking my shoulders.

I open my eyes and see we're in front of my grandparents' apartment building. I spent the entire drive begging him, and I didn't see where he was taking me. But what does this mean? What's going on?

"Things are happening at the Axis right now," Jak warns. "It's not safe. This whole rebel thing has the Director beside himself. He's wild and out of control. Get your grandparents and get out of the dome. Take as many people as you can. That's all I can say."

Jak grabs my hand, gripping it tight as he closes it into a fist, then kisses me. I don't pull away, but I don't kiss him back either. It's a goodbye kiss. His way of letting me go. He lets go of me, his eyes watery, and I watch as he gets in the car and drives away.

My entire body is numb. I stumble into the lobby. With my back against the cold brick I take a few deep breaths. The pain returns to my chest. The pain of rejection and loss. That's when I feel the pain cutting into my clutched hand.

I look down at my palm, where Jak had closed it into a fist, and see Jak's ID card and a note. I look around, half-expecting him to reappear, then unfold the note. My heart drops.

Dearest Nat,

I'm sorry for how I treated you. You'll always be my first love. No matter how hurt I am, I could never intentionally hurt you back. They're taking Evan back down to B3. He will not be released. Here's my key card in case your friends can rescue him. Be safe.

Love, Jak

We may never see one another again. Me and Evan. Me and Jak. Nothing will ever be the same again after today. I need to get back to the Axis as fast as I can. But first there are two people I need to warn. I clutch the card and run upstairs to my old home.

"Grandfather!" I call out as I knock on the apartment door. "Grandmother? Are you home?

My grandfather throws open the door and stands in awe. "Natalia." He has tears in his eyes. "I wasn't sure if we would ever see you again."

I throw myself into his arms, his embrace filling the emptiness I've felt since we were torn apart. When we let go, I see Grandmother standing behind him.

"Why are you here?" she asks.

"I've come to warn you. You need to get out of the dome as soon as possible."

"What do you mean?" Grandfather frowns. "What's going on?"

"It's complicated," I explain. They both stare at me, waiting for an explanation, and I realize it will take more than my pleading to get them to leave.

"You know the people who have gone missing?"

"Why yes, Muriel's son went missing last week. It's really not like him. He was a good boy. I can't believe he would relocate to another part of the dome and not tell his mother. He has a wife and a baby on the way."

"That's because no one is relocating. The Order is taking them."

"Why would you say something as ridiculous as that, Nat?" Grandmother's eyes shoot daggers toward me. She's still afraid.

"They still have the virus. They use it and run test on these people. Not everyone is immune anymore."

"Lies!" Grandmother shouts. "Get out! It's all lies."

"No, it's true." I turn to Grandfather, pleading. "Remember Waldorf? He worked with Mom and Dad. Well, today he confessed to everything. He was the one—the one who—"

"The one who betrayed your parents." A strange voice comes from the living room.

A man steps out in the open. His face has changed over the years, more wrinkled and half-covered by a bushy beard, but I recognize him instantly as the man who was outside the dome. This time I know why he's familiar to me.

"Uncle?" My mouth drops open in shock. "Uncle Alec?"

"Yes, Nat," he says. "It's me."

"How did you get inside?"

"Evan helped me sneak in on the back of one of your expedition trucks," Alec explains. "Since then, I've been in the Outer Forest. When it was safe, I made my way here to Mom and Dad."

"I can't believe it is really you." I run and hug my uncle as tight as I can. I have a decade of hugs to make up for. Over his shoulder, I see Xara and her mother are here as well.

"Is it time to go?" Mrs. Douglass asks. I should have known she would be a rebel.

"It's time." I nod. "I need to get go back."

"I don't understand. Can't Evan and the others handle it from here?" she asks.

"Roe has my mother's proof," I explain. "But everything else is screwed up. I need to get back and save Evan. They're taking him for testing."

"Nat," Alec says, "Evan can take care of himself. He knew this mission was dangerous."

"No." I step back, shaking my head. "You don't understand. There is no way out of there. He's trapped, and I can help him."

I take another step back toward the door. They don't understand. I can't lose Evan. I need him. I grab the door handle behind me.

"I'm going," I say. "You can't stop me."

"Nat, wait!" Xara calls after me as I turn and run from my grandparents' apartment. I make my way to the Axis. I know what needs to be done, and I'm sure there's a way we can do it, and save everyone.

CHAPTER 29

I walk back into the dome, unsure of where to go first. The girl at the front desk looks at me, confused. I need to distract her some way, so she doesn't alert the Order that I've returned.

"Where's Leta? Wasn't she here earlier?"

"She's not on until later," the girl says, eyeing me.

I have Jak's ID card clipped to my shirt, hanging backward, so she can't see the face on it.

"Silly me," I fake a laugh and start walk toward the elevators. I click the button and see the receptionist stare at me in the reflection on the steel. I get onto the elevator and punch in Floor 18. When the doors close I exhale, and my hands shake as I tuck Jak's ID card away. I hope Roe is in her office.

The entire lab is in an uproar. Boxes are on desks, papers are strewn all over the tables, and the scientists are emptying the shelves.

"What's going on?" I look around at the chaos.

"Something happened up in Microbiology," Cardinal says. "Roe didn't say much. All the members were called up there."

"Did you all get the immunity serum?"

"Yes, right before she got the call," Mrs. Richards says.

"Good. I don't know if Roe is coming back. Has anyone notified Sophie?" I need to make a plan, but first I have to catch up.

"She's been hiding Leta since the night shift. Leta was flagged for making illicit ID cards. They're going up to Systems to run the message on the monitors. Thankfully, our contact there is still a supporter. Soon everyone in the dome will be shown the proof," Mr. Richards says.

"Okay," my voice shakes. I can't believe this is really happening. "Can all of you be in charge of the immunity serum? I have something I need to do."

"Don't worry." Cardinal assures me. "We'll get it out safely. But don't wait too long. You don't want to get caught in here when the Axis comes down."

I reach in and grab one vial, putting it in my pocket where the microchip is secured. As much as I despise Waldorf, I plan to carry out his last request for the best of mankind.

I stop at the door of the lab. "My uncle is alive," I shout back. "He's with my grandparents. They're going to start evacuating the dome."

"Alec is alive?" Cardinal's jaw drops. "How is that possible?"

"He escaped that night," I explain. "That's the real reason Evan is here. He came with Alec to carry out my mother's plans."

I leave the lab, but not before noticing excitement build in Cardinal's eyes. I really don't know anything about her; not where she comes from, and not why she's on the Expedition team. Maybe we'll have the opportunity to get to know each other when all of this is over.

The elevator takes me to Floor 2, where I was not long ago. Papers are strewn all over the floor, filing cabinet drawers are left open. But no one is scrambling around; all the people are standing in front of a monitor showing gruesome photos of the infected.

Residents of Dome 1618, you have been lied to. You have been lied to by the Order and you have been lied to by your elected government. They have stolen your loved ones off the streets and used them for biological testing, infecting them with the virus that brought on the Cleansing War. They have kept you inside the dome as prisoners for the last decade. It is safe to go outside the dome.

We are bringing the Director and the Delegates to justice. We are bringing down the Axis. Please evacuate the dome immediately, for your safety.

Join us. Join the rebellion. You no longer need to be divided. No longer do people need to live afraid. Join us on the outside where you can start a new life.

The message repeats from the beginning.

Catherine spots me and runs over. "Last I heard, you were

dragged off to the Learning Institute. I'm glad you're okay. As you can see, things have gotten out of control here."

"What happened on Microbiology?"

"The Delegates went up there with the Director," she explains, quickly whisking me away from the group, down the hallway into the Director's office. "They had a meeting with the Head of Microbiology. All Samson has been able to message me is that there was an attack and the Director has been injured. It sounds bad."

"That's because the Head of Microbiology gave himself the virus before meeting with the Director." I walk behind the Director's desk and press the button for B3.

Catherine stares wide-eyed as the bookcases reveal the hidden elevator.

"I need to go find Evan," I say.

She nods. "Samson and I will help people get out of the dome."

"Ask Jak, too," I say. "He helped me. He really is good inside."

"Take these." Catherine passes me a gun and a small device. "Samson gave me those to protect me. But if you're going where I think you're going, you need them more than me. Use the one to protect yourself and the other to destroy whatever you need to."

I shove the device in my pocket and take the pistol. The cold steel of the gun feels awkward in my palm, without Evan nearby to direct me. I grip it tight, and brace myself as the doors slide shut.

CHAPTER 30

B3 is darker than it was last time I was here. Fluorescent lights still flicker above, but now some bulbs have jagged holes, like open sores where bullets have ripped them apart. The lights cast their uneven glow down the bare walls, reaching across the floor toward the open doors of each cell, as if welcoming my return.

The gun shakes in my hands as I inch my way down the hallway. Gripping it tight, I point the barrel out in front of me and search each cell, one-by-one. Empty. I pause at the last door, letting my breath out in a strangled exhale. There was an infected in there last time I was here.

I pivot through the open doorway, but almost drop the gun immediately. The infected that lunged at the door the last time I was here, now lies slumped on the floor with her head bashed in. Blood pools in her lap, where it's already began to dry. My stomach rebels as I grab the wall, feeling my way out of this horror show. Visions of Evan, trapped down here with these monsters, fill my head, but I push them out and move down the hallway to the right.

Each step I take makes my skin crawl as the screams that fill the hallways of B3 get closer. I try to ignore them and focus on the windows of each room. Each has shelves and furniture knocked over, but only one has an infected. It lies on the floor in a pool of blood, its twisted face staring up at me. I cover my mouth in an attempt to keep down the contents of my stomach, and force my feet to continue to the end of the hall. *What happened down here?*

I peek around the corner, where the long hallway leads to a set of gates. Between the iron pickets, long arms reach for me. Their screams are louder here, bouncing off the walls and piercing the air. I want to hide my face and cover my ears, but I force myself to look. I have to know if Evan is one of them. I need to know if I'm too late.

But I can't see him in the sea of faces, so I keep moving around the bend to the other labs. Here, there are only three rooms, and there are no beds or tables, just empty space. The first two are dark, still I peer through the shadows with a shred of hope that Evan is inside. The third room is lit, and the bodies of three infected lie sprawled across the floor.

I jump back and scream as a bloody hand reaches up and bangs on the window from below. It leaves a long streak of red as it slips down the glass. Scrambling for my gun, I point it at the window, but nothing moves again. *Pull yourself together, Dacie.* I take a deep breath, then shuffle closer to the glass. Evan's face comes into view; his body lies slouched against the wall like nothing more than a rag doll. A cry escapes my lips as I drop my gun and push open the door.

I hold the door open with my foot and stretch out so I can reach him, without locking us in. His mouth hangs slack and his eyes are only open a slit. His hair is matted to his forehead, caked in blood, and his shirt is ripped to threads, barely intact, with one sleeve missing.

"Evan," I whisper. "Evan, it's me, Nat."

"Nat." My name escapes his lips with a murmur.

"Come on," I say a little louder. "I'm here to help you."

"Nat," Evan says again, this time more audibly as he opens his eyes. He groans, trying to push himself up, but his shoulder looks like it might be dislocated. "Is that really you?"

"It is—" I struggle against my tears as I drop to my knees. "Can you push yourself this way? We need to go."

Evan looks at me, as a tear falls to my cheek. He stares a moment, as if finally accepting I'm really here, and then begins to drag himself in my direction, stopping to catch his breath as he winces against the pain. All I can do is stand there, helpless, just as I've felt most my life trapped inside this dome.

He looks up at me, his eyes stronger, and more determined. "Are the guards gone?"

I nod. "Something happened to the Director. All the Members have been called to Microbiology. B3 is empty."

"It's starting." Evan flashes a half-smirk at me as he pulls himself closer.

Once he's within reach, I pull him by his good arm out to the hallway. The door slams shut behind us, echoing in the hallway, where it intermingles with the screams of the infected.

"What happened in there?" I sit next to him, anxious to be close but afraid to touch him.

"They made me fight those—things," he says, choking on his words. "I told them I was immune, and their tests wouldn't work on me, but they still tried to infect me. Once they saw I wouldn't turn, they decided to try other tests. Survival tests. That's what these rooms are for."

My chest tightens as I realize the horror of his words. "They must have done this before, to others."

"The first one was the hardest," Evan says. "It was a woman in a cell. I kept thinking, 'Are you a mother? A daughter? Someone out there misses you.' But I had no choice." His voice breaks. "She came at me, again and again. Finally, I had to kill her or she would have torn me apart." A shudder runs through his body and I put my hand on his good arm to soothe him. "The second was a little easier. It was that one that almost caught you, so I pretended I had to kill it to save you. These last three ... well, I almost gave up, but I remembered you and how they'd taken you to the Learning Institute. How, if I never tried to escape here to come and save you, you might forget me."

I lean over and brush Evan's hair from his face. "I would never forget you." I kiss him softly on the mouth, and his lips part open and move with the weakness and yearning of a broken man who has a second chance at life. In that moment everything dissipates—the fear, the pressures; it's just us like it was always meant to be.

But we're not free yet. I break away, running my thumb along his lips as my palm rests against his cheek. "Alec is inside the dome, and the message has gone across the monitors. I think the Director has been infected by Waldorf. It's time to go."

"We have one last thing to do," Evan says. "We need to get to B1."

"No. We need to get help for your arm."

"Nat, there's no time. You have to put my arm back into place."

"What! I can't do that."

He winces as his good arm moves the dead one out to his side. "Come sit over here."

I reluctantly follow his directions.

"Now, lean over, grab my hand and put your foot against my torso for leverage. Very slowly, pull my arm towards you."

I start to pull and Evan howls out in pain, yelling, "Don't stop!" I keep pulling, and soon the infected drown out Evan's shouts with their shrieks. I'm rewarded with a popping sound.

Evan lies panting on the floor and I let go of his arm. "Thank you." He rotates his arm as if nothing happened. "It's tender, but it will work."

"We don't need to go to B1. Catherine gave me a device to kill the infected down here."

"We need to carry out Alec's plan. We need to shut down the boiler. Not only will it give the resistance a chance to take over, it will shut down all of these terrible experiments."

"The experiments are over, and we weren't able to get to the virus, because Waldorf blocked the freezers. Now we can't shut down the boiler systems. If we do, the virus will release itself on the entire dome."

"Dammit," Evan says. "Take me to the elevator, then. Let's get out of here."

I realize I left Jak's key card on the Director's desk. How stupid. Of all the things to mess up on, after getting this far, a key card is our undoing. "We can't get out." I hold out my empty hands.

"There's another way," Evan says. "Through the dumbwaiter. I found it when I was down here last time. It's how you get food from floor to floor. We will take it up to B1, and leave from there."

"I thought only B3 had an exit?"

"I thought so too, but when Mrs. Watson took our key card up to Engineering, she found the master blueprint. There are exits strategically placed all over this dome."

"Why haven't I heard about this before?"

"Nat, there hasn't been time to explain every little detail. Let's get out of here."

I grab my gun from the floor, and follow him around the remaining curve of the hallway. We're nearly back at the entrance when he points to the small elevator. There's a keypad next to it.

"We have to take turns," he says.

"I'm going first. You're injured. Plus, I have the gun."

"No. I'm going first." His eyes focus on me. There's an urgency in them. I'm sure he just wants to get as far as B3 as quick as he can.

"I'm the one who taught you how to shoot," he continues.

"Plus, I can't climb in without your help."

I want to argue, but I know he's right. After some awkward climbing, he finally situates himself in the small box, with his knees pulled up to his chest. It smells like old metal, rusted to the point I hope it stays together. He flashes me a weak smile, as I key in B1. The dumbwaiter jerks before grinding upward. After a few minutes, the chute groans as the dumbwaiter makes its return.

The tiny device Catherine gave me weighs heavily in my pocket. My job isn't done. I run back to the gated area, past the room where Evan fought for his life against three infected, who were once innocent people, stolen from their homes on the surface. When I arrive at the gates, the infected reach toward me, as if they're begging. There's only one thing I can give them now—peace.

I pull the device from my pocket. It's a tiny sphere of smooth silver metal, with a single button that marks the surface—a tiny little button that controls all of the lives of those in front of me. I look back at the infected. No. Their lives ended a long time ago. It's now or never.

The button presses with surprising ease; I roll the grenade along the floor until it disappears in the middle of hundreds of feet of the infected. I pause one last time, taking the images of their faces and imprinting them into my memories. If no one remembers the mistakes we made here, how will we stop from making them again?

I run as fast as I can back to the dumbwaiter, where it sits like a gaping hole waiting for me to climb inside. I scramble in and reach around, keying in my destination. With a jerk, the dumbwaiter creeps upward and I slide the door shut. But the moment everything goes dark, the dumbwaiter shakes violently. It screeches to a stop, and I brace my arms against the walls of my small enclosure. I know I succeeded—the infected have been eliminated, but I can't help but feel a prickle across the back of my neck as my hairs rise at the thought of being trapped in this tiny box. I bang my hands on the walls beside me. Nothing.

What will Evan do if I'm trapped in here? The entire place is falling apart above us, and I'm stuck in the walls. I can't even go back to B3, which right now doesn't seem like the worst alternative.

Something rattles overhead, and the dumbwaiter jerks back in motion. I rest my head on the steel behind me and wait for my destination. After a few seconds, the dumbwaiter stops. I slide the door open and watch as the unfamiliar floor of B1 comes into view.

Evan is nowhere to be seen. Ahead of me is a maze of pipes running from boilers twice my height. Their motors vibrate the air, whirring in a never-ending loop. Warmth makes the air heavy, but the silence makes it uncomfortable.

"I'm not going to let you hurt her again." Evan's voice cuts through the air from the other side of the machinery.

"That's not why I'm here," Jak replies.

I stumble out of the dumbwaiter. Jak's here? But why? I run between the machinery, trying to follow their voices, but I stumble over a man, slumped on the floor. There's a gash in his head, but he still has a pulse. He's wearing a blue work suit, with B1 on the chest. He's just a worker. Did Evan do this? Or was it Jak?

I step out from behind a row of boilers and see Evan pointing his gun at Jak. Even worse, Jak is pointing a gun back at Evan. Nothing good can come from this.

"What are you doing here?" I ask Jak.

His eyes flicker to me, and then snap back at Evan. "Catherine told me what happened," Jak says. "I came to stop you from blowing up the dome. Think of all the innocent people."

"What?"

"He's lying," Evan says. "We can't trust him."

"I don't understand."

"Nat," Jak pleads. "You know I'm right. I'm sorry about everything that happened between us. I don't know why I did it. I thought the Director was acting in the best interests of the dome. He wasn't. I saw that video. No one can deny the proof now. But all those innocent people above us, haven't they suffered enough?"

"We aren't going to blow up the generator," I explain. "I killed the infected that were downstairs. Where is the Director now?"

"I told him you came to save the Outsider." Jak looks at me again. "He's on his way to stop you so I ran ahead."

"The Director's not dead?"

"Not yet. But he also told me about the plan—Evan's plan. I came down here because I knew I could make you understand."

"What plan? We're just trying to get outside."

"You can't stop us," Evan yells at Jak.

"What's going on Evan?"

"Nat, don't you understand. It's the only way."

My stomach does flip flops as it twists itself into knots. My mind races back to B3, back to why Evan wanted to come here.

"There isn't an exit on B1, is there, Evan?"

"Nat, you know Alec will agree. We have to shut down this dome. You saw what they did down there. All those innocent people turned into those—things."

"No." I shake my head. "You can't do this. You'll hurt those people above. You'll be just like the Director."

Evan's gaze darts between Jak and me, like a wild man trying to decide who to trust. I walk over to him, holding my hands out, not taking my eyes off his.

"Evan. I told Catherine she could trust Jak. He's the one who told me where you were. He helped me save you." Evan's eyes soften, but he still shakes his head. "He can help Samson make this a better place for people to live. You and I can have a life here."

His eyes soften as they search mine, as if he's trying to believe me. Whatever happened to him on B3, I need to make him trust me again. I stare back and manage a smile. "I know it can be better."

He nods, and I put my hand on his gun, lowering it. Jak does the same, as I take Evan's gun into my hands.

That's when I'm grabbed from behind.

"Nat!" Jak yells.

"She's wrecked everything," the Director hisses in my ear. "All our hard work—ruined. Can't you see it, Manning? She's one of them."

His skin burns against my cheek and something sharp touches my neck. Sweat drips off his face onto mine.

"Don't hurt her!" Evan yells.

"She took it all away from me!" the Director yells. "I won't let her leave this floor alive."

"No!" Evan calls out. "You'll spend the rest of your life in prison."

"I'm dying as we speak," the Director growls, loosening his grip for a moment as he shakes his head. He's fighting the virus; I can feel it. Waldorf succeeded.

"She's immune," Jak yells. "You can't hurt her."

I cry out in pain as the sharp instrument pushes against my throat.

"I beg to differ," the Director hisses.

I've got nothing to lose. He'll kill me once he stops Evan. I reach across my side with the gun in my hand and aim it behind me. I'm not sure where his body is, but he's so close, I take a chance, place the gun tight against my side, and pull the trigger.

The Director lets go of me and I spin around to see him reel back a step. As he falls, he kicks my legs out from under me, and I collapse to the floor. His reflexes are surprisingly fast. In one quick movement, he's on top of me, squeezing the breath from my windpipe as he raises a large knife in the air.

A gunshot rings out. The Director's head snaps back and his body crumples on top of me. I can smell his cologne, as his neck presses against my cheek, and memories of our first encounter flood my thoughts. Screams erupt from my throat as I try to push his body off.

Jak appears and pulls the Director's corpse away. Another set of hands grabs me under my arms, pulling me to my feet. "It's okay, Nat," Evan says. "You're safe. Jak saved you."

My body shakes, out of my control, and I struggle to catch my breath. That was close. I huddle against Evan's body as he runs his hand down my hair.

"I'm so sorry I ever brought you to the Axis," Jak says. "I thought you would be safe. I thought it would bring us closer."

I let go of Evan and run over to Jak, throwing my arms around his neck. He wraps his arms around my waist and holds me tight. Jak saved my life. I wish I never had to hurt him, but I have to let him go.

"Won't you stay?" he whispers into my ear. "Stay, and help me rebuild our home."

"It's not my home anymore, Jak," I whisper back. "It hasn't been since the dome took my parents away from me. I have to go and rebuild, so I can start a new life of my own."

"Nat." He leans his forehead against mine, sending a shiver down my back. "I can't stop loving you."

Those final words carry more truth than this dome has provided in decades. Jak kisses my cheek, then lets me go. I release my arms from his neck and realize this is it—this is our goodbye. It's on our own terms this time. No Director, forcing us together. No Order, forcing us apart. This time it's ours alone.

Jak nods to Evan, then walks toward the elevators and waves goodbye. I step forward, about to call out to him as the doors close. I almost ask him to wait for me. But I don't. I hold back my feelings for the safety and security of my past, and watch as the doors close between us.

Evan takes my hand and I turn to the other set of elevators, their doors wide open, waiting for me to accept my new future. Evan squeezes my hands, flashing me his half-grin, and we step forward, together. The doors close on B1, and soon open to the lobby.

Order members run past, moving toward the exits of the Axis. Evan holds his hand up as he peers out the door. But no one is threatening; people are trying to escape. I walk out into the open, and Evan follows, as I make my way through the lobby. The large telescreens continually play the resistance's message, over and over again.

I step out into the street, where screens continue to blast the truth for all to hear. People are carrying suitcases, and pulling their families behind them. Stores have been abandoned. Windows are smashed. I never realized how powerful the truth could be, until today.

As we walk through downtown, the Order detains people. How long will their charade carry on? Will they try to stop us? As the Order grabs an older woman, she cries out, drawing the attention of a group of residents. They drop their bags, picking up debris from the road, and move forward, crowding the Order. I turn away, unable to differentiate the cries between the innocent and those who hunt them. I'm afraid of the outcome, either way.

As we make our way to the Apartment District, I see a familiar face—my Uncle Alec. He spots us at the same time and runs over, hugging Evan, then mussing his hair like he used to do with mine.

"You've done it, kid," he says to Evan. "Your mom will be proud. This Axis is finished."

"We couldn't destroy the boiler," Evan says.

"What?" Alec's eyes grow wide. He clenches his fists at his sides.

Before he loses it, I continue. "The infection will spread to the outside. The freezers are not accessible."

He bites his lip, pausing before he speaks again. "I have another job to finish here, no matter what the consequences. I'm going after the Director and the Delegates."

"No." I grab my uncle's sleeve. "Don't. The Director is dead. The others will have it under control."

"I have to, Nat. They deserve to pay for what they did. Every last one of them."

"We need to get out of here," I plead. "I've got all the information for the vaccine with me. We need to get it outside to safety."

"Do that," Alec says, putting a hand on my shoulder. "And take as many people out there with you. When I'm done, I'll join you. Keep moving forward, Nat. There's nothing left inside here for you anymore."

I look back at the Axis. Alec is right. This place stole my life from me. It served as a vessel for my answers, and now that I've got them it's time for me to move on.

Evan grabs my hand and squeezes it, as I watch Alec disappear inside. The uncle I once lost has returned. But his agenda has changed. He's fueled by hate and vengeance. I'm too tired to care about those things anymore.

We make our way outside the dome. When I feel the open air against my face, I know I'm finally free. The night sky stretches out above me. The moon and stars light my way toward the life my mother wanted me to have. I turn and see other people flowing out of the open dome. In the distance, I can hear music in the air. People are celebrating.

I look out into the skies of the mysterious beyond. My fingers reach over and entwine with Evan's. I whisper, just loud enough so he can hear me.

"Look, Evan. Out here, in the night, you can almost feel the stars shine against your skin."

Evan squeezes my hand, and I never want to let go. I wish we could stay frozen in this moment forever. Under the stars. Free.

THE END

ACKNOWLEDGEMENTS

When I submitted *There Once Were Stars,* I had no idea how much my life would change. There was so much I had to learn, not only about writing, but also about the publishing industry. If it wasn't for Georgia McBride taking a chance on an unagented newbie, this book may have never seen the light of day, and I never would have continued to write the many stories I've completed since (and am still working on). Her belief in this novel means the world to me.

I also have to send my thanks to Kahla Dombowsky, a co-worker, who offered to read *There Once Were Stars,* and upon completion came into my cubicle exclaiming, "This is so good!" That short burst of excitement gave me the confidence I needed to take this novel to the next level. From there I connected with an old friend, Bridget Spicer, who has been an invaluable beta reader, alongside Kahla and my mother Faithe, all helping to make my novel the best it can be. These three make up my team, and I couldn't do what I love without them.

Since the day I signed with Month9Books, nearly two years prior to publication, I have met a world of wonderful writers and learned how to become better at this craft. A sincere thank you to everyone I've connected with, including my first editor,

Sarita Amorim who taught me much more than any class could, on how to improve my manuscript. Amy McNulty, Jennifer Bardsley, Jessica Gunn, Suzanne van Rooyen, Pat Esden, Julia Ember, Louise Gornall, Vicki L. Weavil, Bethany Morrow, Stacey Mosteller, and the rest of the #WO2016 crew have been invaluable in teaching me how to help promote my book, before and after publication. Dorothy Dreyer and Beck Nicholas, both part of the Month9Books family, have pulled me into their inner circles of friendship and experience, showing how one can balance family life with the writer's life. Booktuber Shala (Shaegeeksout) was the first to agree to a beta read without knowing anything about me; I reached out to her through Instagram, and her support since has been amazing.

For a girl who grew up in the middle of the Canadian prairies, this is beyond a dream come true. Thank you to my father and his made-up bedtime stories, and my mother who always pushed me to read.

All of you have helped to make my dream come true.

MELANIE MCFARLANE

Melanie McFarlane is a passionate writer of other-worldly adventures, a little excitable, and a little quirky. Whether it's uncovering the corruption of the future, or traveling to other worlds to save the universe, she jumps in with both hands on her keyboard. Though she can be found obsessing over zombies and orcs from time to time, Melanie has focused her powers on her YA debut There Once Were Stars, and her YA urban fantasy Summoner Rising.

She lives with her husband and two daughters in the Land of Living Skies.

Connect with Melanie:

Website: www.melaniemcfarlane.com
Twitter: @McFarlaneBooks www.twitter.com/mcfarlanebooks
Facebook: www.facebook.com/mcfarlanebooks
Goodreads Author Page: www.goodreads.com/melaniemcfarlane
Instagram: www.instagram.com/mcfarlanebooks
Wattpad: www.wattpad.com/mcfarlanebooks

OTHER MONTH9BOOKS TITLES YOU MIGHT LIKE

LIFER

GENESIS GIRL

FACSIMILE

Find more books like this at http://www.Month9Books.com

Connect with Month9Books online:

Facebook: www.Facebook.com/Month9Books
Twitter: https://twitter.com/Month9Books
You Tube: www.youtube.com/user/Month9Books
Blog: www.month9booksblog.com

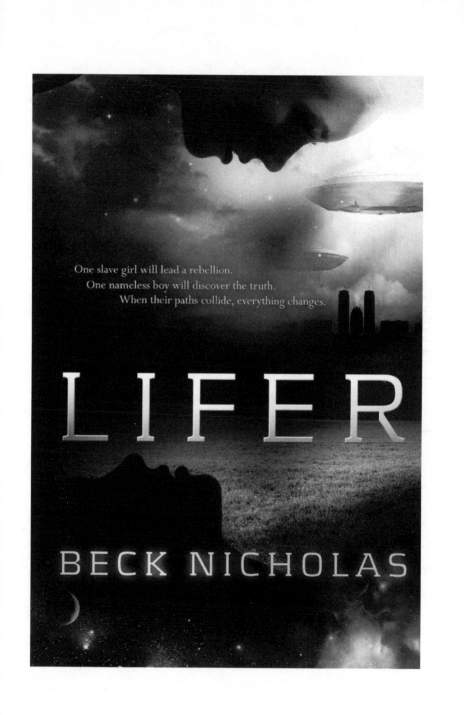

One slave girl will lead a rebellion.
One nameless boy will discover the truth.
When their paths collide, everything changes.

LIFER

BECK NICHOLAS

Their new beginning
may be her end.

BLANK SLATE: BOOK 1

GENESIS
GIRL

JENNIFER BARDSLEY